This book is dedicated to my husband Michael Warren, my life partner.

Acknowledgments

My husband, Michael, took each step of this journey with me. He also contributed his extensive knowledge of antiques; and he encouraged me when I doubted myself. My friend Linda Ferraro, offered valuable (and honest) feedback. She also introduced me to my editor, Laura Logan. Laura is not only skilled; she is patient and supportive. She turned a storyteller into an author. Brenda Izen took me on a virtual tour through the streets of Israel; she allowed me to see Israel through her eyes. My friend, Michael Cavalier, has encouraged me throughout the years. He is a wise and funny man, and I cherish his friendship. I want to thank my dearest friend and cousin, Marie Hoey. She insisted I write years before I found the courage to write my first essay. She has always been in my corner. I am blessed with two beautiful daughters, Rachelle Opman and Cynthia Kurkowski. They cheered me on and supplied endless tech support.

Preface

Threads of the Parachute is a work of fiction. The names, characters, places and incidents portrayed in my book are the product of my imagination or have been used fictitiously. The evolution of this story began in my childhood when I would see the spark in my father's eyes when he spoke of his WWII service. My father served his country on three continents: North America, Africa, and Europe. My father, Technical Sergeant Jerry Miello, was a country boy from Rutland, Vermont. After his death; I was entrusted with his wartime letters to my mother. It took me three years to find the courage to read them. Once I held the first letter, I became obsessed with his words. I knew I wanted to write about WWII.

My mother's family tree is filled with storytellers; and I inherited their love of storytelling. The two components meshed and a story was conceived. I was helped along by a WWII veteran, Jimmy Rizzo. He is a family friend who served in Burma. I used my father's letters and conversations with Jimmy to get a realistic feel for a soldier's life. However, any incorrect portrayals of military life fall directly on my shoulders. Be kind; I am the daughter of a WWII soldier. For historical dates and background, I relied on Wikipedia and firsthand accounts that I researched on-line.

Cervinara, Italy is a real place; it is the ancestral home of my grandfather.

My father did mail home a German flag, and my mother did wash it and hang it on her Brooklyn clothesline. My Uncle Nick ripped it down, and spent the rest of the war praying he would not be deported.

In Rome, 1944, my father and his Army buddies did climb up the balcony where Mussolini had previously given his speeches. Each of them, including my father, gave their own wine induced speeches to the crowds below.

One final mention: The name Joseph (Jody) Fish appears in my story. Jody was my cousin and a Marine who lost his life in Vietnam.

"Older men declare war. But it is youth that must fight and die. And it is youth who must inherit the tribulations, the sorrow and the triumphs that are the aftermath of war."

—Herbert Hoover

Threads of the Parachute
Chapter 1
New York City
October 2018

The taxi door closed with a nervous rattle. She surveyed the driver, the caustic music, the stale air, and seat belts that hadn't been touched since they rolled off the assembly line. "Bryant Park," she said. Her body language announced, *there will be no further interaction.* Her eyes were riveted on the pages of a book; she did not smile or talk on her phone. Cia hated small talk—especially with strangers. The driver got the message; he was silent.

His eyes, however, had their own agenda. They veered to the rear view mirror at every opportunity. The woman in his back seat was beautiful. Her hair was dark and thick, and it framed her face; but it was the eyes that transfixed him. The eyes that reminded him of the black stones he collected by the river in his homeland. He knew her type: the *pretty girls.* They didn't bother with cosmetics, sexy clothes or silly games to attract men. Men lined up. He took his time through the Manhattan traffic; he was in no hurry to end this ride. "May I drop you at 42nd Street?" he asked.

"Yes," she said. The woman paid the fare and added a respectable tip. She headed for the steps of the 42nd Street entrance to Bryant Park. The driver lingered at the curb for an extra minute to watch her walk. Her loose clothes did not fool him; there were curves hidden beneath.

As she walked, the aroma surrounded her. The waffle kiosk sent the smell of freshly baked waffles into the air. It was the smell of childhood, comfort, and happiness blended into a small, square, dented baked good. She inhaled and tried to capture the sweet air.

Cia acknowledged she had little alone time in her life; she missed it. The crisp autumn air relaxed her and she welcomed the sun's rays on her face. The sun lingered for just a few minutes before it retreated behind a cloud.

Cia was relieved; she had arrived before her mother. It gave her a few minutes alone. Her husband had quipped, "Are you meeting on neutral ground?" "My brother has research to finish at the library," she replied, "and he offered to drive Mom in from Brooklyn to meet me."

Sophia Trotta, her mother, plowed her way through the tourists at exactly 11:30 am and headed straight for the park bench and her daughter. Cia knew that posture: stiff and determined. Mom was not happy. She did look younger than her 64 years. Her hair, now a

8

reddish brown, flattered her face. She was no longer thin, but her mother's strong personality commanded a larger frame.

Cia did not rush over; in Manhattan, you did not surrender your prized position on a park bench to the tourists.

"How are you Mom?"

"I'm good," Sophia replied. "Busy as always; how was your business meeting?"

"Okay," said Cia. "Jacob wanted me to check out some bronzes." *My mother is not listening to me.*

"Why do they do that?" her mother asked. "What makes them want to look like clowns?"

"Mom, did I miss something?"

"Over there" she jerked her head to the left. "Why does that girl have the sides of her head shaved and why is her scrawny ponytail purple?"

"I don't know, Mom. Maybe she has lice." There it was— another failed attempt at a mother/daughter Hallmark moment. They sat in silence. They stared at pigeons.

"I made us sandwiches," said Cia's mother. "Your favorite— chicken cutlet with roasted peppers."

"Thank you, Mom. And I brought us coffee."

"We need to talk, Cia. You know that Ancestry DNA kit you gave me? At the time I said I had enough family, but you insisted. Today I have a new match. A close match."

"Mom, it's probably a cousin. I manage your account; I'll check it out when I get home. What time is Nicholas picking you up?"

"Not until two; it will give me time to shop. Would you like to join me? Your birthday is in a few weeks. I'd like to buy you earrings."

"Thank you, but I think I'll head back to Long Island. Jacob could use my help with inventory." They ate their sandwiches with slow determined bites. They sipped their coffee. They stared at tourists. It was mandatory to listen to updates of the extended family whenever she spoke with her mother, and today was no exception. When Cia provided all the acceptable responses and enough time had lapsed, she stood. "Mom, I need to get back to Levittown." They left the park together, gave each other a quick kiss, and walked in opposite directions.

Chapter Two
Naples, Italy
January 1944

Bella Napoli. It was no longer *bella*; it was a rat hole. The Port of Naples had been bombed mercilessly by the Allies and the Germans. However, once the port was in the Allies' control, it reopened to traffic within a week. Carmine studied his surroundings; this was his family's ancestral home. He was glad his parents were back in Brooklyn and could not witness what he was witnessing. The place was filthy, the people were filthy, and the smoke, dust, and smells of decay assaulted his senses. But he was happy to be here. He hated North Africa, his last deployment. Carmine had tolerated its scorching sun, its isolation; but his 24-year-old body was no match for the malaria that had tormented and debilitated him.

Now he was in Naples. He spoke the language; the culture was his culture. His parents had often said they would take him to Italy. They had promised him that he would make his confirmation in Italy; but there was never enough time or money. And so his first pilgrimage back home was today—to a land in ruins. The truck ride to the Army base told him all he needed to know. Some of the civilians waved and smiled to the American soldiers, while others projected their hatred through searing eyes. J.J. pointed and said, "Look at that signorina, I wouldn't mind getting some *amore* from her." Carmine wanted some of that, too. He was a married man, but he was fighting a war and he was far from home. Carmine could easily rationalize the betrayal of his vows. He wanted to taste different women, but he liked them *fresh*. *Fresh* was a rare commodity in a war zone.

The truck coughed and choked its way through the torn-up roads until it reached the Army base. Naples was a crucial landing base for the Allies; it was crowded with soldiers that soon would be pushing north through enemy lines. The boys jumped off the truck and ran for the mess tent. It was January and they were freezing. They huddled around the stove and poured themselves cup after cup of bitter coffee.

A corporal walked in and asked, "Where is Sergeant Carmine Trotta?" Carmine raised his coffee cup in the air. "The captain wants to see you now." The two men headed for the office. The corporal introduced him to Captain Wadsworth. The captain said, "You'll be reporting to me while you're here in Naples. Have a seat Sergeant." Carmine would never get use to taking orders. He sat there stiffly in his chair and waited. He struggled to maintain an expressionless face.

"It is my understanding that you speak the southern Italian dialect," said the captain. "Tell me about your family, Sergeant."

Carmine was not sure what this captain wanted to hear. He kept it brief. "My parents left Naples in 1915. They settled in Brooklyn, New York. My mother spoke only Italian to me; I learned English from the nuns. My father speaks some English. He's a carpenter. He loves America." *And he's not a Fascist sympathizer.*

"The Army needs soldiers who can speak to the Italians in their own language," said the captain. "It puts the civilians at ease, and they will share information that could help the war effort. I hear you're organized. The warehouse is a mess; fix it."

"Yes, sir," said Carmine.

Captain Wadsworth sized up his new quartermaster. *He's sharp; but his dark Italian good looks could be a problem.* The captain had learned that you don't mix swarthy good looks, the Italian language, and a quartermaster together. A quartermaster managed the warehouse. If the war was to be won, the soldiers had to be supplied. In a place where people have nothing, this soldier could get any woman for a sack of groceries.

In the past, the quartermasters the Army had assigned him had all been corrupted by the black market. The black market paid or traded the quartermasters for supplies in the warehouse. Beer, whiskey, medicine, cigarettes, food—it was all negotiable. The captain had not found an honest one yet, and this guy was potentially worse: he spoke the language of the black market men. They would swarm around him and capitalize on his Italian roots.

13

No trouble communicating their shopping list; and those good looks would attract all the signorinas.

He'll be trading with the black market for perfume and women's clothes, and feeding the signorina's whole goddamn family. I can read black market all over his face. But I have no choice; Army Command assigns them to me. They say it's vital that we communicate with the civilians. We need them to trust us. I can tell the sergeant is intelligent; at least the inventory will get done and the warehouse will have some order.

Carmine watched the captain closely; his instincts told him this guy didn't like him. The captain was going to ride his ass. "We'll have a meeting about the civilians once you get settled. The women from town sometimes cook food for us; it will feel like home."

The boys followed Carmine to their quarters; the Army had reinforced it with lumber and there was sawdust everywhere. It assaulted their eyes and noses, and the soldiers coughed and groused about the smell; but Carmine—the son of a carpenter— found it welcoming. It reminded him of his childhood. Each night when his father came home from work, a stream of sawdust would fall from his clothes. Sawdust smelled like *home*. Like *family*.

Carmine cleared his throat and immediately assigned specific cots to Fish, J.J., Otter, and Mac. He reserved the cot closest to the stove for himself. After chow, they headed for the Red Cross

14

center. Mac decided to leave his trumpet behind; he wasn't ready to take requests from drunks.

The atmosphere at the Red Cross lifted their spirits. There was a bottle of Ruppert's beer in every soldier's hand. There were some G.I.'s in the corner singing *Pistol Packin' Mama, Lay That Pistol Down.* The sound of people laughing put Carmine and his men at ease. After a few more hours and a few more beers, tongues loosened and words slurred.

Many of those slurred words infuriated Carmine. The men referred to the Neapolitans as animals. It was clear to him that these soldiers thought the civilians were childlike, ignorant, and corrupt. They laughed about the smell of the naked Italian women. When Carmine was back in Brooklyn, he prided himself on being an American; he was born in America. Italy was the enemy; he accepted that reality. But he lived in a predominately Italian-American neighborhood. People were respectful. Carmine could listen no longer; he stood with such force that he knocked his chair over, and walked out.

He saw a shadow when he opened the door to his quarters.

He was drunk; he imagined it. No, he saw a slender figure near a footlocker. In one leap he was on the guy; the intruder had Mac's trumpet in his hands. Carmine grabbed for his neck and sent him crashing into a cot. He leaned over him and pulled the tightly held trumpet from the thief's clutches. Now he was looking right into his face. He was a kid, no more than sixteen. Carmine picked him up, dragged him to the door and threw him out. He was just a hungry Italian boy; he looked like Carmine's cousin Sal.

In North Africa, Carmine didn't look like the locals. Here, the locals could be his distant relatives. He wanted to kick the ass of all the soldiers at the Red Cross. For the first time since he left home, he cried. He never mentioned the trumpet incident to his men.

***

The pounding of hammers made their heads burst with flashes of pain. Maybe building bed frames after a heavy night of drinking wasn't a good idea; but it was what Carmine had ordered. He had eyed the extra pieces of lumber piled outside; he knew the larger pieces could be used to make bed frames. He assigned Fish as the team leader. Fish's father was also a carpenter; Carmine knew Fish could build or mend anything. He wasn't a craftsman like his own father; but this country boy from Rutland, Vermont would get the job done. Their quarters would feel more like a home. The boys now called their quarters *L.Q.*—after the new night club in New York City called *Latin Quarter.* Carmine would build his own bed frame tonight while the boys were out playing cards.

Bright and early the next morning he got to work in his new warehouse. The captain was right: it was a mess. Carmine could never deal with disorder; to him it was chaos. He needed everything in its place. He ordered the boys to sweep it out and get rid of the trash. They tried to eliminate the odor by opening the doors; but the outside air had a worse acrid smell. *I'm surprised the captain put up with this shit.*

Carmine got satisfaction from organizing and stocking the shelves. The work was comforting; something in him craved order. In a short time, Carmine had completely transformed the warehouse. It was efficiently organized and clean, and his paperwork was accurate and legible. The next morning, after breakfast, Carmine reported to the captain's office. The combination of seeing the sun for the first time in three days, plus his pride in transforming the warehouse, put Carmine in a good mood.

"I have to hand it to you, Sergeant Trotta," said the captain, not bothering to look up. "You did a good job organizing the warehouse. To show my appreciation, take a look at the film I have; will any of it fit your camera?

Carmine surveyed the pile and picked up one roll of film. "This one will work, thank you."

"Besides managing the warehouse," said the captain, "your other job is to get to know the locals. Gain their confidence. We bombed the shit out of this place, so they find it hard to trust us. But the locals hear things. We want to know what they know."

"How do I gain their trust?" asked Carmine.

The captain drummed his fingers on his desk and said, "Find a way."

"Yes, sir," said Carmine.

"There is one more thing," said the captain. "One of your men is being transferred; here's the paper work. He's needed as a translator. Send him to me. That's all."

Carmine's boots pounded the ground crushing small stones that added to the dust as he made his way back to L.Q. There was something about the captain that unsettled him. It wasn't his size; the guy was short, skinny, and almost bald. Carmine always trusted his instincts; he knew this man was a threat to him.

Back at the barracks, Carmine passed along the orders. "Otter, report to the captain. You're being transferred." As the door closed behind Otter, Carmine surveyed Fish's handiwork. The bed frames looked sturdy; Fish got the job done. "Those bed frames really look good, Fish. Good job."

"Thanks, Sergeant. Your bed doesn't look too shabby either." The two men smiled.

Moments later, Otter stormed back in, leaving the door to rattle uncontrollably and announced, "They're sending me north; but not for another week. I'll be moving around; so I'll get back once in a while for our card games."

Carmine just stared at him; he had no real use for this guy. *Instead of Otter they should have called him Weasel.* After lunch,

18

when the corporal delivered their mail, Carmine asked the corporal to take pictures of him and his four buddies. Wives and girlfriends ate that shit up.

It was late. It was quiet. The boys were still out playing cards. Carmine lay in his newly constructed bed. He was proud of his work; his father would have approved. He had received two letters today. One from his wife, Rachel—he read that one as soon as it arrived. Now he would take his time and read the one from his friend who was fighting in the Pacific.

***

Burma, 1944

Hello Carmine,

There is nothing good to say about Burma. I'm in a jungle; the bugs are as big as half dollars. Remember how we complained about the roaches in Brooklyn? My buddy was bitten by a scorpion. When I cut down trees to use as poles for the phone lines, leeches get under my clothes. They suck so much of my blood that they burst— and my clothes are filled with my own blood. One guy was on guard duty and heard a noise; he shined a light on the spot. There was a tiger in his sights. Fortunately he was a marksman and he shot it dead. What they do now is line the tanks up at night and make a lot of noise with them so that the tigers stay back. There is nothing to do here, no place to spend your money. There are a few boys who know about jewelry—and there's a lot of it here. They buy it up and send it home. If you can believe them, they say they're making a fortune. At night I have to sleep with netting over my cot and every morning I check the inside of my shoes for bugs. But I do sleep on silk sheets. I found a ripped parachute and asked the quartermaster if I could have it and he said, "Yes, we have no use for it." So I cut it up and made myself silk sheets. I listened to that song you heard in North Africa, Lili Marlene. I can't believe it's a German song and the Americans like it. Whoever wrote it must have been a soldier. It haunts you.

I'll turn in now.

Your friend,

Jimmy

***

Carmine put down the letter and said, "Parachutes . . . I can get parachutes."

***

"I saw a damaged parachute in here. I don't care if you have to rip the warehouse apart. Find it." Carmine had to work through his hangover and it wasn't easy with all the outside noise invading his head. Engines roared, tires crushed the gravel, and soldiers' voices rose to compete with the loud chaos.

One voice got his attention—all his attention. "*Buongiorno*, Sergeant Trotta," said Captain Wadsworth. "Good morning, Captain," answered Carmine. Carmine refused to speak Italian to him. The captain was mocking him; and he was sure he hated all Italians.

"Sergeant, there is a lot of work ahead. We are getting extra supplies; there must be something big planned. Make sure your inventory is pristine or you and your boys will be missing out on a lot of sleep. Did the jacket supplies get here? The boys are freezing; they need warmer clothes. The closer we get to Germany, the colder the climate." Before Carmine could answer, the captain turned to face the door. "You see the farmers and peddlers talking to the boys?"

Carmine followed his gaze. "Yes, sir," he answered.

"The fat one is a black market entrepreneur," said the captain. It seemed to Carmine that the farmers and peddlers were trying to keep their distance from the fat guy. "Should I chase him away, Captain?" asked Carmine.

The captain shook his head. "I would like nothing more; but it is not in our best interest. We can get useful information from him. He and his type hear more information than the poor locals. We'll get into bed with the devil himself to end this war. We're all one big happy goddamn family." The captain repeated his favorite mantra.

Carmine had been around enough *wise guys* back in Brooklyn to read this entrepreneur; the wise guy was sizing him up, too. Carmine had the map of Italy written all over his face. Did the fat guy guess he was Italian-American? In all probability he already knew his last name, the Italian town his family came from, and who his relatives were. He was an easy mark; and for the first time, Carmine understood the captain's unease with him. *The captain must think my loyalties are going to lie with the local Italians; plus I learned in Africa just how lucrative a quartermaster's job could be. But I still don't like him.*

"This is what I want you to do," said Wadsworth. "I'll go back to my office while you hang around outside. He'll approach you. Make nice—just speak your momma's dialect to him."

Carmine's face tightened but he returned a rote "Yes sir," before Wadsworth abruptly turned and walked away. He hung outside alone and smoked a Camel cigarette; within minutes, the fat man's grinning face was two feet from his. "Buongiorno Carmine, di dove sei?" Carmine answered, "Cervinara, but I am an American. My parents no longer live in Cervinara; and I will speak English."

The fat one began his speech; it was well rehearsed. Carmine listened intently. "Allow me to introduce myself. My name is Bruno Falco. This war has brought such troubles to our people. The Allies bombed our hospital, the Santa Maria di Loreto, and our church, the Santa Chiara." His voice cracked and he made the sign of the cross when he spoke of the church. *Nice touch.* "Our people have barely enough to survive. There is little food for the children. You can help your father's people. We can help each other; but we will talk later. You look busy. Many supplies are on the trucks."

Carmine did not speak. Then he turned his back to Falco and walked inside. That last remark bothered him. *Was this piece of shit hinting that the supply trucks might get hijacked? Would they hijack trucks guarded by soldiers?* He would pass this nugget on to the captain.

Inside he found the damaged parachute under some crates; that was a good sign. He had learned how to exploit the warehouse for his own personal use from a sergeant in North Africa. His mentor had used the words *creative inventory.* "Don't show anyone the inventory sheets until I look at them," said Carmine.

It was time to get back to work. If the soldiers couldn't see Sergeant Trotta in the warehouse, they could hear him. The metallic sounds of new shelves being assembled, supply containers being ripped open, crates scraping across the floor, filled his time. He needed to fix, assemble, organize; he couldn't be idle and he expected the boys to follow his lead.

The boys were cold and sweaty at the same time. They were exhausted; the trucks had to be unloaded and sent back to the port to be loaded again. They had to work fast. At the end of the day, they took what they wanted for themselves and left the warehouse. There was beer, cigarettes, chocolate bars, soap, blankets, and a damaged parachute with them when their weary young bodies fell into L.Q. Carmine had *adjusted* the inventory sheets; and now with a dramatic half bow he made an announcement. "Tonight, all of us will sleep on white silk sheets." Before the boys could say a word, he threw the parachute at their feet. "My friend, Jimmy Rizzo, gave me the idea. This parachute is good to no one in the air, but we can use it. Mac, get started cutting."

Excitement and amusement overtook their exhaustion and they began making sheets. The scene resembled mischievous little boys at play; and then they took pleasure in making their beds. The boys wiped the sawdust from their new bed frames, added the silk sheets then piled blankets on top with an exaggerated flair. J.J. gathered all the scrap silk pieces and threw them by his bed. "Tomorrow boys, we'll take the scraps and make pillows."

J.J., like Carmine, was Italian-American; but his parents would not teach him Italian. J.J.'s parents wanted him to be all American; they believed that speaking the Italian language would make him less American. They also understood that America's enemy spoke Italian. J.J.'s parents were in the U.S. legally, but they were not American citizens. There were people in their hometown in upstate New York who were suspicious of their loyalty, even though their son was fighting in the U.S. Army. J.J.'s parents went to bed each night in fear. They feared their son would be wounded and they feared they would be deported. The fact that Italy had surrendered to the Allies did little to ease their fear.

In the morning, J.J. was up before the others. He washed, shaved, combed his hair and took a few extra minutes getting dressed. He was waiting for the farmer to arrive. The word *farmer* was an exaggeration; the man had chicken coops and planted vegetables in the spring. His chickens supplied eggs for anyone willing to pay 20 cents each for an egg. The egg man was an old guy who reminded J.J. of the shop owners back home. But it was the egg man's two granddaughters who propelled him out of bed at this early hour.

This morning he was in luck; all three of them showed up. J.J. bought eggs. Carmine also bought eggs. The girls were very talkative, their voices rising and falling, sounding determined. J.J. turned to Carmine and said, "What are they saying?" Carmine smirked. "They're fighting over who will have you first."

"Very funny," said J.J., "What are they really saying?" Carmine didn't respond. Instead, he became part of a four-way conversation that excluded J.J. Finally, the old man and his granddaughters left without saying one word to him.

"It seems," said Carmine, "I may be entering into a business venture with the egg man and his granddaughters. The girls are seamstresses and they wanted the silk fabric. They saw the silk parachute pieces in the corner. They will trade eggs, preserved mushrooms and peppers for the parachute pieces. They will also knit us warm socks." J.J. threw Carmine a sideways glance and wondered aloud what else the granddaughters might do for him? Carmine clutched his fists and said, "The girls are not *puttane*. I will take you along for a meeting at their house—but you will show them respect."

***

"Take your M1 with you," Carmine told J.J. "Who the hell knows what's out there. Germans are still around." The MI Garand rifle was heavy—almost 10 pounds. The first time Carmine fired the damn thing, the stock kicked back with such force that his shoulder was black and blue for two weeks.

J.J. and Carmine headed to the egg man's house late Sunday morning; the rest of the boys were still nursing hangovers from the night before. They drove north away from the port. Carmine studied the houses along the road; they looked more impoverished than bombed out. Most of the bombs had hit east and west of the port. In the east were the rails and petroleum facilities; the west had steel mills. North of the port was spared for the most part; it didn't warrant the cost of a bomb.

The overcast frigid day added to Carmine's sense of gloom. His mother had said that the southern villagers were always poor; but they took pride in repairing their tiny houses. The women planted flowers and swept the walk. Today the roofs of the houses are patched with whatever scraps they could find; and some of the windows are boarded up. Maybe it would look better in the spring? Maybe the women had stored their seeds and would plant brightly colored flowers? J.J. is smiling and waving to an old man; he is immune to the sadness Carmine is seeing. Now here's a familiar site, a fig tree wrapped in tarp; fig trees in Brooklyn also wore winter coats of tarp. Italians loved their figs.

"What is that?" said J.J., pointing to a small figure by the side of the road. They slowed down to get a closer look. It was a skinny kid about 10 years old who was picking up twigs. Carmine began speaking to him in Italian. Finally, Carmine cut off a large chunk of the salami and said, "Mangia." The boy took a big bite of the salami, grinning at Carmine.

"Sergeant," said J.J., "we're going to be late. What are you doing?"

"I told the kid I wanted him to eat the salami in front of me; otherwise he'd have to share it or someone would steal it from him." Carmine gave the boy some money; then he and J.J. drove off.

J.J. asked, "The kid did a lot of talking back there; what else did he say?" Carmine did not answer; he sat silently and stared at the road.

The house was small and old—very old. The roof had been patched and there were clean curtains covering the windows. It was the most inviting place Carmine had seen since he left Brooklyn. It certainly beat North Africa. However, they did see the harsh realities of war all around them. The chicken coops, their main source of survival, were in need of repair. Farm equipment was abandoned and left to rust; and there was an inadequate supply of firewood piled against a dilapidated barn; but these images faded away when the door opened to them. The aroma of Italian food filled their senses; and it brought tears to their eyes. Tomato sauce—or gravy, as they called it in New York—was cooking on a wood burning stove; there were long strands of spaghetti drying on racks. Only one word came into J.J.'s head: *Momma*.

That was the last word J.J. wanted to think about right now, not when there were two beautiful girls standing in front of him. He waved shyly and gave them the chocolate, flour, and the rest of the salami. The egg man welcomed the two of them and introduced himself as Nonno. He said his Christian name is Mario; but the soldiers heard his granddaughters call him Nonno, which is *grandfather* in Italian. Now every soldier calls him Nonno.

The older granddaughter spoke up. "My name is Tessa and this is my younger sister Pina; her Christian name is Giuseppina. We speak English and our Nonno speaks some English." Tessa was even more beautiful than Carmine had remembered; her curves were more apparent today. He assumed Nonno wanted them covered up when the girls accompanied him to the Army base. Carmine wanted to run his hands through Tessa's long thick dark hair and bury his nose in it and carry her scent with him back to the base. Her skin looked like it had been dipped in honey, sweet, golden, and ripe. She had large dark eyes and full lips that Carmine was determined to kiss—but not today. Today they would share their common heritage and enter into a business relationship.

Before the meal, they bowed their heads and gave thanks. Carmine wondered, *what the hell are they thankful for*? Then Tessa and Pina served their homemade spaghetti made with fresh eggs. There was also chicken; but Carmine ate just enough so as not to offend them. He left most of it for the hosts to eat another day; J.J. got the message and ate sparingly. Nonno poured homemade wine, and the conversation slowly flowed into Italian. J.J. didn't mind that he was excluded from the conversation; he managed to catch a few words here and there, and that was enough for him. Later, Tessa and Pina served the chocolate that the two men had brought for the sweet table.

29

The wine and the Italian language had loosened the tongues of the hosts and they began to tell their story. The girls' father had drowned in a boating accident. At the time, Tessa was a young child; her mother was pregnant with Pina. Her mother died giving birth to Pina. Her mother's parents, Nonno and his wife, raised them. Their grandmother died two years ago. Carmine picked up subtle clues from Tessa. Pina's birth was difficult for both mother and child. Pina survived, but she was childlike for a woman of 18 years. Tessa, at 22, was more like Pina's mother than her sister. Pina had a woman's body and a pretty, doll-like face; she would need protection from soldiers and the locals. Pina added to their conversation where she could. She told the men that after her mother died, Nonno gave the children his last name. No paperwork was filed; he told the priest that their names were Tessa and Giuseppina Salvatore.

Now it was time for business. Nonno's wife, Lily, had been a dressmaker. She designed and sewed wedding dresses and she was well known throughout Naples. Lily taught her granddaughters to sew. Tessa was an expert seamstress; Pina was still an apprentice. They learned English by speaking with merchants and English-speaking customers. Now there was little fabric for clothes. Their grandmother Lily had stockpiled thread, yarn, and other notions; but the fabric was gone. They had heard from women at church that parachutes could supply silk fabric, but they had no way to acquire such treasure.

They had seen the remnants near J.J.'s bed and had begged Nonno to intercede for them. "If I could get the silk, I could make women's fancy undergarments; even in war they would sell," said Tessa. "The soldiers were always looking for gifts to send home to their wives and girlfriends. The local women would buy them, too." Tessa blushed when she spoke those last words. Carmine understood she was talking about prostitutes.

Pina added, "I once made a baptismal dress for Signora Russo and she paid me with her homemade cheese; maybe other women would hire me. We could help Nonno."

Carmine listened to their plea; but there was no need to convince him. He would find parachutes—as many as they wanted—no matter what he had to do. In return for the parachutes, they would provide food and knitted socks. Carmine really missed clean, warm socks. His feet were always cold; and as many times as he had asked Rachel for warm socks, they never came. Rachel insisted on sending soap and cookies. He had plenty of soap, and the cookies arrived stale, moldy or both. Carmine nodded to the women; but today, his nod was different. He was happy.

He had heard stories of American uniforms being sold on the black market. Tailors would dye the fabric and make outfits for civilian use. Carmine rationalized that stealing uniforms was wrong because soldiers needed them; but damaged parachutes were useless to the paratroopers. He was a happy man today. He had eaten an Italian meal, he'd sipped homemade wine like his

31

father made in his Brooklyn cellar, and he had looked into the eyes of a beautiful woman. He knew Tessa would soon share his bed. He and J.J. headed back to the base feeling content and optimistic.

"So what do you think?" Carmine posed the question to J.J. on the ride back to L.Q.

"I think," said J.J., "that you're going to drive the boys crazy looking for parachutes."

"How difficult can it be, J.J.? You forget I'm the quartermaster. I can make dreams come true. I can make the boys happy; they'll just need to find some parachutes in return. They don't have to be new ones; in fact, damaged ones are better. No one will wonder what happened to them."

They rode on for awhile in silence. Then J.J. asked, "So Sergeant, what do you think of Tessa?" Carmine did not answer. After they parked the jeep, Carmine hopped out and headed over to the warehouse alone, leaving the question hanging in the air.

CHAPTER THREE
New York
October-November 2018

Cia liked to board an off-peak train; it meant fewer commuters would be invading her space. The Long Island Railroad, with all its tribulations, was crucial to Long Islanders. If Cia boarded the 12:49 pm express train out of Hicksville, she could arrive at Penn Station at 1:33 pm. Of course, that was assuming all the variables cooperated. New York wasn't famous for its cooperation. At this moment in time, she was on a train headed back to Hicksville, Long Island. Jacob would pick her up at the station. She used her alone time, (*alone* if you did not count the hundreds of passengers, the ticket collector and the conductor), to talk herself out of her bad mood. Cia had given this mood a name: *pasta purgatory.* *Pasta purgatory* was coined one stressful night when she returned from a visit with her mother. At her mother's house, the pasta was always served up with a healthy portion of torment. Any mother/daughter visit would inevitably lead to a bad mood. She looked out the grimy window at Jamaica Station, and recited her mantra: *I will not bring this baggage home to Jacob. I will not give her power over me.*

Jacob came from a different world. His parents adored their only child; but it was a healthy love, and they respected each other's boundaries. Cia's mother respected no boundaries. Her brother, Nicholas, was self-absorbed; her father was dead. She missed her grandfather, also dead. Whenever her aunts said, "You look like Grandpa Carmine," it made her happy. Grandpa Carmine had been her fortress.

The train pulled into the Hicksville station; but Cia did not see Jacob. She sat down on a bench and waited for him, pulling calm into her mind to spare Jacob the stress of the trip. Finally, she saw him. She walked over to the curb and got into the car. "I had to circle the block; I couldn't find a place to park," Jacob said cautiously. He knew she would be wound up and short-tempered.

She smiled a rehearsed smile and commanded, "Take me home."

***

Back home and now wearing sweats, Cia was relaxed and ready to talk about the business of the day. "Jacob, I think the bronzes are real. But you'll have to look at them yourself; the reproductions are getting better each year," said Cia. "The pieces were heavy and you would have approved of the patina, but not her prices. I can't see how we could sell them at the pier show. I told Linda you were the expert and that you would need to see them. I added that our customers wanted animal or Native American bronzes. Sorry, I didn't see any art deco statues."

Jacob sighed. "That is what I really wanted, Cia; but they are becoming impossible to find. Okay, I'll set something up; maybe she'll be open to a trade deal. Let's not go back to the shop tonight. Inventory can wait. Instead let's go to the deli, pick up sandwiches, and drive to Jones Beach."

"I'm in," she said. The ocean waves relaxed her, the food nourished her, and Jacob comforted her. The night was good.

***

Jacob, coffee in hand, opened the door to the antique shop early the next morning. He had just disarmed the alarm system when the phone rang. It was his mother-in-law. *I don't know if I can deal with her before a substantial infusion of caffeine.* "Yes, Sophia, that will be fine. No, she isn't suspicious. Yes, she would want Uncle Tony invited and also your ex-husband's sisters," said Jacob. "Of course, I want your help to plan your daughter's surprise party. You can work on the menu and flower arrangements. No, she is not depressed; 30 is not old. Sophia, she just pulled into the parking lot; I have to go." He hung up the phone.

Jacob stood by the window and watched Cia walk toward the antique shop, C. J.'s Antiques & Fine Furnishings. What did that beautiful woman see in him? He was average: average looks,

35

average height, average weight, and average receding hairline. He knew that at 35 he should give some serious thought to a gym membership.

He greeted her as she walked into the shop. "Good morning, Cia mia! There's a collection for sale in the Hamptons; do you think you can hold down the fort for a few hours?" Cia smiled. "I think I can handle the mob, as long as there's a salad with extra olives in your hand when you walk back through the door."

He left; Cia began to dust and organize. She was adamant that the shop not resemble a musty warehouse. They had both given up careers in finance to follow a simpler life with an aesthetic component. They had a clear plan in place when they opened their store, and their business acumen had brought them success. Jacob had found ways to expand their business and attract high-end clients. He hooked up with wedding planners and hotel staff who wanted to stage their premises with vintage furniture. Renting furniture was a lucrative money stream for the store. Cia's contribution was her *eye*. She appreciated detail and form; she chose pieces that would bring in the right buyers. Life was good; of course her mother wanted to know when she was going to have a little reproduction of her own. She stared at the pendulum clocks that marked time all around her; their synchronized movements brought her own biological clock into focus. *Tick tock, tick tock.* She pushed that reality aside.

Cia refocused her energy on the digital hunt for some interesting pieces; eBay was a good place to start. *What was for sale and at what price?* Cia and Jacob kept on top of trends. Yes, even antiques were subject to trends. Of course, if you asked most antique dealers what was selling, they would answer, "Nothing." She poured herself a fresh cup of coffee and switched gears. She pulled up the Ancestry DNA site and looked up her mother's page. She managed her mother's Ancestry DNA account and had signed her mom up under her real name, Sophia Trotta, and not a code name. Her mother had returned to her maiden name—Trotta—after she divorced her husband, Cia's father. Her mother said she had found a close match when she logged into the account; most likely it was a second cousin. She probably attended the woman's wedding 30 years ago and complained about the food. Cia would investigate and report back, and mother and daughter would attempt an uncomplicated conversation.

Her mother's page did not make sense. There was a profile labeled *extremely high*, meaning it was a close relative. *I need to focus*, thought Cia. The sun's rays streamed through the window and caused a glare. *That must be it, I'll close the blinds.* Cia returned to her desk, sat down, and with her shoulders back, stared at the screen . . .

"Holy shit!" she said aloud. "They share 1900 centimorgans; DNA doesn't lie. Who was this match? I need to research this at home, not at work—too many interruptions. Jacob will help me."

Cia clicked off the Ancestry page, closed the computer and went back to dusting.

***

"Okay, Cia mia," said Jacob, "Now that it's a new day, are you ready to find out if you're related to Mussolini? Maybe *Il Duce* left you his fortune; I bet he owned a bronze of Marcus Aurelius or Mercury. I know he commissioned bronzes of himself. Let's outline what we know. The Ancestry chart dictates that if your mother has 1900 centimorgans in common with this DNA match, then the match is Sophia's grandmother, aunt or half sister. Sophia is 64, so this woman, using the code name *Nevada3,* is not her grandmother; that leaves aunt or half sister. She could be an aunt, but half sister is more likely. Was there an affair or a former marriage? I worked with a woman who found out at 50 that she had a half brother. After both her parents died, her aunt told her that her father had been married before and had had a child with his first wife. She was never told about the brother or her father's previous marriage. I guess that saying is true—all families have their secrets. You are also related to *Nevada3*; but not as close a match as your mother."

"I know," said Cia. "I'll send this woman an inquiry on Ancestry's message board."

***

Dear Nevada3,

I am Cia Crispo. I manage my mother's Ancestry page. She uses her full real name, Sophia Trotta. Ancestry has matched you and my mother as close relatives. According to its findings, the two of you share an extremely high DNA connection. Family names are Borgia and Trotta. I am excited to learn more.

Sincerely,

Cia Crispo

***

"Now we wait," she said. Jacob put his arm around her.

"Cia, you seem calmer now. Please consider that Sophia may not know about this person. To be candid, she isn't the type to hold back. I think you should talk to your brother; maybe Nicholas could supply some insight."

"If I go in to see him my mother will get involved," she said.

Jacob held up his hand. "Let me handle that. I'll tell him I picked up a collection that included some old textbooks. I'll ask him to drive out here to see them. Trust me; I'll set it up. Once he's out here we'll clue him in on the latest Sophia chronicles. By the way, I loved the way you wrote to *Nevada3* that you were *excited* to learn more."

Cia pulled back her hair, twisted it into a tangled ponytail, stared at Jacob . . . and said, "I know this amuses you; I bet I'm related to the Addams Family. It all makes sense to me now. Morticia cuts the heads off roses; my mother cuts the blooms off basil plants. And my aunts have worn black for 40 years. I can't wait to meet Cousin Itt."

***

The truck was filled with lamps, vases, and small tables. Jacob was dropping off antiques to a client in Westchester County. It was a crisp, clear autumn morning, and the drive north offered him a chance to take in foliage that was more vibrant than what Long Island had to offer. Driving by himself allowed him the opportunity to speak to Nicholas without the risk of Cia overhearing him. He reached Nicholas on his office phone and lured him to his house with the promise of rare books for sale.

"Okay Nicholas, I see my exit coming up; I'll speak with you soon. Goodbye." He parked his truck and surveyed the quant, little town; it made him wish he had taken Cia with him. She would have loved walking along Main Street and stopping in at the bakery and stained glass shop. *Not my best plan after all.*

Cia spoke softly into her phone; she wanted her words to only reach Jacob's ears. Cia was not one of those passengers who spoke loudly and wanted everyone on the train to hear her. She needn't be concerned today; three seats ahead sat two college students who were preparing for a test. Their noisy Q & A session, sprinkled with obscenities, drowned out all other conversations. She was on her way to Manhattan to meet with an antique dealer who had parlor furniture for sale: a love seat, chairs, lamps and five small tables. Jacob was cautious when buying vintage furniture. "The price of reupholstering with quality fabric," he argued, "often wipes out any profit." So far his phone call hadn't mentioned the dealer, the furniture or the reupholstering. Cia imagined he was calling to caution her about the bottom line. Finally he said, "Don't commit to buying the furniture until we research the price of the finished product. I also want to check with the hotels to see what type of furniture clients are requesting." Cia felt a sting of annoyance; Jacob was questioning her business sense. She decided to change the subject.

"It's been three days and no response from *Nevada3*. I had Mom sign up to find new cousins. *Nevada3* probably did the same," said Cia, "but a close match like this—she must have some interest."

Jacob was not really listening to his wife. He was waiting for an opening to announce his parents' visit. He had practiced a casual comment, but it stuck in his throat. In the end, he cut her off mid -sentence and blurted out the words. "Cia, before you hang up, I have something to tell you. My parents are flying up for Thanksgiving. They said they miss us and they want to see the Macy's Thanksgiving Day parade. Their friends will be in

Arizona, so my parents can stay in their Manhattan apartment. I invited them here, but Mom said she didn't want to inconvenience us; plus she wants to visit the art museums."

"Okay" his wife said, "but you know how I feel about spending Thanksgiving in a restaurant. I need home-cooked food. I need to smell roasted turkey, and I need to be away from strangers. I'll cook. Mom can be a guest; I hate to see her so worn out by the end of the day. I'll ask Nicholas to invite his new girlfriend. I like this; I'll start making lists." She hung up and started planning the feast, making a preliminary list in her head.

The Long Island train arrived at Forest Hills, her favorite station. If she didn't know she was in Queens, she would imagine she was in Old World London. Stately Tudor homes lined the streets and the station itself was a piece of history—circa 1900. For years she had looked out at the station from her train window; then one day she just stood up and walked off the train. She forgot about her appointment and walked around the area. It transported her back to a time when her antiques would have been new purchases for the local homeowners. Yes, she missed her appointment; but she was proud of her rare moment of spontaneity.

It was odd that her in-laws would fly north at the end of November. Now that they were Floridians, they shunned any temperature below 60 degrees. She tensed when she remembered the real reason she sent away for Jacob's Ancestry kit. She had lied to her husband; she had told him it would be fun to research his

42

European roots. She suspected his DNA test would reveal he was adopted. He was different from his parents. Jacob was amicable and low-key; he preferred small backyard parties and beer. In contrast, his parents were the center of attention at every party; the more extravagant the event, the more they grabbed the spotlight. His parents were tall and thin; Jacob was neither. When Jacob's Ancestry results came back, there were no surprises; he was their child. She found it ironic that now her mother could be an adopted child. Her idea to have their DNA tested backfired. Come to think of it, her mother had been opposed to the whole idea. She pushed that out of her mind, and allowed herself to focus on her meeting with the dealer.

***

Nicholas spotted Jacob's car as he walked down the steps of the Hicksville Train Station. He opened the door and sat down; his upper body slouched. After an awkward silence, Nicholas spoke. "Thank you for picking me up. I don't know how these commuters do this all week; it's a job in itself. I spent the day at the New York Library; but I did take time out to walk over to Bryant Park and feed the pigeons. Nikola Tesla would feed the pigeons in Bryant Park. People say there is an energy force in the trees that sparks creative thought." Nicholas did not add that in his more metaphysical moments, he looked for Tesla's face in the crowd. Nicholas Crispo, 35, a published professor of Roman history—and also a believer in ghosts.

"No problem," said Jacob. "Before we walk in the door, I want to go over the surprise party. Can you come up with a Plan B? It's not ideal to have your mother at our home for Thanksgiving just two days before the party. The odds of a slip-up are high. Your mother is already upset that I invited your father's family; but your sister fought to have them at our wedding. Cia would be hurt, especially if Uncle Tony wasn't there to celebrate her day. Any ideas?"

Nicholas sat there silently . . . then spoke at a higher pitch, his hands waving in the air. "I've got it. I'll tell her my new girlfriend, Marion, would like to invite us to her apartment for Thanksgiving. My mother would not miss the opportunity to see her apartment and evaluate her culinary skills. At the last minute I'll say Marion's oven broke down and the three of us will go out to a Brooklyn restaurant."

"Sounds like a plan," said Jacob, as they pulled into the driveway.

Cia greeted her two men and they sat down to her brother's favorite meal: ravioli, meatballs, stuffed potatoes and cannoli. Jacob watched the sibling interaction. They were more at ease with each other when their visits did not include Sophia. This was obvious to Jacob but he never shared his observation with either of them, not his place. His guess was that the tension began in their childhood. They certainly looked alike with their dark thick hair and dark eyes; but Nicholas' thick glasses and quiet disposition

44

made him look like the serious professor that his students and the rest of humanity saw.

"I brought you here under false pretenses," said Cia, "I need to talk to you about mom's parents. You refused to have your DNA tested, so you don't know that there's a new family development. It appears that Mom has a half sister." Cia shared the DNA results with Nicholas. In true Nicholas style, he did not respond; instead he sat in silence. Next he wanted to see the Ancestry post himself. Her brother sat at the computer and requested privacy to study the DNA results. Cia acquiesced. Jacob suggested the two of them go for a walk; he said there was a full moon in the Long Island sky. Cia grabbed a sweater and was out the door before her husband.

They walked in silence. It was cold, but the chill, the full moon, and the smell of grass cut for the last time this season filled her senses and cleared her mind. Eventually, like two drones navigated by a single distant master, Jacob and Cia were drawn back to their house. They had walked for over an hour. Nicholas waited for them to take off their sweaters and sit by the fire; he then delivered the news like he was presenting a lecture on the effects of methane emissions.

"Mom does have a close match; a half sister makes the most sense. Here's the thing . . . only cousins related to Grandpa Carmine are also related to *Nevada3*. Add in that Mom and *Nevada3* share 1900 centimorgans, and you have a close match. Simply stating it . . . Grandpa Carmine would have some serious explaining to do to Grandma Rachel. The research points to Mom and *Nevada3* being half sisters. There's good news and bad news. The good news, Cia, is that Grandpa Carmine is our biological grandfather. The bad news is . . . how the hell are we going to tell Mom?"

Cia, for once, mimicked her brother's demeanor; she sat with her hands on her lap and stared. She tried to absorb the words that, on this day, had rocked her world. Like a small child trying to catch bubbles, Cia grasped for memories and DNA facts that would satisfy her confusion.

"*Nevada3* hasn't responded," were her only spoken words.

"Okay," said Nicholas. "We'll wait a little longer; then we have two options. We can look up the Trotta name in Nevada or use the Ancestry message board to write to people who are matched to Mom and *Nevada3*—new cousins we don't know."

Jacob began to speak in a hurried voice. "I think we should wait until after Christmas to break the news to Sophia. According to Cia, your mother had a strained relationship with her father; and she shouldn't process all this in the middle of the biggest family event of the year." Nicholas understood that Jacob wanted to protect the surprise party and in a larger frame, he wanted to protect Cia. He didn't want Sophia to go all Neapolitan Medieval at the birthday party. Nicholas asked for and received Cia's agreement that they wouldn't ruin their mother's life until after Christmas.

***

The party plans were taking shape. Jacob's mother orchestrated every minute detail and the responses were e-mailed to her. Mindy, Jacob's mother was a born event planner and her son gave her *carte blanche* with one exception: Sophia. His mother reminded him that it was her daughter's party and Sophia should have a prominent role. Sophia collaborated with the chef on all aspects of the menu. Jacob added the flower arrangements to Sophia's to-do list to keep her more involved. The party would be at his parents' favorite Manhattan restaurant, *Sammy's*. He had hired a singer and a piano player; and the restaurant owner, a good friend of his parents, had promised that Cia would not suspect a thing until she was ushered past the bar.

Cia was not suspicious because she was experiencing OCD meltdowns planning a Thanksgiving dinner for four. She had been disappointed that her mother and brother weren't joining them; but at least Sophia would not be in the kitchen for three days. It concerned Cia that each year the holidays took a greater toll on her mother.

***

The blended aroma of coffee and a roasting turkey greeted Jacob as he opened his eyes Thanksgiving morning. This was not a day to get in his wife's way. Between the pride she took in her cooking and her obsession with details, her kitchen rivaled the efficiency of the Kennedy Space Center. He walked into the kitchen, kissed her on the cheek and poured himself a cup of coffee, which he drank in his office.

It wasn't until his parents arrived that a festive tone took over the house. His mom, Mindy, looked beautiful and cold; and his father, Louis, said, "I can't wait to eat." At that point, Cia breezed out of the kitchen to greet her guests. Cia was no longer an overcharged android; she had transformed back into his lovely, cheerful wife. As they relaxed and enjoyed pre-dinner drinks, Jacob sat in silence and listened to his parents weave stories about the Thanksgiving Day parade. In reality, they had watched the parade on a flat screen TV in their friends' Upper East Side apartment. They went to great lengths to keep the story line accurate. They had come to New York to see the children and to go to the parade. It was obvious that they not only loved Cia; they loved her spirit. They were happy to be part of the conspiracy.

Jacob remembered that awkward dinner, with his parents, years ago when he and Cia were first engaged—when he announced that Cia would keep her last name, and not change her name to Greenman. The comment did not even register with them; they understood that strong-willed Cia would not change her name.

At five o'clock, the two couples sat down to their Thanksgiving feast. The preparations had gone off without a hitch.

That was classic Cia—nothing was ever left to chance. Antipasto, rigatoni, turkey, gravy, stuffing, potatoes, broccoli soufflé, homemade pies and anisette cookies were prepared with Sophia's recipes. Mindy and Louis complimented their daughter-in-law's efforts with each new course. Mindy was also a good cook; she loved to host dinner parties. She understood all the love and attention Jacob's wife had put into the meal. Cia had fretted for days to make this meal perfect.

Louis raised his glass of wine and said, "This has been a wonderful day; I'm blessed with a beautiful family. The meal was delicious, and of course I ate too much of everything. I will admit that I am even enjoying the cold weather. Mom and I would like to have you join us for dinner at Sammy's restaurant this Saturday." "We'd loved to join you," said Cia.

"Excellent," said Louis. "But we will need to make a late dinner reservation—8:30. Is that okay?"

"Its fine," said Cia.

Okay, my father sounded casual, thought Jacob. "Dad, since the weather meets with your approval, why don't the two of us take a walk? I remember as a little boy, the two of us would walk by the reservoir after our Thanksgiving dinner."

His father laughed as he stood up. "Good idea, Jacob. I can walk off some calories. Oh, and Cia, could you write down

Sophia's cookie recipe for Mindy? Once a year is not often enough to have those delicious cookies."

"My pleasure," said Cia. "That recipe is very old—it comes from her father, my Grandpa Carmine."

***

Out on their post-dinner walk, Jacob smiled at his father. "That was quite a performance in there; you and Mom seemed to be enjoying the conspiracy. I really appreciate that you traveled to the frozen tundra to be with us."

Louis shrugged and smiled. "We're looking forward to celebrating with you and Cia."

After a few minutes, Jacob dug his hands deep into his pockets and hesitantly announced, "Mom looks happy." Louis stared at his son but did not comment. Jacob was thankful for the noise level on Hempstead Turnpike; it made their silence less obvious. His father understood the implication in his son's words. He would not be vilified by his son. His wife accepted him as he was; and it was none of Jacob's business. They walked the rest of the way back to the house in silence.

***

Mindy and Sophia met at Sammy's restaurant at 3:30 the afternoon of the party to oversee the event planner's progress. There was no theme, no 30th decorations in sight. Purple was Cia's favorite color, so the napkins and flowers were a vibrant deep

50

purple. Mindy had to give it to her—Sophia could blend tulle, flowers and satin ribbon and make it all look festive and smart. The room was taking shape. Mindy liked Sophia; she accepted her unfiltered words because they were never mean-spirited. The two women, from two different cultures, respected each other; their friendship flowed easily. It didn't hurt that they lived on opposite ends of the east coast, and saw each other only twice a year. Mindy was also relieved that Sophia loved her son. "Sophia, I'm happy you took me up on my offer to dress at the apartment; it will save you a trip back to Brooklyn. Let's go, it's time to make ourselves ravishing."

***

"Cia," said Jacob, "you're wearing that black dress?"

Cia looked at her dress, then back at Jacob. "Yes, don't you approve?"

"You look beautiful." said Jacob. "It's just that my favorite color is blue and I'd love to see you in something besides black once in a while."

Cia looked in the mirror and adjusted her hair ever so slightly. "Well, not tonight. Besides, you know what my friends say. We're from New York; we're going to wear black until they come out with something darker. Besides, I wore blue Catholic school uniforms my entire childhood. To me blue is a prison color."

"Now," said Jacob, feigning anguish, "I have to think about you in your Catholic school uniform. Not fair."

Cia laughed. "Keep that dream alive; it's better than the harsh reality of me with braces and teenage acne. Come on. Let's go meet your folks." They locked the house and walked to the car.

Jacob knew he could not arrive before 8:30.The good news was that the midtown traffic was awful. He was nervous; but he was confident his mother would handle any loose ends. Jacob had suggested to Cia that they should plan a trip to Cape Cod to celebrate her thirtieth birthday by themselves. She liked the idea of a trip for just the two of them; he did not think she had any suspicions about what the night held for her.

It was a New York miracle. There was one parking space right outside the restaurant! *Who was responsible for this miracle, Mom or Sammy?* Cia and Jacob walked inside. The owner was a man of his word; nothing looked off. No one scurried to the back; waiters didn't send messages with their eyes. It was all good.

They walked to the back, turned a corner, and heard a thunderous roar: S U R P R I S E! Jacob studied her face carefully; she looked confused, even scared. Friends and family encircled her, competing for her attention. She kissed Jacob and said, "What do I do now?"

"Did you really think my parents went to the parade? You are gullible." He gave her a wink and a hug. Cia took a deep breath and prepared to make the rounds. Cia made it a point to seek out her mother first. Sophia kissed her, wished her a Happy Birthday and asked her daughter why she hadn't worn high heels. Cia moved on to greet the other guests and make attempts at small talk. Small talk that came so easily to others was a painful effort for her. It was an aspect of her personality that she had always kept to herself. *How should I present myself—light and airy? Should I gush with excitement or look humbled by the turnout? I don't know who the guests want me to be.*

Cia began to hug and kiss all the people who approached her. Hugs and kisses took the place of words. She had no words.

Jacob made a short speech. He thanked everyone for coming, and introduced the singer and piano player. The waiters began to circulate the appetizer trays. Cia heard her Uncle Tony's laughter. The shoes of her mid-sized heels marched to his side. She could find words with her Uncle Tony. Her own father had been quiet and cold. In contrast, her father's brother, Uncle Tony, was affectionate and happy. He was the family storyteller. He made everyone laugh.

She sat down next to him; after two glasses of wine, Cia confided in Uncle Tony about the Ancestry find. Uncle Tony leaned close to her and declared, "Well, if *Nevada3* has money, then she found herself a family." Maybe it was the wine. Maybe it was the music. Maybe it was the prospect of an impending catastrophe. Whatever it was, it made her hold on to her uncle's arm and laugh a deep, teary, throaty laugh. It was the release she needed. Uncle Tony did not need her to be charming and witty; she would not receive a failing grade from him.

Cia's eyes became riveted on her father's three sisters. The sisters stood near her mother, but purposely ignored her. Then they moved closer and stared at Sophia's large frame. Yes, she had gained weight. Sophia had tried to camouflage her curves; she was probably wearing two sets of spanks. No, on second thought, she was wearing a 1980s girdle, and at that very moment the bones of that woman-hating device were digging into her and leaving snake-like indentions in her flesh. Cia continued to watch the *three witches of East Flatbush*. The birthday girl had seen enough. She enlisted the aid of her brother; she simply told him, "Fix it." Nicholas elbowed his way past the sisters to his mother's side. In the next moment, Sophia, in the arms of her son, danced her way to the other side of the room.

Jacob also experienced familiar family drama. He watched as his father danced with an assortment of women. Louis whispered in their ears and rubbed their backs. Jacob noticed that the women, some of them married, smiled and blushed. He couldn't look at the old fool; he wanted to find his mother. She was at the gift table, her back to the dance floor. Jacob's mother kept herself busy to avoid the humiliation. She diverted her eyes from the stares of Louis' dance partners.

All through his childhood Jacob had heard the arguments and the slammed doors, followed by his mother's tears. Father, mother and son never discussed the betrayal. Jacob tried to keep it from Cia. The memories of Cia with the Ancestry DNA kit rushed back to him. He didn't know how to tell her that he probably had half siblings sprinkled all through the metro area. The results, fortunately, did not raise any inquiries.

Sophia's DNA results made him shiver; he knew that she would find a way to blame Cia for her new betrayal. Jacob secretly harbored an intense dislike for the woman. She tormented Cia. Early on she resented the attention her father gave to his granddaughter. Now Cia was a beautiful, independent woman with an adoring husband. *She's jealous of her own daughter. Now this DNA news, we'll have to put up with her meltdown.* Jacob forced himself to take measured steps out of the party room; he wanted to sprint. He reached the bar and with his elbows forcibly leaning on the bar, ordered a beer. When a party guest walked past him, he pointed to the sports channel to explain his stepping out of the party room. This night was important to Cia; he would get through it.

He glanced into the party room and saw his father dancing with yet another woman who was not his wife. *Why does she stay with that pig?* He gulped down his beer and looked for his own wife.

The last hour of the party was the best. The alcohol accomplished its goal: people loosened up and Uncle Tony performed for the inebriated guests. They urged him to tell more family stories, and he kept them entertained.

The party ended at two. Jacob drove the birthday girl home. They kissed each other goodnight and slept soundly. The next morning she called her mother and mother-in-law and thanked them for their participation. Then, for no special reason, she called Uncle Tony and told him she loved him. They promised to get together for Christmas. Cia hung up and went to the computer; Uncle Tony had encouraged her to check the Ancestry message board every day.

And there it was—a message from *Nevada3*.

"Happy Birthday to me."

CHAPTER FOUR
Naples, Italy
January-February1944

He was cold.

He was tired.

He was hungry.

Carmine couldn't wait for the workday to end. He wanted to hit his bed and not move; but hunger won out. The boys said the cook was making chicken tonight, and that was one of his favorite meals. He waited his turn on the chow line; then looked around for a place to sit. He hoped no one would strike up a conversation; he was not in the mood. The chicken tasted good; it wasn't burnt or cold. The cook served peas. He liked peas; they reminded him of home. When his mom made him *piselli* with onions, she added a little tomato sauce and grated cheese.

He had a plan: eat fast and get back to L.Q., no shower or letter writing tonight—just sleep. He tried to ignore the soldier at the back table; but it wasn't working and it added to his misery by giving him a headache. To make matters worse, the soldier had a southern drawl that was hitting Carmine's ears like a subway train screeching into the Canal Street station. The guy was trying to make the boys laugh with jokes about the food. It was working. He heard the laughter through his pounding head.

He was halfway through his meal when the soldier said something out loud and the soldiers around him laughed. The guy made the mistake of repeating his words. . .

"See these peas? I can get 20 minutes with a 15-year-old whore for a can of peas." Carmine just reacted; he didn't consider his next action. He stood up with his plate, walked quietly over to the asshole, and dumped his peas over the guy's head. Then he picked up the soldier's tray and dumped those peas over his head.

Carmine's only words to the guy were, "Go fuck yourself, cowboy." He walked out. No one said a word. No one was laughing. He sat on his bed and pushed all thoughts of his behavior out of his mind. Carmine made only one decision that night; he was going to get drunk.

***

The next morning Carmine had a hangover that was pushing down on his head. He imagined it could march down to his toes and torture him until the war ended or he died, whichever came first. At this moment in time, he thought he'd opt for dying. He hadn't felt this awful since his last malaria siege. "Just find some ripped up parachutes. There are enough of them landing on this

58

goddamn country to turn the hills snow white. Just find them," barked Carmine.

While his warehouse crew set to work, Carmine headed back to his desk to review the inventory. Even the slightest rustling of papers made his head pound. As he worked his way slowly and carefully through the inventory list, he heard footsteps. The steps were steady and light. They weren't coming from one of the boys in the warehouse; this was someone else. With a smile on his Irish face, the chaplain pulled up a chair next to Carmine.

"Good morning Father Carey, are you going to say mass in the warehouse? I can round up two altar boys for you; just hear their confessions first."

Father Carey smiled and put a sympathetic hand on Carmine's arm. "You look ragged this morning, Carmine. I hear there was a disturbance last night at chow; I thought you could use a friend." Sergeant Carmine Trotta stared down at his hands in silence, and a welcomed calmness washed over him. Was it the priest's collar or the word *friend* that touched him?

He began to whisper. "Father, I don't know if you can understand what I am going to tell you. Back home, most of the kids in my neighborhood were born in Brooklyn, but we loved our Italian culture. Our parents were Italian immigrants. It all changed the day Italy sided with Hitler. Then I saw myself as a proud American. Italy was the enemy and I would fight for the country of

59

my birth. But there was always an unspoken Italian pride somewhere in that mix.

"I know the Army looks upon the Italians as inferior beings. I did not imagine I would witness such disrespect in Europe. Who am I kidding? They believe the Italians are inferior to the French and even the Germans. Does that make any sense? These civilians did not ask to be bombed or to have their meager livelihoods disrupted. Even before the war, they were shunned by northern Italians. The *Mezzogiorno*, or southern Italians, were kept poor and uneducated. If my father hadn't immigrated to America, I would be one of these starving Neapolitan peasants.

"Father, have you ever noticed that back in America, most of the Italians you meet are from Naples or Sicily? Have you ever asked yourself why? The northerners had money; they had jobs and education. There was no reason to leave their beautiful homeland. The *Mezzogiorno* were starving; they wanted jobs and a better life. They were forced to leave all that was familiar and enter a strange new country. And Father, they loved their children just as much as the people in Milan."

"I'm sure that's true," said Father Carey.

Carmine gestured as he spoke. "I can handle the talk about the Fascists—hell, I agree with them; but the disrespect for the women puts me in a rage. These poor souls are trying to feed their families; they humiliate themselves to survive. They are not animals. The children are suffering; I see it as if it's my family being treated like scavengers. Father, in your next sermon, I want you to lash out at the use of young girls as pieces of trash. Will you give me your word?"

Now it was the priest's turn to stare in silence. When he spoke you could hear the uncertainty in his words. He was there to bring comfort; how could he comfort this soul?

"Carmine, you have every right to feel as you do; I cannot argue against the injustices that surround us. You were sent to this place because you have a skill the Army needs. You speak the language of these, poor, conquered people. It would be more to your liking to be deployed to the Pacific where the locals do not look like you; but that would not help the war effort. Speaking to the civilians, gathering information is crucial to getting the Italians to trust us. Carmine, most of the soldiers are decent young men who are far from home."

Carmine looked at the priest with a look that half said, *Are you kidding me?*

Father Carey took a deep breath. "Of course, there are those in need of God's grace; but Carmine, you need to control your temper. I will work on my sermons. Would you be surprised to hear that the captain sent me to see you? He will deal with that soldier. Trying to find God's grace is a tall order in wartime; but I

61

know you are a righteous man. The horror around you would not cut so deeply if you were not righteous."

"I try to do the right thing," whispered Carmine. "The war has forced me to bend a few rules; but I have lines I will not cross. My vows to my wife have taken a beating; but I'm a young man and I'm far from home." Father Carey touched his cross and opened his mouth to respond to Carmine's confession; but he remained silent. Instead, the priest scanned the warehouse and said, "There are enticing goods stored in this building; do not give in to temptation."

"I take what the boys need and I try to help the starving children and families that have nothing to eat. I never make a profit. And Father, so we're clear, I don't visit prostitutes."

"Carmine, I understand the temptations to break God's commandments are all around you; pray for the strength to remain in God's graces. Let me give you my blessing before I return to my office."

"Thank you, Father; I will pray not only for myself but for these poor civilians. They never cared about politics. They just want to feed their family and live in peace." Out of respect for the priest he stood and walked him to the door. He was calmer now; he went back to his inventory with razor sharp clarity.

***

Carmine was ravenous by noon. In the mess hall, he piled his tray high with food. He ate soggy frankfurters and limp French fries and imagined he was eating at Nathan's in Coney Island. The only component missing from his imagination was the smell of the sea air. His hangover had subsided and his morning talk with Father Carey had lifted his depression. After lunch, he went back to the warehouse and made some inquiries. The parachutes were coming his way. Whiskey, soap and chocolate were the commodities he traded for the parachutes. Everyone had their hand out; all of Naples was a trading post. Locals and soldiers tried to steer him to the black market, but he resisted. Bruno and his thugs preyed on their own people's misery. He hated them. In Carmine's way of thinking, if he bartered for damaged parachutes and fed the hungry children with warehouse supplies, he could hold his head high. If he sold supplies to the black market he was being dishonorable.

One good thing that was coming out of this mess was that he was beginning to gain the trust of the civilians. Was it his refusal to do business with the black market? Was it his reputation for feeding the children? Carmine saw that he was accepted and trusted, which led to loosened tongues. Tongues that spoke *the southern Italian dialect;* and when those words reached his ears he understood their meaning. A cloak and dagger spy? No, but he heard enough to satisfy Captain Wadsworth. There were whispers of Germans spotted in the northern hills and rumors of supplies being hijacked from the port.

The look of disdain that the captain had worn in Carmine's presence was now gone. The captain still didn't like Sergeant Trotta; but he admitted—only to himself—that the sergeant was getting the job done. Captain Wadsworth wasn't a fool. He knew his quartermaster was wheeling and dealing in the warehouse; but it wasn't out of hand, and his boys respected him. Now if Trotta could only control that goddamn temper.

Sunday morning Carmine and his boys went to mass. He owed it to Father Carey to fill up those empty seats. The priest was a good man and the only man on European soil he trusted. Carmine could confide in him, unburden his weaknesses, and confess his many sins without fear of betrayal or retribution. He realized that a confidant was the missing component in this sewer by the sea. He trusted his buddy, Jimmy Rizzo, but all letters were scrutinized by the censors—and censors didn't have a sense of humor. Only once did he break protocol. Back when he was training at Camp Gordon, Georgia, he asked a seaman to deliver a letter to Brooklyn. The seaman was heading for the New York port and he agreed to hand-deliver a letter to the Brooklyn store owned by Carmine's father-in-law. He should not have ignored censorship rules; but he wanted Rachel to know he was being shipped overseas. He was upset; he hoped that telling his wife would reduce his level of fear. Carmine needed a confidant.

As soon as mass ended, he packed the two parachutes and some food and drove to Tessa's house. He went alone; he left J.J. on base. When he took that sharp curve in the road, he looked for the skinny kid collecting twigs; but the road was empty. At the house with the sweet aromas, clean curtains, and chickens clucking, he accepted that he would rather be standing here than anywhere else on earth. The realization startled him. Tessa opened the door. *"Buongiorno,"* she said. She looked like an angel; and she was smiling at him—smiling at him! He greeted Nonno and offered him the salami Rachel had sent in her last package. Pina looked up at him like a young child waiting her turn. He presented her with a wartime prize: a small bag of sugar. At first she thought it was flour but then she noticed the granules and her face glowed.

"I will bake, I will bake," she said, as she danced with the sack of sugar held to her bosom. The parachutes he presented to Tessa. She thanked him and placed them on a clean rug. "Join us for our Sunday meal," Tessa and Nonno said in unison.

At the table, Tessa and Pina had begun to speak in Italian; but Nonno put an end to it. He wanted them to practice English. The war would end someday, and their ability to speak English would make their survival easier. Carmine casually mentioned the Sunday morning mass he had attended; he wanted to impress Tessa. Today the meal was meager—only pasta, no chicken. That infuriated him—but not because he felt slighted. He wanted them to have a bountiful feast every day of the week. He made a mental note to get them more food.

After the meal, he caught a break. Nonno apologized and excused himself, saying he needed to attend to chicken coop repairs. Pina was busying herself in the kitchen, pulling out baking pans and making the Neapolitan cookies.

Tessa spoke first; it seemed to him that she had rehearsed her words. She began, "The parachutes will bring in money and the money will help Nonno. I will sew beautiful undergarments for the ladies." She hesitated and then said, "Is there a way to get new parachutes?"

"Why do you need new parachutes?" asked Carmine. "A parachute has yards of fabric."

Tessa gestured toward the pile of parachute silk. "I can only use clean pieces of the ripped parachutes; it is impossible to wash silk and still make it look new. Sometimes it smells of war. If I had new yards of fabric, I could sew dresses—and women would pay well for them. If we had more money, Nonno could rest." Tessa looked down at the floor, embarrassed by her family's poverty.

If Carmine was in his right mind and not ruled by his male needs, he would have laughed at her. Instead he smiled and said, "I will bring them to you." Tessa ran to him and embraced him. Carmine embraced her but did not rush in for a kiss, not even on her cheek. He would wait until she was feeling more than gratitude.

They parted and stood back from each other; Tessa folded the parachute silk. Did he sense a spark of interest in him? Was his parents' homeland bringing him this happiness? He would dream tonight. Nonno was walking back to the house as Carmine walked out with his exchange of knitted socks and jarred peppers. They bid each other good day as they passed each other. When Carmine reached the jeep he whispered to himself, *Bella Napoli.*

On the way back to the camp, he recounted every moment he had spent with Tessa. He was so deep in thought that he almost drove past the twig boy. The boy was in the road where he had been last time. Carmine stopped the jeep and pulled off the road.

"What's your name?" The boy said his name was Giovanni. They spoke for 10 minutes and Carmine understood that Giovanni was on the lookout for salami. He told the boy all he could give him today was socks, peppers and some coins. Then he told the boy to be at this spot next Sunday at noon and he would have food for him. Carmine knew his mother would have wanted him to fatten up this scrawny kid.

***

That night, after chow, he called a meeting. The boys figured they were screwed; the sergeant never called a meeting. He said they needed to find new parachutes. They brainstormed: maybe

67

someone knew a paratrooper; maybe another quartermaster had one; what could be traded? It was finally J.J. who said what the others were thinking.

"Sergeant, you're a quartermaster. This is Naples—you can get anything on the black market." There it was, out in the open. Carmine stared straight ahead. He knew two things: he would not deal with the black market, and he would find a parachute even if he had to join a paratrooper unit and jump out of a goddamn plane himself.

He looked at his men. "I want to get this done and I need your help." They knew they would turn over every bush and Mount Vesuvius lava rock to find what their sergeant needed. J. J., Mac, and Fish were keenly aware of the importance of this mission; and they knew that they would be quartered in hell if they failed. They respected the sergeant; but they knew he would ride their asses and makes their lives even more miserable if they didn't come through.

All week Carmine squirreled away extra supplies for Tessa and Giovanni. When he checked in a large quantity of the same food in the warehouse, he moved a portion of the food to a designated corner. The food in that corner space would be delivered to Tessa and Giovanni. Carmine's generosity also extended to the children who gathered outside the warehouse. He offered them food out in the open. His rationale was that by feeding the children he would gain the trust of their parents; in return, the parents would pass along information. But the truth was that he simply wanted to feed the children. The realization that the children would be hungry again when he moved north to Rome saddened him.

***

The next night Carmine ate sparingly; the pork chops tasted like rubber and he imagined if he closed his eyes he would not be able to distinguish the pork chops from the carrots. He dumped most of the chow and went back to his quarters. He found a can of sardines his wife had sent him; that would be his dinner. The sardines ignited thoughts of his wife waiting for him back home.

Before they married, Carmine had never held down a job that paid a weekly wage. His father did side jobs for people in the neighborhood, and Carmine was his assistant. Once he married, Rachel's family brought him into their produce business. Her family owned a fruit and vegetable market and hired Carmine to wait on the customers. Rachel said he had no people skills; he gave customers one-word answers and shrugged his shoulders. His father-in-law finally relegated him to loading and unloading the produce trucks. When the draft board had asked about his employment, he wrote *store clerk*.

That was his ticket out of combat; a lucky break. He went to Camp Gordon Georgia for training; then shipped overseas to North Africa. He was a warehouseman in Algiers; but in reality he was useless to the war effort. Shortly after he arrived he contracted malaria and spent more time in the hospital than in the warehouse.

Here he was now, trying to charm other sergeants into trading new parachutes for desired goods. He was not going to disappoint Tessa; he wanted her to think of him as a successful military officer. He would not walk away from her. Each night, he drilled the boys: What leads did they hunt down? They could no longer look him in the eye. Day after day, they came up empty. Carmine tried to remain optimistic.

***

After two days of rain, the sun's rays followed Carmine to Sunday mass. After mass he prepared to head to Tessa's house. He drove north with J.J. Carmine knew that J.J. wanted to talk but was hesitant; Carmine would not help him unburden himself. *He'll tell me when he has the balls.* J.J. finally got up the nerve to say what was on his mind. J.J. took a deep breath and forged ahead.

"Sergeant, I know you will not get involved with the black market; but would you object to helping the boys find a night of true love? There is a place, you know—a *signorina casa*—the boys would like to visit the prostitutes there. The black market runs the place and all they're asking for is some beer. Hell, we can get plenty of beer."

Carmine pulled off the road and brought the jeep to an abrupt stop. He turned to face J.J. "J.J., do you want to walk back to the base?" J.J. tensed and sat mutely in his seat. He shook his head *no*. "No, J.J., I will not help you, Fish or Mac; and when was the last time you saw a V.D. film? I will not deal with these men; they treat the local prostitutes like dirty rags. These men are scum with no souls. You want to visit a prostitute? Not here. Wait until we reach Rome; disrespect the Romans. The Romans look down their noses at the Neapolitans, our people. I understand that soldiers need to visit prostitutes; but I don't want you to visit the young prostitutes around here. J.J., these hungry girls speak the same dialect that our mothers speak even today! Maybe it makes no sense to you; but that's where I stand. One more thing, these black market men will not let it go; they will keep setting traps for all of us. You watch yourself." J.J. gave a jerky nod and kept his eyes facing forward.

Carmine was proud of how he handled J.J.; he knew J.J. was just a lonely kid looking for comfort. And J.J. understood that the topic was closed. Maybe the priest was getting through to Carmine. He had walked out of mass less than an hour ago; he could still taste the communion wafer on his tongue.

J.J. was relieved to see the boy on the road; he would be a welcome distraction from his sergeant's wrath. Giovanni was waiting, this time with a smile on his dirty face. Carmine was also smiling when he noticed the multi-colored socks on Giovanni's feet. Tessa only had small scraps of yarn, so she knitted socks using remnants in many colors. Hell, Carmine slept in the pretty socks and he didn't give a damn what color they were; they were warm.

They pulled the jeep to the side of the road. "Giovanni, I brought you many surprises," said Carmine. As he turned to get the supplies, he stopped and looked back at the boy. "Today you will go for a ride." Giovanni's face opened in a wide smile as he hopped into the back of the jeep.

When they reached Tessa's house, Giovanni desperately wanted to make himself useful. He gathered the supplies high in his arms and struggled to walk toward Tessa's door. J.J. came to his rescue and took some of the boxes that were teetering perilously in Giovanni's stack. If Tessa was surprised to see three visitors, she gave no indication; she waved and held the door for them. Carmine glanced over at Tessa and said he would need a little more time to locate the parachutes; but in the meantime, he hoped she would be happy with the supplies he'd been able to get for her, Pina, and Nonno.

As Giovanni set the boxes down on the kitchen floor, his eyes lingered over each parcel of food; he hoped he would be offered something to eat. Carmine had brought with him: chocolate, flour, pork chops, sugar, sausage, and cans of shrimp and sardines. Giovanni was in luck; as if it were an afterthought, Tessa instructed Pina to get down two extra plates, one more wine glass plus a water glass for the boy. Giovanni smiled to himself.

Tessa busied herself with the meal preparation and storing the treasures Carmine had brought with him. He could invite anyone to dinner at Nonno's house; after all, he supplied the food. J.J. has had dinner with them before, but not the boy. Carmine has a good heart; she had heard the church ladies say he feeds the children. Tessa was humming as she worked in the kitchen.

Before they sat down, Tessa took Giovanni to the sink to have him wash his hands and face. As before, they bowed their heads and offered a prayer. Carmine noticed that Giovanni did not pray; he filed that observation away to ponder later. The prized entrée was pork chops, compliments of the U.S. Army. Tessa served the pork chops with mushrooms and spaghetti; it was as good as any Sunday meal Carmine's mother served back home. Giovanni ate like this would be his only opportunity to eat for a long time; Pina had to slow him down.

If anyone took the time to notice, something had come over Carmine. He had boldly sat himself next to Tessa just before the Sunday prayer began. Carmine reached under the table and held her hand. She squeezed it tightly and did not let go until she served Giovanni more spaghetti. Carmine would not be standing up anytime soon; his manhood was on display. He avoided looking directly at Tessa and this lack of attention did not escape J.J.'s scrutiny. After dinner, Carmine walked out to the chicken coops with Nonno; Giovanni stayed at the kitchen table, relishing a rare treat of chocolate. "Nonno," said Carmine, "what can you tell me about this boy?"

Nonno shrugged and said, "He lives by the old church with a big family; but he is not one of them. He was not there before the war. Maybe he is a cousin who no longer has a home?"

Carmine took a deep breath and asked, "If I supply his food and clothing, would you keep him here with you? He could help you with chores, and I think he would like tending the chickens. Would that family agree to give him up?"

Nonno smirked. "Of course they would agree to have one less mouth to feed. I will have him here with me; I think he would be a good companion for Pina; and I would like a boy to help me. Yes, it will be good and a blessing." They turned to head back into the house.

Nonno talked to Tessa and Pina and they gave Carmine their approval. Now it was Carmine's turn to talk to Giovanni. The two walked outside and sat in the jeep. Carmine laid out the plan and waited for the boy's response; it was not the response he anticipated. Giovanni cried; he made deep mournful sounds that touched Carmine's soul. Carmine fought back his own tears. The boy eagerly accepted the offer. He said there was no need to tell the others; they would not look for him.

Giovanni asked him one question. "Will you come back and visit me here?"

"Yes," said Carmine. "I must check to see how good a worker you are; and I will begin to teach you the American language." He covered the boy with a blanket and ushered him back inside. Carmine wished he could stay here, mend the chicken coops and live with Tessa. It was going to be a bittersweet drive back to L.Q.

***

Carmine waited until it was lights out before savoring the events of the day. Tessa had squeezed his hand. He would have to say something next time; she had given him a signal. Did she know he was married? He pushed that question out of his mind; tonight was for him and Tessa. Maybe God was thanking him for helping the boy. Carmine wanted to be the best man he could for her. Damn it, he had to get parachutes. Maybe someday he and Tessa would be married and she would wear a parachute gown. He closed his eyes and relived the day's pleasures.

Monday came and went with the same disappointment as last week—no parachutes. He was going to have to make the ripped ones pass the smell test. Maybe some of them landed in a field of lilacs. He finally said to the guy on the phone, "Just tell me your price; I'll pay it."

At the end of the day he took out a cigarette, lit up, and headed back to L.Q. The good mood that had followed him from Nonno's house yesterday suddenly evaporated. Bruno Falco was waiting for him outside the L.Q. like a predator ready to pounce. "Hello Carmine," he said.

"What the hell do you want?" snapped Carmine.

A practiced smile spread across Bruno's face. "I want to help you. I hear you are in need of virgin parachutes. Virgins are a rare commodity."

Carmine didn't appreciate the double meaning. "I'll repeat my question, Bruno: what the hell do you want?"

"I want us to both get what we want," said Bruno. "You want parachutes; and I have a list of what you can get for me. Our deals can be more than just trade for parachutes; I will pay you in American dollars for the things I need. You can go back to America a rich man."

"Sorry Bruno, my soul is not for sale."

"I have no need for a soul," said Bruno. "You get me what I need and I will get you so many parachutes you can sail the sky until the war ends."

"No dice. And stay out of my business."

"Carmine Trotta from Cervinara, don't you know you *are* my business?" Carmine glared at Bruno, made a half circle around him, and walked away.

He had another unpleasant surprise when he walked into L.Q. Otter was there playing cards with the boys.

"Hello Otter, what are you doing here?"

"The Army moves me around, and I was near here," said Otter. "I figured I'd stop in for a friendly game of poker. In some towns, we give the civilians a dollar a pot and they let us use their kitchen to play cards. They even sell us wine; we play all night and nobody bothers us."

Carmine shook his head. "Well, take your card game there tonight. I'm going for some chow; you be gone by the time I get back." As much as he disliked Otter, he did give him an idea. He would talk to Nonno on Sunday.

The quartermaster had no time to pursue his quest for parachutes. The Army was keeping him very busy. Supplies were being shipped in everyday and they had to be unloaded, inventoried, and stored. The captain guessed that something big was going to happen soon.

Carmine put everything aside and concentrated on getting the supplies out to the troops. The soldiers were depending on him. There were long hours and little sleep; every muscle in his body ached. He worked through Sunday, but he had Monday off. After breakfast, he was exhausted, but he missed Tessa and Giovanni. He made up his mind to drive out to their house.

Giovanni opened the door; he looked like a million bucks. His hair was cut, he had color in his cheeks, and he was wearing clean clothes that Tessa had gotten from a woman in exchange for eggs. Nonno greeted him and apologized for not staying. He said he and the boy had to help a neighbor patch a roof. Pina was out delivering eggs to the neighbors.

Carmine did not work out a strategy; he moved up to Tessa and kissed her, hard. Tessa kissed him back and pulled him closer. Carmine's head was spinning; he picked her up and carried her in a movement that resembled a waltz. These were not the moves of the stoic Carmine. He had never been this happy in his life; and his happiest moments were here in a war zone. They kissed again.

"Will you spend time alone with me?" he asked.

"Yes," she said, without hesitation. "But what will we say?"

"The woman who sells the boys pasta meals at the Red Cross has French ribbon to sell; I will take you to see her. Then I know a soldier who will give us privacy in his girlfriend's house. Will you be with me?" He looked at her with hope and desire in his eyes.

She answered quickly. "Yes, Carmine, I will be with you. But you are from New York; you like fancy women."

Carmine smiled and drew her closer. "You *are* my fancy woman; no one has your beauty. Now I need to move away from you or Nonno will see what I am feeling." He reluctantly let her go and turned toward the door.

Carmine walked to the jeep and unloaded a ham, flour, chocolate, and a jar of honey. For Giovanni he brought Army socks, a toothbrush and a sweater, plus a small gift. Mac liked to carve animals out of pieces of wood. Carmine had convinced him to donate his carved bear to the kid. "He's ten years old; he should have a toy," Carmine had argued. Mac caved in and gave him the bear.

When Nonno and the boy came home, Carmine handed Giovanni the wooden bear wrapped in brown paper. He rocked back and forth as he held it, then ran to Carmine and hugged him, shouting, "Grazie!"

"*Thank you*, say *thank you*," said Carmine, smiling. Nonno looked younger now that he had an apprentice; it was obvious that the two of them were forming a bond.

Carmine took Nonno aside and told him, "There is a way for you to make extra money that would not take your energy. The soldiers could have card games at your table. They will chip in one dollar for each pot. I will make sure they behave, and they will bring their own food. What do you think?"

Nonno was conflicted. "I have heard of other families having card games; they say the soldiers get drunk. I don't want drunks in my house; I have granddaughters to protect. I will have them in my house only if you come, and I will not allow alcohol. What do *you* think?" Nonno asked.

Carmine knew he would have to sell the soldiers on the alcohol-free zone, but he would get them to agree. "Okay," he said. "And I have more good news. I have found a woman who has French ribbon to sell; I will take Tessa to her on my next day off. Also, I must ask you, is the boy a help to you?"

Nonno smiled. "He is a good boy and very smart. I do not ask him about his parents; maybe one day. God has given me a son: he is a blessing in my old age."

Carmine clapped Nonno warmly on the shoulder. "I'm glad," he said. He made his goodbyes and promised to return on Sunday, casually mentioning to Tessa that he would take her on Sunday to see the ribbon.

He had kissed Tessa. Yes, he had kissed Tessa. He tried to convince himself that it had actually happened.

Tuesday was another busy day at the warehouse; the shipments just kept coming. He read *Stars and Stripes* for some hint of what was in store, but there was nothing he could find. There was an announcement that Bing Crosby would be coming to Italy to entertain the troops. Very nice; but he hadn't seen one entertainer since he'd been drafted. Rachel would write him with news of big stars entertaining the troops in Italy. *Well, where the hell are they?* Maybe when he's in Rome, he'll see a movie star. The only star he really wanted to see was Marlene Dietrich—yes, that would be swell.

Whenever the captain was out of the warehouse, Carmine continued his search for flying silk; but always, he came up empty handed. At the moment, he was putting together a deal for two hams. A guy wanted two bottles of scotch in trade for the hams. J.J. could negotiate a better deal; he had a way of getting supply clerks to like him. "If they liked you, they'd be more willing to call around and help you make a trade deal," J.J. told him. Still, even J.J. couldn't get new parachutes .Carmine knew he couldn't put Tessa off much longer. On Friday, Bruno approached him with the news that he had found a parachute.

"I'm listening," said Carmine.

Chapter Five
Naples, Italy
February/March 1944

"I need fuel."

"Not unless you pour it on your whorehouse."

"Why do you speak to me with such anger?" Bruno asked.

Carmine looked to see if there were soldiers close by before he continued. "I'll get the girls out of the house. You pour the fuel, and I'll light the match. That is the only way I will get you fuel. But the truth is, I don't supply fuel."

Bruno looked past Carmine. His muscles were tight and his face red. When he spoke, his words were deliberate and strained. "Sergeant Trotta, look around you. The Americans have bombed us without mercy; do you think I am so different from you? I need to eat; I need to survive. Look at what they have done to my ancestors' land. I will not go back to poverty. I do not have the luxury of being a good Christian; but I am not the only one here with sin on his soul. Let me ask you why you want the new parachutes? Is it to send back to your wife in Brooklyn or is it for the egg man's daughter?"

Carmine's first urge was to slam his fist into Bruno's face; but he kept his hands deep into his pockets and said, "Get out of my sight." Bruno shrugged and headed off.

Carmine walked to the warehouse and started his paperwork, but his concentration was off. At first he blamed it on Bruno, but then he began to sweat. He knew the symptoms. He went to the dispensary; they immediately checked him into the hospital.

***

Naples, Italy

February 1944

Dear Rachel,

Well darling, I'm in the hospital; the malaria is back. Boys from Brooklyn don't get malaria in North Africa. We can thank the Germans for this. It looks like I may be here for awhile. They are trying to cure me of this damn disease. The doctor acts like it's my fault for not taking the quinine pills. I just can't take them anymore; they make my head swim. Truthfully, honey, I was only feeling sick the first day outside of being a little weak. I needed a rest.

You asked about the food in Naples. If it was peacetime and the people could farm

83

and fish, the food would be as good as what our mothers make. People here are poor and food is scarce, but they do their best. The Army has food—we're never hungry. Sometimes local women sell us food, mostly pasta. The hospital food is better than at the mess tent—at least it's hot. And the coffee is good.

I broke out in fever blisters so I couldn't shave. Now I have a mustache; but I am already tired of it. Did you get the orchid I sent you through the Army Exchange Service? I'm sorry you don't like the V-mail; I know they shrink the letters down. I don't have choices.

I'm glad you liked the picture of me and the boys. Save it—maybe someday we'll have a reunion and we'll all look young. There's really not much to do here, so I play cards and write to everyone. Now I need to find an officer to censor the letters. Please send me more salami, not the small ones. I also like cans of stuff like sardines. Do you need points to buy them? There's a 10-year-old boy here who could use some warm clothes; maybe your neighbors could donate some?

Don't tell my mother I'm in the hospital.

Well, I'm feeling tired, so I'll just sign off for now.

All my love, your husband,

Carmine

***

It was fine with him when the boys showed up at the hospital in the middle of his poker game; he had lost 18 dollars. He didn't bother introducing his boys to the three wounded soldiers; he didn't see the point. He finished his hand and walked back to his clean bed. "Fish, is that what I think it is?" Carmine saw the package in Fish's hand.

"Yes, Sergeant, its Suzanne's maple cake all the way from Proctor, Vermont."

Carmine smiled. "Fish, you better marry that girl when you get back home. So what have I missed?"

They looked at each other. No one spoke. "Now we're getting to the real reason for the visit. What's going on?"

It was J.J.'s words that rushed out at him. "There are a lot of supplies missing from the warehouse. We got a large shipment of warm clothes, including the heavy jackets the captain requested.

They're gone. The shipment arrived at the Bagnoli depot just three days ago. We trucked it all to the warehouse within 24 hours; the supplies are already gone. Wadsworth is on the warpath. He started an investigation. We wanted you to know before you had a visit from him."

Carmine's face remained statue-stiff. "Thank you. Keep me updated."

The hospital needed some of Carmine's blood, so the boys took off, leaving him the cake. He felt obligated to flirt with the nurse as she siphoned his blood. Next, he opened the cake from Proctor, Vermont and shared it with soldiers on his floor. He knew Bruno was behind the missing supplies; and he was confident his boys were not involved. The captain's bald head probably exploded like a land mine. Carmine smirked; he was glad he was here and not there.

After 10 days, his test results came back negative and he walked out of the hospital. The rancid Naples air engulfed his face like a filthy sack tied too tightly around his head. He already needed a shower. He had been in a clean environment for over a week; now the familiar foul smells returned.

Over the next few days he had three visitors to the warehouse: Nonno, Captain Wadsworth, and Bruno—who loitered by the entrance. Nonno brought him hard boiled eggs, a loaf of Pina's bread, and thick socks knitted by Tessa. Captain Wadsworth's visit was less compassionate, but not too bad.

"Are you taking your quinine pills?" he asked. "I spoke with the dispensary and the doctors. I need you right here—not between clean sheets with hospital corners. I am not blaming you for the black market theft. I think it is in your favor that they waited for you to be out of commission before the rats moved in. I will get to the bottom of it on my own; your job is to get the supplies replaced."

***

Bruno was waiting for him as he left the warehouse. His pretense, of course, was concern for Carmine's health. Carmine was having none of it.

"I know your men stole the supplies—supplies the Army needs to win this war. Do you remember the war? Maybe you would like a return of the Germans and the black shirts? Get out of my face." Carmine glared at Bruno.

Bruno raised his hands in a gesture of offering. "Carmine Trotta I want to bring you what you call a compromise. If you want new parachutes, I will trade them for good whiskey. You cannot say I am an enemy of the Americans; the soldiers are stronger without whiskey."

Carmine was speechless. He wanted to walk away from this pig, but he wanted to please Tessa even more. The words came out of his mouth as though they were spoken by his shadow. "Okay, Bruno, I will do your deal. I can't get fuel anyway, but I can get whiskey. There is one thing I want besides the parachutes. There is a boy living with the egg man; he needs good shoes. When I see the shoes on his feet then I will know you are serious."

"That is no problem," said Bruno. "The boy will have his shoes." The two men stood there awkwardly, not knowing what else to add. It was Carmine who nodded first, then Bruno. There were no more words needed; they turned and walked in opposite directions.

***

There were still no new parachutes. The sergeant called another meeting. His men steeled themselves around the stove and waited for his words. "I am no longer looking for new parachutes; the old ones will do. The push now is for bottles of scotch. We must be careful, though. Captain Wadsworth keeps a close eye on the inventory. We can wheel and deal; just be careful and cover your tracks." Carmine could feel his men's gaze bore into him. As uncomfortable with himself as he was with them in that moment, he pushed open the door and headed back to the warehouse.

J.J. might still be a virgin, but he wasn't a stupid virgin. He knew that the sergeant had made an unholy alliance with the black market. He looked over at Mac and Fish; they were stone-faced.

***

88

It had been three weeks since Carmine had driven out to Nonno's house. On Sunday morning, he went to mass and then packed up his gifts—compliments of the United States Army—and headed out. Giovanni looked like he had grown taller in that short time. He ran to the jeep and helped unload the food. First on his agenda was to check Giovanni's feet. The boy was wearing what looked like top-quality Italian leather shoes. *Bruno could requisition the crown jewels from the Tower of London,* Carmine thought. He sighed; he knew he could no longer turn back. As the saying goes, he was *sleeping with the enemy.*

Tessa was in the doorway, her cheeks flushed. Was she anticipating the arrival of a new parachute? She would soon be disappointed. Dinner would need to wait until the pork roast was cooked; it had just arrived with Carmine. Nonno used the time to confer with his American guest. "If you think the card games will make money for us, then how can I refuse? But no alcohol, and you must be here. I will not have my granddaughters left alone with soldiers. I am an old man I can no longer fight off young men."

The last thing Carmine wanted to do was to chaperone a card game, but he agreed to the conditions. Nonno was a proud man; this was a means of earning American dollars. In the near future, Nonno could repair his barn and build new chicken coops.

Carmine turned the conversation to Giovanni. "Giovanni looks like he has a full stomach; is he any trouble?" Carmine asked.

89

Nonno shook his head. "No trouble, every day I love him more. His dialect is from the north. He is very smart: he can count, read and write—but he doesn't know his prayers. Tessa and Pina teach him. He still has not mentioned his parents. It is also peculiar that he shrugs when I ask him his last name. But I don't push him. He seems happy here. I should have rescued him before you asked.

"Now Giovanni is the rescuer; he found a cat. He found it the day Bruno presented him with his new shoes, so he named the cat *Bruno*."

Carmine was curious about how Bruno held up his part of the bargain. "Nonno, tell me about his shoes."

"Bruno came alone, at first I thought he wanted to take my chickens," said Nonno. "He was kind; he tried different shoes on Giovanni. The child liked him. Bruno asked if he should call me Mario or Nonno; I said Nonno, since that is how the American soldiers greet me. Then he left. Carmine I think you paid him a lot for the shoes."

"Yes, I did." Nonno gave Carmine a questioning look, but Carmine had nothing more to say about the shoes.

**

At dinner time, Carmine took in the portrait before him: four family members busy with their work, all with contentment on their faces and food in their stomachs. Tessa gave him a

90

conspiratorial nod but nothing more. They all took their places at the table, and once more he noticed that the boy did not pray.

Carmine cleared his throat and tried to sound casual in Nonno's presence. "Tessa, that woman has agreed to sell her ribbon; I will take you there next Sunday." Before Tessa could answer, Pina interrupted. "Tessa has made beautiful garments for the ladies; the ribbon will be used for drawstrings and straps. Last week a woman came to our door to ask about our work; she had heard of our silks." Tessa and Nonno encouraged Pina to continue. "The church will have First Communion in the spring; the girls will need communion dresses. Tessa will sew the dresses and I will make the veils."

After dinner Carmine petted the cat and gave one universal good-bye to the family. On his drive back to camp, all he could think of was Tessa.

***

"I have been called a rat but never a cat," Bruno said with a rare smile. "That boy is in my heart. He is a good boy; you tell me what gift I can deliver to him."

"Okay," said Carmine. "I'll think of something. Let us talk about parachutes now. What is your price? Remember: I am a quartermaster, not General Eisenhower."

"Five unopened bottles of good scotch will work," offered Bruno.

Carmine scoffed. "I cannot and will not do that; come up with another number."

"Okay, Carmine—two cases of French wine."

Carmine winced. "When the Army marches into Paris that will be a ransom I can deliver—but not in Bella Napoli. Two bottles of scotch and that is my final offer."

Bruno accepted the offer.

Carmine was happy to have that settled. "Tell me where the parachute is; I can pick it up myself."

"That will be impossible" said Bruno. "It is still in the hands of the owner. But we will find a place to make the exchange."

Carmine was still thinking about Giovanni. "Bruno, Giovanni can use some books. He is smart. He can read and write. I think his parents were educated people; I don't understand why they did not teach him his prayers."

Bruno reacted with red-hot rage. He spoke through clenched teeth. "Never repeat that he does not know his prayers. Teach him *Padre Nostro and Ave Maria* and shut the fuck up." Bruno's vehement reaction took Carmine by surprise. He responded with equal, if silent, gruffness. Carmine placed a cigarette between his lips, lit it with his right hand and shook the match three times. Then he dropped the match and with exaggerated force ground it down with his boot. Without a word he walked back to L.Q.

Carmine had not said anything in response to Bruno's outburst. He reasoned that he was in Naples now, and superstition was a main staple. His Zia Nunciata wore a *curniciello* or horn around her neck to ward off the *malocchio*, the evil eye. Was Bruno fearful of some evil curse on the boy if he did not speak to God? He knew two things: he needed the parachutes; and he did not want *malocchio* to assail Giovanni. Bruno had been adamant that Carmine not speak of this to anyone.

***

The exchange was finalized. Bruno came alone, the heavy parachute held roughly in his arms. He examined the scotch and gave his approval. "I have brought you gifts: three cameos from Sorrento. The books I have delivered to the boy. It was a good thing I showed up when I did; the cat had run away. I helped the boy find him. My wife laughed when I told her I was out of breath from chasing a cat."

Carmine walked away feeling unclean. What had he done? What would the priest think of him? He pushed all of it out of his mind and examined the cameos. Bruno was shrewd; one for his wife, one for Tessa, and one for his mother. Bruno had tapped into every raw nerve in his body.

Now the challenge before him . . .Tessa had agreed to be in his bed. He was not the confident lover that his Italian good looks and strong body suggested; he never learned the art of lovemaking. He was awkward and rushed. His wife was a virgin on their wedding night. Rachel had sent him clues of her disappointment; after the wedding night she feigned poor health and looked for any excuse to avoid him. Since he entered the war he had been with women, but he did not care if they were satisfied. It was his relief that was important. Could he be the man Tessa desired? Maybe she was a virgin and would not expect Valentino. Now, when he thought of their private moments, his body did not respond. This would be a good time for a malaria episode; but he would risk humiliation to have her naked body near him.

***

"Look soldier, when you needed the chocolate and perfume to impress your *signorina*, who made your dreams come through? Now I want to take you up on your offer to use her home. It would just be between two and three on Sunday afternoon. You are not the only one who needs to shack up. To sweeten the deal, do you think she would like a pair of silk drawers?" That cinched their gentlemen's agreement.

He arranged to visit the ribbon woman with Tessa. He would pay her with American dollars; no looting the warehouse with this one. If they made a deal that would be good; but it was just a ruse to put Nonno off the scent. What did Nonno suspect? He would deal with that at a later time if he had to. At night his thoughts were filled with Sunday afternoon. How could he be over-the-moon excited and fearful at the same time?

If the priest was looking for Sergeant Trotta at services Sunday morning, he would be disappointed. Between the parachute from the black market and the shattered marital vows, Carmine opted for the coward's way out. He avoided the priest and got an early start out to Nonno's house. Giovanni waved and held the cat with the other hand. That stray hungry cat had given the boy an endless supply of love and affection. Carmine's attention was now focused on the boy's neck: he was wearing a crude wooden cross that hung from rough cord. Nonno approached and asked the boy to tell the women their guest had arrived.

Nonno spoke hurriedly while his eyes watched the door for the boy's return. Nonno repeated the words Bruno had said to him. "*I have given the boy a cross; he is to wear it every day. It is a piece of shit so no one will take it. A gold cross would last as long as it would take someone to reach his neck. Here is his baptismal certificate, dated 1934; I have given him your last name and I am the godfather. Make sure he learns to pray and you and your family are forbidden by me to talk about him to anyone except Carmine.*"

"Nonno," said Carmine, "What is this all about?" Nonno gave him an exaggerated shrug. His head flopped to one side, his shoulders raised as if controlled by a marionette master, and the palms of his hands faced the sky like the scales of justice. Carmine had seen this Italian gesture before. He saw it executed at the

Brooklyn docks more times than he cared to remember. Its meaning ranged from: *Who knows? I do not care!* to *What do you want from me?* Carmine shook his head and said, "Bruno should have married my Zia Nunciata; they could have consolidated their witchcraft and killed off Hitler."

The two men walked into the house; in their arms they cradled meat, cheese, and wine. Tessa blushed and averted her eyes; Pina was reading a Christian book to Giovanni. Carmine placed the parachute near Tessa's worktable and winked at her. "Tessa, we must go now, the woman did not allow much time for our visit, bring one of your small garments as a partial payment." Tessa found her coat and kissed Nonno on both cheeks.

***

They sat in silence in the jeep for the first 10 minutes of the trip; then Carmine made some small talk about the ribbon. "I should bargain over payment while you examine the quality of the ribbon. Do not give her reasons for the purchase, or she will pull back the ribbon and sew her own garments. The garment I asked you to bring is for a soldier's girlfriend." They talked about other things on their way—but not one word about their rendezvous.

There were introductions and the offer of caffè and biscotti. They declined. He could see that Tessa was pleased with the quality of the ribbon; this was an easy conquest for him. The woman wanted Camel cigarettes for the ribbon; but Carmine was adamant, "you can make your own bargain for American cigarettes." Carmine offered her five American dollars. She agreed and wrapped the ribbon in paper. They left.

The soldier met them at the designated spot, and Carmine handed over the silk drawers. If there was a girlfriend anywhere, Carmine did not see her. The soldier walked to the road and the couple entered the room. The room was not scandalous. He did not know what he had expected. It was not the room of a prostitute; it was the room of a young woman who was doing her best to get through this nightmare. There was a purple scarf draped over a lamp shade; dried—not fake—purple flowers filling three vases; and a picture of Saint Gennaro, patron saint of Naples, prominently displayed over the bed—along with the mandatory woven palm cross.

The room actually had a pleasant fragrance—a rare commodity in this rat hole. He surmised that she was a disillusioned 20-year-old who had hopes that the American soldier would carry her off to Teaneck, New Jersey, or a similar American town. Suddenly, the realization that they were alone struck them at the same time and they rushed to each other, laughing, talking, embracing and kissing in no particular order. He sat down on an overstuffed chair and pulled her onto his lap.

"Tessa tell me about you, I know nothing."

"There is not much you do not know. My parents are dead. I care for my Nonno, Pina and Giovanni. That is my life. You have given me two blessings: the joy of sewing beautiful clothes and the affection of you, my American soldier." She nuzzled her head into his neck.

Carmine would have no worries about his manhood cooperating; he was so hard he hurt. He planned to sweet talk her and then pull her into his arms and carry her to a bed with clean sheets. Instead he kissed her and clumsily began removing her dress; she was struggling to maintain her balance. He was then motionless. She was wearing a slip she had sewn with his silk and her grandmother's lace. It was beautiful; she was beautiful. With great care he removed the slip and saw the outline of her womanhood. He could have burst right there in this stranger's room. She delicately removed her bra and undergarment, all the time meeting his eyes.

She had larger, rounder breasts than he estimated and her mound of black curls glistened from moisture. In a New York minute he was out of his clothes and guiding her to their bed. He lowered his body on her; and the way her legs responded, he knew he was not her first. He slid down and kissed the inside of her thighs and rested his head; he wanted to be in this room with this woman in this position for the rest of his life. There was no war, no Brooklyn, no fear. He touched her mound and gently licked it; he prayed it would not be over at that moment. He moved his body up and slowly entered her; his head was exploding. Tessa was moaning softly and moved with his rhythm; he could hold off no longer. They lay together with uneven breath; neither willing to separate.

When some time had passed, he gently turned over and stood up. He found a wash basin and cleaned their union from his groin. She was wearing her slip when he returned to her. They were quiet; he offered her a cigarette—and to his surprise, she accepted. That was something else she had done before. They dressed not in silence; but in laughter. Tessa had been relieved that she had satisfied him.

She was not a virgin. That would have angered most Italian men; but she could not go back, could she? Her first was a boy she knew from school; he had begged her to give him her virginity; she was 16 and in love. Her second lover was a fisherman; she liked him and she liked lying in the boat with him. Today was different. She was no longer a girl; she was a desired woman. She knew Carmine had belonged to her for the last hour; he was not thinking of the war or of his wife in America. She had all his attention; she controlled him with her body. Tessa wanted him to take her to America. Nonno, Pina and Giovanni would join them in Brooklyn. She wondered if that could be more than just a dream.

They stripped the bed, left no sign of their presence, and closed the door behind them. The ride home was filled with conversation and laughter. He pulled the jeep over before they reached the house and handed her a gift. "I wanted you to have this today, to remember our first time together. Please wear it all the time. When I saw the cameo it reminded me of your smooth and perfectly etched face. She climbed on his lap and kissed him; he could feel her tears on his face. He walked her to the door; placed the ribbon package on the table and announced that he had just enough time to get back to the company. He walked outside into the raw February air and climbed into the jeep.

***

He would have time tonight to replay the joy of Tessa in his bed; he could relive it moment by moment. Tonight he had guard duty; he would have Tessa's image to push away the fear of the darkness. He thought about his buddy Jimmy Rizzo serving in Burma; when he had guard duty he had to worry about being carried off by tigers. *I don't know that kind of fear; I bet it's even worse than he lets on*, Carmine thought.

One good thing about guard duty was that he could sleep late the next morning. Monday at noon, the corporal informed him that Captain Wadsworth wanted him to report to his office. The captain was hunched over a frayed map of Italy when Carmine entered. "Good afternoon Sergeant Trotta. You look healthy again. The boys are pushing the Germans back; but they are not ready to give up. We will need to get supplies to the north, and I think your days in your ancestral province are numbered. You did good work and soon you will be moving toward Rome. I'm sending you north with four extra men; you will need more work horses to get the supplies to the soldiers. Hell, supplying the boys takes an army of men in itself. That's all for now." Carmine wanted to ask him for a timetable; but that was a stupid question. Captain Wadsworth was probably in the dark, too; even if he did hear something, he wouldn't be sharing it with his favorite *paisano*.

***

"All schedules for the card games will be approved by me; and no one is to bring alcohol. I don't want to see as much as one sorry-ass bottle of Ruppert's beer."

Mac protested, "But Sergeant, that will be a tall order with some of the other boys, especially the ones who have to travel."

Carmine shook his head. "It wasn't my idea. Nonno has been a friend to all of us and I want to help him; I would consider it a personal favor if you drummed up some business."

The first game was scheduled for the following Saturday afternoon. Carmine arrived early with two pizzas from the ribbon lady and four bottles of Coca Cola. Maybe that would quench their thirst. Besides J.J., Mac, and Fish, there were three other soldiers ready for the low stakes poker games. Carmine would not play; he reasoned he would spend the time with Giovanni. Tessa and Pina moved their sewing into the bedroom; only Nonno and Giovanni would be on-lookers.

There was a clean white sheet covering the table, with ashtrays set up by each place. Carmine said, "The house gets one dollar for each card game. There will be no alcohol, and I will collect all side arms at the beginning of the night. Anyone who causes trouble will be thrown out and refused entry to future games. Bring your own food if you think you might get hungry. Today there will be two pizzas from me. I was lucky to find a few bottles of Coca Cola; I'll get some glasses. Any questions?" The games began.

The sergeant sat down next to Giovanni, who was playing with a carved wooden dog that Mac had brought for him. Carmine handed the boy his own bottle of Coca Cola and a slice of pizza. The boy smiled when he touched the soda bottle and drank it down in a few large gulps. Then he belched loudly and everyone laughed. Giovanni eyed the package beside his American hero; he did not reach for it but his eyes remained transfixed. Carmine handed the boy the package. The boy tore it open and stared at two blank books. Carmine explained that they were stamp albums.

"Giovanni, my father sent you these stamp books all the way from America. Now each stamp I give you, I want you to write down all the information about it. I will show you what you should write. I am going to give you stamps from other countries too." Giovanni would have hugged him if the books, the wooden dog and the cat weren't dominating his hands. Carmine noticed that even the cat looked healthier now.

"Well you must be some horse's ass; where did you learn to play poker, in a schoolyard?" This was followed by the crashing sound of a chair hitting the floor. Carmine had the soldier by his neck in less than a minute. He made it clear that he did not give a rat's ass about the details. They would be respectful or leave. The sergeant made one discovery—the G.I. had alcohol on his breath; beer to be exact. This was a whole new set of problems. He could ban alcohol, but how could he stop them from drinking before they showed up?

He announced a new edict: "You will arrive here sober or find another game." It had a hollow ring even to Carmine. He took Nonno to the side and apologized. "I have my eye on that *pineapple*; his time here may be short-lived."

Nonno looked serious and asked, "What is this *pineapple;* he is a*ananas?"*

"Nonno, I don't know why the soldiers call men they don't like *pineapples*; even my friend in the Pacific calls men that name. Nonno, your granddaughters will be safe, you have my word; and I am keeping a watch over the money in the pot. You will have money for repairs, even a new roof."

When the games ended, Carmine handed the soldiers their side arms and they left. They probably hadn't been this sober since the general's visit three weeks earlier. Naples might be a pigsty, but when a general rolls into an Army camp, everything—including

103

the soldiers—needs to be in tip-top shape. Even the latrine was scrubbed down and smelled at least a little better. Nonno and Carmine cleaned up and counted the money: 27 American dollars—that was real money. Carmine took a look around; pleased with himself, he went back to camp.

Chapter Six
Naples, Italy
March/April 1944

If there was such a thing as a wartime routine, Carmine was living it. The routine fluctuated at times, but it was reliable enough that Carmine could try to make weekly plans. He had no illusions about the future; he would soon be headed north. If Hitler's army was to be defeated, the Allies had to push north from the Port of Naples all the way to the Rhine. *Hallo Deutschland.*

He was no fool; he saw the supplies arrive at the depot in Bagnoli. The soldiers were getting extra gear and the officers were usually huddled around maps. Carmine hoped it would be the beginning of the end. It would not be easy; the Germans were dug in. The Resistance reported their presence just north of Naples; that is why the boys never traveled anywhere without their weapons.

It was Sunday. He went to mass. Later, he packed up the jeep with sugar, flour, salami (compliments of Rachel), chocolate, and a ham. Rachel had also sent a package of clothes for Giovanni, including socks, pajamas, and underwear. Tucked away out of sight was the second new parachute for Tessa. Even Bruno was finding the silk difficult to "acquire"; Tessa, however, was not disappointed by the delay.

"Carmine," she had said, "I have yards of silk. I do not wish to sew dresses or wedding gowns; it is too much sewing and the women make impossible demands. The small garments take little time to sew and I have many customers. Also, most of the women are not fussy. They need to order again and again; the garments wear out."

Tessa no longer blushed when she spoke of such things. This was great news; the damaged parachutes would suffice, and soon he could cut his ties to Bruno and the black market. He still owed Bruno two bottles of scotch for this last new parachute in his jeep. Carmine had been empty-handed when Bruno delivered the parachute. He had told Bruno he needed a few more days to get the bottles. Bruno had trusted him; was he honored or ashamed?

Nonno's house looked less shabby; with the money from the card games he was able to make repairs. He was a proud man; now he could begin to regain his pride in his home.

Giovanni surprised him by speaking a complete English sentence: *"Uncle Carmine, I made you a toy."* He then handed Carmine a carved wooden animal. It was evident that it had been whittled by young hands, and he was hesitant to identify the animal. He thanked and hugged his newly labeled nephew and began to unload the jeep. With arms full, he walked through the door. *If this is war, then I have found a refuge.*

He greeted Nonno and urged the boy to open his package, also compliments of Rachel. Giovanni grabbed for the package and ripped the wrapper off. The scene reminded him of Christmas morning back in Brooklyn. Carmine loved this boy. Giovanni held up the clothes and thanked Carmine. Imagine a boy being excited to receive used pajamas, socks, and underwear! Carmine hadn't originally noticed that there were cowboys in big hats printed on the pajamas; Rachel's clothes had brought America to this beautiful child.

Pina and Tessa were huddled over a piece of silk. Tessa roughly snatched the fabric away and ordered Pina to rip out the last row of stitches. Pina, with her face tightly fixed, complied with her sister's demand. Carmine walked over to the women and spoke to Tessa. "I have brought your new parachute; we must leave now if you wish to buy the woman's pearl beads." She dutifully kissed Nonno, smiled weakly at Pina, and opened the door. Carmine helped her into the jeep.

"I have tiny pearl beads with me from the ribbon woman; this way you can show them to Nonno when you return. We can go straight to our hidden bedroom." Carmine glanced across at Tessa. "Pina was upset today; she almost always has a smile."

"Pina is not a child; she must improve her sewing if I am to sell her garments. She is no longer selling to Signora Russo; her stitches must be straighter. I promised her that if her work improves I will give her a beautiful silk garment to wear to the rosary club next Saturday." Tessa changed the subject. "Carmine, I have a garment with me for the soldier's girlfriend. This one she will like. It has purple lace; I think that is her favorite color."

Carmine nodded his approval. "That is a very nice thing for you to do."

When they reached the rendezvous point, the two men spoke a few words and then Carmine handed the other man the silk drawers. The soldier lit a cigarette as he left. Alone in the room, Carmine and Tessa undressed without any pretense of seduction. Naked, Tessa walked around the room touching the woman's possessions; then she sat at the side of the bed and waited.

She had picked up his cues. He wanted no talk, no embraces, and no foreplay. Carmine approached, laid her down and lowered his body on her. They fell into a rhythm; each body took what it needed. Then it was over. He stood up and dressed. She lay naked in the bed and smoked a cigarette. He desired her body and cared deeply for her; but he had heard enough soldiers' stories to know he failed to excite women. If he could be truthful, if only to himself, he would admit that his young body wanted only release, not romance.

Tessa felt satisfied. No, Carmine was not the fisherman who would make her scream out in beautiful agony; but he was her salvation. He would deliver her from chicken coops; she decided that their next time would be better. She would fake all the passion of an opera star; she would use her mouth to make him moan and then she would scream in ecstasy.

When they arrived back at the house, Carmine handed her the tiny pearl beads. Nonno came out and helped Tessa out of the jeep. "Nonno, I cannot stay; I need to get back. I want you to know that the Saturday card game will have 12 soldiers. Some are coming from a distance; if they are hungry, that is their problem; J. J. told them to bring food. I will come early and help you set up. They will arrive sober or they will get out. Try to find a second table; we will have two card games and you will collect double the dollars."

The old man said, "Okay." But his frown and lack of eye contact bothered Carmine. They said goodbye.

***

J.J. was pacing, pausing just to warm his hands by the stove. "It's his third meeting of the war; the sergeant has been in a foul mood for two days. I wish he'd *get a bag on* and try to forget where he is for a few hours. He wants us all here at twenty-one hundred hours." The other men shrugged their understanding. Having delivered Carmine's orders, J.J. headed over to the Red Cross for a beer.

The men were gathered around the stove at the appointed time. Carmine laid out the ground rules for the card game. "Only two of you at a time will play cards; one at each table. The third one will be with me; we'll be the peacekeepers," said Carmine. "The card games will start at sixteen hundred hours; sniff around for the smell of liquor on their breath. Remember: they get no food, even if they offer to pay. I don't care how far they traveled to be there, no food. Any questions?" There were none.

Carmine thanked his men, displaying a rare smile. On top of the card games, there was another piece of business he had to attend to on Saturday. Bruno would be at the house Saturday to collect his two bottles of scotch. Carmine was adamant: he would not welcome Bruno into Nonno's home. He hoped Nonno would not overrule him; soldiers playing cards and a black market dealer did not make for a good mix.

Saturday brought gray skies and the threat of rain. He and the boys arrived an hour early to help Nonno set up. Everyone's hands were busy, and there was laughter in the house. The boys set up the second table and Giovanni added the tablecloths. Carmine announced that there would be a change in plans. He asked Nonno to boil eggs. "If they're hungry," he said, "sell them two hard boiled eggs for a dollar." Nonno must have approved of the plan because without a word he filled a large pot with water.

Pina had just entered the room and she looked fresh and pretty in her new silk dress. Her hair had a large old-fashioned comb in it

110

that pulled the hair off her face. Tessa followed her out with scissors in her hand. "Pina come back into the bedroom, I need to cut the loose threads off your new clothes." Not only had Tessa made her sister a simple but pretty silk dress, she had also made Pina her very first silk slip and undergarments. Pina walked differently today. She was not used to the feel of the parachute silk; Tessa had surprised her by sewing tiny pearl beads on all three garments.

The two women came back out after Tessa put the finishing touches on Pina's new silk garments. Carmine walked over to Tessa and kissed her on both cheeks. Was it a brave move? Maybe, but he was pleased that Tessa had found it in her to reward Pina's work. He complimented Tessa on the fine work she'd done on the dress, and admired the comb in Pina's hair. "It was my mother's; she wore it on her wedding day. I wear it today because I will say my rosary for her." Carmine smiled at Pina; then turned back to the preparations for the card game. The house was full of conversation and activity; no one noticed when Pina left the house.

A few soldiers started to trickle in; it was time to meet Bruno outside. Carmine placed the two bottles of scotch in Bruno's truck. Bruno was holding a package in his hand. Carmine refused to inquire after the item; he didn't want to give him the satisfaction. "Pinocchio, the Italian puppet, I got it for the boy." Carmine noticed that he never used the word *bought*.

Before he could bring the boy outside, Tessa approached. She handed Carmine a coat and said, "Please catch up with Pina, it's starting to rain and she will be all wet by the time she arrives at the prayer group. She will get upset. I warned her about going to Signora Russo's house through the back; but she will not listen to me."

Carmine handed her the package from Bruno. "Okay. Here . . . this is for Giovanni. Now, where am I going?" Tessa was about to answer, but Bruno cut in and said to follow him; they walked off with the coat. When it began to rain more heavily, they picked up their pace.

After 10 minutes something was registering on Bruno's face and he started to scream Pina's name. "Signora Russo's house is straight from here; we should be able to see her. I don't like this."

"Maybe she is there already," Carmine answered, without alarm in his voice. "There's an old shed over there. Maybe she took cover there when the rain came." They headed for the shed.

It was Carmine who saw them first. There was a man on top of her and her clothes were ripped off. She was still, not making a sound. "Oh my God, is she dead?" Carmine let out a guttural scream. With one savage move, Carmine pulled the man off Pina. Since the man's pants were around his knees, Carmine easily turned him over and straddled him. Carmine's left knee pressed into sharp pieces of wet metal on the ground; he welcomed the pain. Bruno crouched and pinned the guy down at his shoulders.

Carmine's fist reached the man's face with such force that he knew his nose was broken; his fist continued pounding his face. The man had tried to fight back but he was no match for Carmine and Bruno's Herculean strength. The only words Carmine uttered to the man were, "*You fucking Nazi.*" The man came back at him with a gurgled sound. Then Carmine reached for his sidearm; but he heard Bruno's words. "No, go to Pina. I will do the rest; my men will see that he is never found."

Pina tried to cover her body. Her dress was torn at the neckline, pushed up around her waist, and covered in mud; the new silk underwear was ripped and silk threads with tiny pearl beads hung grotesquely from her thighs. Carmine wrapped her coat around her with more tenderness than he had ever felt in his life. She said not a word but it was her eyes that would haunt him for the rest of his life. Her eyes that said, "What happened to me?" Carmine, with Pina in his arms, walked away. They heard two gunshots behind them.

Bruno caught up to them and took Pina in his arms. He was out of breath when he spoke, "I will go to the road; get your jeep and meet us. We will take her to my house. My Yolanda is a midwife; she will know what to do." A few minutes later, they gently placed Pina into the jeep, and without a word, drove to Bruno's house. Carmine carried Pina into a bedroom and covered her with two blankets. Yolanda, Bruno's wife, carried hot water, rags, and clean clothes into the bedroom; and with deliberate body language, sent him out and closed the door.

The men were broken; they spoke in whispers for hours. Finally Bruno said, "Remember, we tell Nonno and Tessa that the man took off. That is the end. My men will do the rest. Bring Tessa here." Tonight Carmine took his orders from Bruno; he left to get Tessa.

He walked into the house and spoke to J.J. "You are in charge; I have to leave again. After I go, tell the soldiers the games are over, the sergeant wants them gone now. You, Fish, and Mac need to stay until I get back with the jeep later tonight. Clean everything up for Nonno, and spend some time with Giovanni." J.J. said he'd take care of things until Carmine got back.

Carmine turned to Tessa. "Tessa, please put your coat on. Pina had an accident; I'll take you to her. Let's go." In the jeep he told her that they would be going to Bruno's house; Carmine wanted Yolanda to tell Tessa what he could not. Fear stopped Tessa from asking questions. When he looked over he saw that she was praying.

When they got to Bruno's, Tessa walked straight toward the bedroom; but Yolanda turned her around and walked her into the kitchen. "Tessa," Yolanda began, "a man grabbed her and attacked her."

"Did he . . . ?" Yolanda shook her head yes. Tessa's scream was primeval.

"S-h-h-h, you can cry with her, but do not make it worse. I washed her. She is bruised, but there are no broken bones. You should sleep here with her tonight; and do not think to tell priests or nuns, they will shame her." Tonight Tessa took her orders from Yolanda. Tessa went to her sister, her 18-year-old childlike sister, who had no understanding of the cruelty of some men. They lay together in each other's arms.

There was noise at the front door. Bruno's men had brought back his truck and the two bottles of scotch. Bruno said, "Vito, you go back and tell the egg man that Pina is not well; and that she and Tessa will be with Signora Yolanda Falco tonight so she can care for Pina. They will be home tomorrow." There was also an unspoken message that passed between Bruno and his men. A message that conveyed, *We took care of the body and it will never be found.*

Yolanda left the sisters alone; she brought the men wine and food. Carmine asked Yolanda to say goodnight to Tessa for him, and he and Bruno walked to the jeep. Bruno said he would take the sisters home tomorrow and they agreed Tessa should be the one to talk to her grandfather. She would know how much hurt his heart could carry.

Carmine drove to Nonno's house; he was relieved when the men saw the jeep and came out. He could not bear to see Nonno's face. The boys spoke among themselves; they were smart enough not to direct any words in the Sergeant's direction. The drive back to camp seemed endless, the road paved with pain. Carmine walked into L.Q. and fell into bed fully dressed. Sleep quickly claimed him.

The next day was Sunday. Carmine would not be headed over to mass. He was angry with God; He should have protected that beautiful child on her way to say the rosary for her mother. How could God allow that to happen? The war had changed for him last night. Even if he were to be wounded, nothing would cut as deeply as the nightmare that had unfolded before him. He wished Pina had walked out through the front door; he would have driven her. He blamed himself for all of it; that guilt would never leave him. Pina thought like a child at play; she never considered danger. Carmine did not want to go to Nonno's house; but he was obligated to face them. He went to the dispensary first and persuaded them to give him medication to treat bruises. They asked him if was taking his quinine. He didn't answer.

If he was surprised that Signora Yolanda Falco came to the door it did not register on his face. He handed her the medication and interpreted the English directions for her; he then thanked her for her kindness. Nonno and Bruno sat at the table and drank strong black coffee with anisette. Carmine didn't know how to read the scene being played out before him. If he were home, he would think someone had died and that the men had recently returned from the cemetery. The mood was somber. Carmine sat down and the signora brought him his own cup of black coffee. If this brew was any stronger the spoon would have stood straight up in the cup. The three men sat at the table, sipping their coffee in sadness and silence.

When Giovanni walked into the room the tension lessened; they all smiled. He carried Pinocchio in his arms and demonstrated how each limb moved and how the feet turned all the way around. They reacted with laughter and hand clapping. Bruno stood up and Carmine followed behind him in military fashion.

Outside Bruno said, "Tessa told Nonno that he had tried to attack her but he ran off when he saw us."

Carmine was still worried. "Bruno, I tried to read his face; but it told me nothing. Has he spoken to you?"

"Just a few words, he is heartbroken for this child; he blames himself. Carmine, you need to understand—he has lived through two wars; it has hardened him. He will go on and be strong for his family. I will watch over them; they will eat and be protected. Someday soon, we will talk about Giovanni; but not today. I see Tessa is outside; I will go back." Bruno went back in the house.

Near the chicken coops, Carmine kissed Tessa lightly on her mouth and embraced her; they clung to each other for solace. "How is she?" he asked.

Tessa's eyes welled up. "She keeps saying a bad man hurt her; she doesn't understand. She is afraid to go outside and she cries because she lost Mama's comb. Bruno said he will send his men to find it. Bruno and his wife have been like a *zio* and *zia* to us. They are very kind; and the signora said she will visit us every day until Pina is strong. Carmine, Pina said you called the man a Nazi and she heard two shots."

Carmine nodded. "Yes, he was a German and the two shots missed him when he was running away. Tessa, it happened; there is no more to say. Let it go. Should I say hello to Pina?" Tessa nodded her head yes.

He walked into the house and froze; he had no idea what to say to Pina. Her bruises were not on her face; she looked weak but not beaten. He would not bring himself to think of the hidden bruises. He had brought her chocolate and was grateful to have something to do with his hands. She looked up and said, "Thank you for helping me."

Carmine could only nod; he held back tears. "Oh, I forgot, I have something else for you. I'll be right back." In the jeep he found the shawl from France that a soldier had sold him. At the time, he had planned to send it to Rachel; but it would help Pina heal, if only a little. He held it out for her; she touched the silk and Tessa helped her place it over her shoulders. "I like the pretty flowers on it." She smiled the tiniest bit.

Carmine took a deep breath, steeling himself before delivering the next bit of news. "Tessa, Pina, the Army is giving my men and me more work to help the war effort. We're going to be really busy for awhile; I don't know for how long. I will be back as soon as the Army gives me a break." He walked over to Nonno and awkwardly kissed him on both cheeks; his only words to the older man were, "I will be back; do you need anything?" Nonno shook his head no. Once he was back on the road, Carmine was thankful he was alone in the jeep; he cried angry tears and screamed into the cold air.

Supplies arrived faster than the boys could inventory and store it all. Captain Wadsworth barked orders relentlessly. Carmine embraced every moment of the long hours. He kept sending word out to Nonno that he wanted to be out there, but he was needed at the warehouse. Lies, all lies. That was the last place he wanted to be. He could not face Nonno, Tessa or Pina; but he did long to see Giovanni.

He fell into a routine of working long hours, eating, and then waiting for the boys to go out so he could be alone with his tears. They were not silent tears; sometimes he moaned or pounded his fists until he told himself he was doing too much harm to his hands. A week later, the malaria returned and he walked into the dispensary and announced. "Here I am, boys."

Malaria had come back at the best time for him and the worse time for the captain. J.J. said that when Wadsworth got the news that he was hospitalized, he kicked over his chair. "What can I tell you J.J.," said Carmine, "I'm indispensable." Malaria was not a curse at this time; it was a lifesaver. He was well fed, got plenty of rest, and the nurses made a fuss over him. Most importantly, the doctors ordered him to stay put. Carmine could hide out and no one could rely on him. He was sick.

***

Naples, Italy

March 1944

Hello Jimmy,

Well, did a tiger get you yet? I guess you won't be going to the Bronx Zoo when you get back. That silk sheet you made out of the parachute gave me the idea to do the same thing here. The boys really liked writing to their wives that they sleep on silk sheets. When this is over, we need to go fishing in Canarsie. I will tell you stories that I need to get off my chest. The censors don't need to hear what I have to say. I can tell you I sort of adopted a 10-year-old boy; his name is Giovanni. I saw him by the road a few times—skinny as a rail. Then one day I got the idea to bring him to this family I know; and they kept him. He wants to see America. Maybe the three of us will fish in Canarsie or Sheepshead Bay. Then my mother will clean and cook the fish and we'll eat like kings. Anyway, there is this guy that wants to talk to me about Giovanni. With all the bad stuff I have seen lately, I hope the boy isn't sick; what else could go wrong? I don't know about you but sometimes I just can't take anymore. I want to go home to Rachel. Some soldiers say they lost interest in their wives since they've been away. Not me, I think I want to be with her more than ever. She was fresh when I married her, no other guy got there before me. I think I may have gotten myself too involved with a local girl; but this war can't last forever and I want to go home to Rachel and my parents and the only goddamn former soldier I want to see is you. I guess you hear the same stories as me about the war; but if I start writing that stuff, this letter will look like Swiss cheese. I have time to write now because the malaria came back and I'm in the hospital.

Don't be stupid like me. Take the quinine.

I guess I'll end this now. Remember, the first one to get home buys the beer at Coney Island.

Your friend,

Carmine

***

Carmine played cards for hours. He found he liked the boys in the hospital; they were on the mend so they were humble. They had seen too much of this war. One of the boys said, "You won my last 10 dollars, but I can give you a Nazi flag if I lose. I wanted to take home some trophies, but now I just want to take myself home." Carmine won the flag. A nurse brought him paper and he wrote to his wife.

***

Naples, Italy

March 1944

Dear Rachel,

Well I'm back in the hospital. Yes the malaria came back. If I was back home, I know you would take good care of me and this illness would be just one more bad memory of our time apart. I miss you darling. I promise you we will have a good life when I get back and you will be proud of your husband. Did you get the cameos I sent? I had to buy two of them so give one to my mother. The boys and I like to go to the local spots where men sell jewelry, tablecloths, bedspreads and other stuff. I stand on the side and say nothing; I just listen to the sellers talking Italian to each other. After the sellers give us their prices, I start talking the Italian dialect and they know I heard them say what they really paid for everything. Then I can get the boys a better price. Tell your father that Naples may have been beautiful when he was here; but not now. Also tell him it is impossible for me to look up his cousins; but when I meet civilians I repeat the family names. I have to be careful; the people here are so poor that they will say they are my people so that I'll give them food. If I can, I give them food even though I know they're lying to me.

Darling, I am sending you a souvenir, a Nazi flag. I ripped it off a building when I fought the Germans. Keep it until I get home; but I'm not sure I want to be reminded of this place. I was able to get four bottles of Coca Cola; that made me homesick. Those lucky stiffs back home can get whatever they want. Yes, I know there are points on some things. One soldier told me his wife had to buy his baby a wooden pacifier and the baby spit it out.

I like that song "As Time Goes By"—I sing it and think of you. Mac has a trumpet and he plays that song for me. He also plays the old songs from home; I don't know the new ones, except "Pistol Packin' Mama"— even the Italians sing that one.

Please don't be upset if you don't hear from me like before; things are moving fast now and my letters might not get through.

125

Read the papers. That will tell you what is
going on over here.

   Love, your husband,

   Carmine

***

He said goodbye to the soldiers and walked out of the hospital eight days later; he was stronger and 87 dollars richer, thanks to poker. At least he was honest with himself; he had been hiding out. He left the tears and aftermath of the rape for Bruno and Yolanda Falco to handle.

A surprise was waiting for him at his bunk. The boys had hung a *WELCOME HOME SERGEANT* sign over the door. Carmine could not fathom that a handwritten, childish sign had touched him; he was getting soft. Before he could take off his boots, the corporal came in and announced that he was to report to the captain. Carmine sighed, turned, and went back out the door.

"Well good day, Sergeant Trotta, did you have a good rest? The Army is fighting its way up the peninsula, the goddamn Germans are dug in, and we need to supply the troops. You will be gone from here in 48 hours. Pack up."

Carmine said, "Okay, it's happening, I'm ready." Carmine's words had actually included a slightly personal touch. The captain and he had not become buddies; but they had found a middle ground.

Carmine and his boys got drunk that night. They could be heard singing *"Show Me the Way to Go Home."* Carmine let go of all the bottled up pain and forgot where he was and what he had witnessed. For that night he was a guy barely out of his teens.

***

Determined to fit it all in, Carmine worked, barked orders, packed the jeep, and carved out time to see Tessa and her family. He would just have to show up; this time he could not get a message through to them ahead of time. When he got there, Tessa walked out to the jeep and helped him unload. If she was suspicious of why he brought more food than before, she gave no indication. They were alone. Nonno and Giovanni had taken Pina to Signora Yolanda's house; Tessa did not know when they would be back.

Carmine scooped her up and set her down on the bed. They undressed hurriedly and fell into each other's arms without the slightest hint of passion. Their bodies rushed through a rhythm that ended in a synchronized climax. They dressed; Tessa combed her hair. They went into the kitchen and sat down at the table.

Carmine took a deep breath and began. "The Army is pushing north through Italy; I need to supply the men. Tessa, I will be gone by tomorrow. I have asked a few of the boys to give Nonno extra food when he comes to sell his eggs. I don't know if I will get back here, and I am not permitted to say more. Bruno has promised to

127

protect your family. I trust him; and he loves Giovanni. Take good care of the boy; I'm sorry I won't be here to help you with him."

It was Tessa's turn to speak, "I knew this day would come; we have had more time than many lovers. Carmine, when the war ends you will go home; but will you come back for me? Will you marry me and bring me to America? I will earn money for us by sewing beautiful gowns for the rich women in New York."

Carmine's body slumped, his head drooping; he was looking at the floor. He imagined that this question might come up one day. He looked up. "I am a married man. I will return to my wife; we were married in the Catholic Church. It is what my parents expect from me. I will not return. You are young and beautiful and many men will want such a bride. I made you no promise."

No words. Then her soft tears and loud words, "You will leave me here with the chickens, a sick sister, an old man and a boy? This is who you are? Go away. I will start over and I will be rich, richer than you. Go to your Rachel—yes, I saw her name on Giovanni's package."

Their final farewell was brief. Carmine sat in the jeep. He knew he was a bastard; but he had made her no promises. He drove to Bruno's house. He swerved to miss Giovanni—the kid was so excited to see him that he ran straight at the jeep. He loved this boy, this beautiful child he had found by the side of the road like a stray cat. Carmine presented him with a full-size American flag.

He thought the boy would hug him; but instead he saluted the flag. Carmine should have carried a handkerchief with him.

They walked inside and Signora Falco was a hurricane of activity. She reminded Carmine of his Brooklyn aunts preparing the Christmas Eve fish dinner. He walked over to Nonno and kissed him on both cheeks. He looked weary; but he rose to greet Carmine. He approached Pina; but he did not know whether to kiss her; instead, he smiled broadly and handed her chocolate. It was Signora Yolanda who put everyone at ease, "I am teaching Pina how to be the best baker in Naples. After the war, we will open a bakery together and we will make everyone fat."

Bruno motioned for Carmine to follow him into another room. "Bruno. First tell me—how are Pina and Nonno?"

Bruno smiled. "My Yolanda keeps Pina busy and she is never alone. She no longer wishes to sew silk garments; she wishes to bake. She bakes bread and anisette cookies now; but after the war she will make the famous Neapolitan pastry. Pina is afraid to go outside alone; Yolanda does not think she will ever marry. She sleeps here; I think Yolanda is now her mother, not Tessa. Tessa is young herself and too heartbroken. Nonno says little. He works, he eats, and he plays with Giovanni."

For the second time that day, Carmine prepared to deliver bad news. "Bruno, I am leaving in the morning. The Allies are pushing north; I must supply them. You said you would protect the family;

129

I believe you. The boys will give Nonno food when he comes to sell his eggs."

Bruno nodded. "I will take care of them. Yolanda, a midwife, never had children; this family makes her a mother. With all the sadness, there is also joy in this house now."

Bruno touched Carmine's arm lightly, "We are out of time; I need to tell you Giovanni's story. Do you remember the day Giovanni and I chased after the cat? We were out back and the boy needed to pee. He was modest; he told me to turn around. I did not turn around; I took a good look. That is when I knew." Carmine just stared at him, confused.

"I will explain, Carmine. Giovanni was a puzzle: he spoke northern Italian, he was educated, but he did not know his prayers. He would not repeat his last name. Yes, he was a puzzle—until I saw his little penis. The boy was circumcised. Peasant boys are not circumcised. This boy is Jewish. There, I said the word out loud for the first time. That is why I gave him a baptismal certificate dated 1934. His last name is now Salvatore.

"I don't know what the boy remembers. I will ask him when the war is over and it is safe to ask. I am afraid to ask around as to how he arrived here. My guess is his rich parents had workers with ties to this area; they wanted him to blend in with us. I have told no one, not even Yolanda. The boy is safer in the south with the Allies in command. I would like him with me; but he keeps Nonno alive with his affection.

"I have convinced Nonno to have the four of them live under my roof until the war ends. I reminded him that Pina's assailant got away and could still be around; Tessa could also be in danger. Nonno can work his chicken coops and sell his eggs; my men will watch over his house. It was easier than I expected to convince Nonno; I am certain he wanted his family protected. They will move here on Sunday."

Carmine struggled to absorb it all. Bruno was not so bad after all; he was a wise man. The bottom line was that Bruno would protect them. "Bruno, I have two requests. After the war, please help Giovanni find his parents or his relatives. If you are unsuccessful, please keep him away from your line of work."

Bruno smiled and nodded. "I will help him find his family; if he stays with me I will send him to the university."

They walked back into the kitchen and Carmine announced, "I need to help fight this war; I will be gone for awhile." He embraced Nonno, Giovanni, Yolanda and Bruno. Then he saluted Giovanni and Pina. He walked into the unknown future, wiping his tears.

***

The captain and Carmine huddled over maps all evening. Then the captain said, "There are four new soldiers joining you; you'll

131

need the extra help. The Army is advancing faster than the supplies can reach them. You didn't do a bad job. Work hard; maybe we'll be home by Christmas." Carmine thanked him and left. He clung to the captain's words: *"You didn't do a bad job."* Seeing Carmine leave, the captain could only imagine the degree of hell Carmine would be facing at his new post.

With everything prepared, Carmine, J.J., Mac, and Fish reminisced about their time in Naples; then the four men had a few drinks and called it a night. Carmine wanted to be focused and alert with the next sunrise. Morning came, and they headed north.

Chapter Seven
Somewhere Between Naples and Rome
April-August1944

"Spartacus was crucified on that road." The reaction to his statement varied. The boys had been on the truck less than an hour before this guy, known as Prof, short for Professor, began his lecture. The new boys knew each other and knew Prof. One rolled his eyes, one glared, and one laughed in his face. Carmine ignored all of them, but J.J. wanted to hear more. It took J.J.'s mind off the war—even if the guy was talking about ancient battles, it was a diversion. J.J. was one of the soldiers who had accompanied the sergeant on the truck, so no one challenged him.

J.J. urged the Prof to continue. "There are two main roads from here to Rome: Route Six and Route Seven. Route Seven is better known as the Appian Way. It was built in 312 B.C. as a route from Naples to Rome. The road was built to transport military troops and supplies. The Allies are using it today for the same reasons, nothing changes. Spartacus, the famous slave leader, was crucified on the road in 71 B.C. Julius Caesar and saints also walked on that road. I thought we might be headed for that route; but we're headed for Route Six. It makes sense. I was told that farther up on

Route Seven there are marshes loaded down with malaria mosquitoes." That last comment caught Carmine's attention. Carmine was quiet but not asleep. He was afraid of what lay ahead; but on the flip side, he wanted to get out of Naples. Pina haunted his thoughts. She was always there; there was no relief from his anguish and guilt. He also wanted to avoid thinking about Tessa and Nonno. Tessa was bitter, and Nonno's face made him feel guilty.

He studied the new boys on the truck; it was too soon to know who would hold up. Until they reached Rome, there would be little time to rest; and who knows how much mail would catch up to them. Their job was to supply the troops. As soon as a town fell and was in the hands of the Allies, Carmine would set up a warehouse. Then the next town would fall and Carmine would pack up and set up a new warehouse. He wanted to push past Rome to the northern Italian border, enter France and get to Germany. He looked around at the hilly terrain; now that spring was here they would have to deal with rain and mud.

They ate in the truck; Carmine had hard boiled eggs and salami to pass around. He wanted to win favor with the four new boys—and they were *boys*. Carmine was the oldest soldier there; the new men looked like babies—no more than 19. These boys would turn to him for direction even emotional support. Jesus, J.J. looked like General Patton next to some of these guys. How was he to keep these men from breaking? It was too much for his shoulders to carry.

When Carmine walked off to look for a spot to pee, the boys turned to J.J. and said, "Hey Private, what can we expect from the sergeant?"

J.J. shrugged, and then added, "Don't cross him; but he'll take care of his men. Be respectful of the Italian women, and watch your mouth. He doesn't say too much; he nods, turns, and leaves when he's finished with you. Try not to start up conversations with him; he'll shut you down."

***

When they pulled into camp, the soldiers there looked happy to see the truck arrive; but they all looked exhausted and dirty. The captain pointed out the living quarters to the new arrivals and said, "Get settled in." All eight men started to unload the truck. Carmine surveyed the supplies and ordered soap, beer, and chocolate to be given out that night; they had their own cigarettes. When he could no longer stand up, he walked into his quarters and fell into his cot fully clothed. There would be no beds or silk sheets now; they wouldn't be in any one place for long.

The next night the captain invited him to his quarters to finish off a half full bottle of bourbon. After the bourbon was gone, the captain opened up to Carmine. He had a lot to say; it was really a one-sided conversation. "Whose idea was it to push up through the

Italian spine? The Germans are dug in and they know the terrain. Have you ever seen so much rain and mud? It will take me two years back in the states to get the dirt and smell off my skin. The Germans will fight like hell to block off Rome, and they don't want us setting up air bases within striking range of the German border. We need more troops, more everything. Where are the troops? I hope they know what the hell they're doing. We have been trying to push through to Monte Cassino. We need to take it, then we can get to Rome. Rome is an open city—*yeah, open to the Germans.* We are taking on heavy casualties. Don't expect to get much sleep; the air raids will scare the shit out of you."

That was more than enough information for one night. "Thank you for the bourbon, Captain; I think I can find my quarters on my own. Good night."The next two weeks were filled with exhausting work, no mail from home, and many air raids. Then Carmine and his boys were moved to another Italian town to repeat the same routine.

At the next town they noticed civilians going about their lives with as much normalcy as they could struggle to maintain. They had to survive this day; that was their immediate goal. They wanted the money in the soldiers' pockets: they offered women, wine, and black market trinkets. It was on the second night that the boys' young bodies went to the town bar—or more precisely, the front room of someone's house. The proprietor, a man of about 60, offered the soldiers wine and hard biscuits made with wine. As

Carmine scanned the room, he had one observation: the men just wanted to get drunk as quickly as possible. There would be no party atmosphere.

The fight started over one soldier demanding to be paid the 20 dollars the other soldier owed him. The other soldier was emphatic that he only owed him seven dollars; and besides he had no money. They took a few swings, mostly missing their target because of too much wine. Soldier *A* picked up a chair and broke it over soldier *B*'s head. Here, there are two things to keep in mind: 1) the chair was a piece of shit; and 2) soldier *B* was so drunk he never thought to move out of the way of the flying chair. Carmine reluctantly interceded by speaking Italian, waving his hands in the air and shrugging his shoulders just like the locals. He then gave the proprietor five American dollars for the piece-of-shit chair. The soldiers sat back down and the night almost ended peacefully.

The proprietor announced that a local talent would sing a few songs for the patrons. The singer maneuvered her way around the room singing and occasionally stopping to place a tip in her brassiere. It wasn't until she stopped by the last table that things went terribly wrong. One of the soldiers put his hand under the woman's skirt and lifted it up. The Italian locals leaped to defend the woman's honor; there was fighting and more broken furniture. Carmine decided that if this soldier, a stranger to Carmine, wanted to be a horse's ass; him and his buddies could fight it out. Carmine rounded up his own men and left. His boys fell into the jeep singing: *Show Me the Way to Go Home*. Back in their quarters, the men, including Carmine, rehashed the night's events and laughed the laugh of carefree boys back home in the States.

***

They packed up, traveled, unloaded and set up. The northern battles dictated that the soldiers needed to be fed and equipped. Carmine and his boys had little sleep. They didn't know where they were most of the time; but they could read a compass. They were inching north, closer to Rome.

Prof and J.J. established a friendship. Prof liked to talk history and J.J. wanted to learn. The two had little else in common. J.J. was from Upstate New York; Prof grew up in Oregon. J.J. was never much of a student; Prof read books by the stack. But the one thing they had in common was their struggle taking that final step into manhood. Their shyness around the other more experienced soldiers created a bond between them.

Prof began today's topic: the Abbey of Benedict of Nursia. "It's not far from here, at Monte Cassino; I should say the ruins of the abbey are not far from here. The abbey was built in 529 A.D. to serve Benedict of Nursia. He wrote the *Rules of Saint Benedict*, which is the format for monastery life that is still used today. Popes have prayed inside its walls. It was bombed in January."

"The Germans don't care about religious landmarks," said J.J., "They'll bomb anything holy."

"Sorry J.J., the American bombers destroyed this holy site that was over 1,400 years old. The abbey was in a protected historical zone but we bombed it anyway. Our boys must have known the Germans were using it. After the war, the truth will come out; but it is a damn shame."

There wasn't much movement in the weeks ahead; each morning they awoke to more rain which, in turn, made more mud. Carmine told his boys, "Get some rest, write to your families; I'll ask the base censor to get your letters read and moved out." Carmine also found rest; he had a malaria flare-up and was placed on hospital bed rest. The doctors prescribed twelve pills a day.

***

Italy

May 1944

Dear Rachel,

I know you're mad at me; but darling I have been writing religiously. But I am on the move now so the letters are backed up. You'll get a bunch at one time. I'm not getting all your letters either; but I know you are writing to me.

Well, I'm back in the hospital. No darling, I'm not wounded. It's the same old thing—the malaria. They have me on 12 pills a day, and boy is my head swimming. I have one of your letters in front of me so I'll try to answer your questions. No Rachel, the Germans did not retreat from Italy—not by a long shot. Remember I can't say too much or you'll get another one of those Swiss cheese letters. No, nothing happened the night I wrote to you while on guard duty. But the time after that, a few German planes were overhead and kept it up for a few hours but there was no damage. It sure makes Coney Island fireworks look sick when you see an air raid. I won't lie, it scares me and I can't get back to sleep.

Something big has to happen this summer in order to finish this damn war. I'm afraid even if this war ends, it will be six months before I get home. I need to come home. If I just knew when it would end I wouldn't mind the wait. Speaking of Coney Island, I promise you I'll take you to the beach all summer when I get back. I'm sorry I never wanted to go; but being away from you makes me realize that I need to do better. Besides, I don't want your family to think you made a mistake and married a bum.

I'm going to play some poker now; the hospital here has a lot of soldiers and they're all looking for a card game. I hope they have their pay with them; I feel lucky tonight.

I Love you. This can't last forever. Next Easter I'll buy you an orchid and escort you to church.

Love, your husband,

***

"Just pay up, soldier." Carmine's luck had not materialized tonight. His head hurt, and his sharp edge was failing him. He paid up and went back to his hospital bed. A priest stopped by.

"Good evening, Sergeant. It says here you're a Catholic; I'd like to give you my blessing." Carmine was sitting up in bed. He whispered, "Thank you," and the priest recited his prayer in Latin.

"My eyes are old Sergeant; but I can see a troubled man in front of me." Carmine's first inclination was to say he was fine in the most dismissive voice he could pull off; but instead a flood of words poured out of him.

"Father, usually I like a hospital stay; I get rest and I don't have to make decisions or bark orders. Since I've been here, I just want to get my boots on and leave. Some of these soldiers are badly wounded. At night I hear them moan. It's more than a moan—it's a sorrow that tears at my skin. They have limbs missing, and heads bandaged, and worst of all—they look like they should be playing stickball in the schoolyard. I close my eyes and all I see is blood. I just want to get up and run—just run and never stop." Carmine leaned his head back against the wall.

The priest spoke softly. "Sergeant that is your humanity I hear. You are not blinded by the carnage. But we must defeat this German scourge; I hear whispers of their most ungodly barbarism not only against the military but on civilians. They must be defeated before humanity can be restored. It will end and this twentieth century madman will burn in hell. I will put in a request for a sleep aid for you. Good night, my son." Carmine felt better; he wasn't sure if it was the priest's words or that he had managed to release his unspoken anguish. He took pills, he took blood tests; he ate and slept. For the next eight days the routine continued. Finally, his tests came back clean and he walked out.

The boys were packed and ready to leave by the time he returned. They were different now. They were solemn; they had seen too much and been worked too hard. Carmine kept in mind that his boys were not in the battles; they weren't fighting to capture Anzio. They supplied the troops; but they were still in physical danger from air raids. If the mail was dependable, that would have lifted their spirits. At least they hadn't reached the point of fighting with each other; but Carmine noticed that they kept more to themselves now.

By the next town, the heavy rains had returned, and the boys rested. They got drunk, sang, and played cards. They stayed close to camp. But they were never in one town for too long.

They packed up and move to different towns, each one farther north. The Germans were on the run; but the push was slow and the casualty count high.

The Allies liberated Rome from German occupation on June 5, 1944.The troops rolled into Rome and were welcomed by cheering Romans who celebrated for days. Carmine and his boys rolled into Rome two weeks later. They were awestruck. Rome was not in shambles; and the majesty of ancient Vatican City had taken minimal damage. They went to St. Peter's Square and saw Pope Pius XII on his balcony! Wait until Carmine's mother heard that news. Rome was exciting and the women were beautiful, friendly, and not in rags. Carmine did not know how long he would remain here; but he was not going to waste one minute of his time. They needed to supply the troops, and they executed their duty with precision. They worked efficiently so they could get their jobs finished and have fun. Fun had been in short supply in recent months.

Objective number one was to take hot showers. Objective two was to eat hot Italian food; that had the side effect of lifting their spirits. Objective three was to get drunk in real bars, not in the front room of someone's house. With the objectives met and executed, Carmine and his boys moved on to the Piazza Venezia. Benito Mussolini had given historic speeches on the Piazza Venezia's balcony which overlooked a public square.

No one knew how it had begun or whose idea it had been; but they decided to climb up to the balcony. One by one the intoxicated soldiers gave speeches to the crowd below. They all agreed Carmine's speech was the best because it was in English and Italian; the Roman civilians cheered wildly. The next morning the boys had only a vague recollection of their speech-giving performances. Their captain, however, banned any return engagements.

More work, more play. Objective four was to endear themselves to the Roman ladies. There were already rumors that they would soon be moving north, so there was no time to waste. They asked the other soldiers for the best places to find prostitutes. The boys made plans to all go to the same place of business; and on Carmine's advice they did not carry their entire pay with them. Carmine would join them, but he made no comment to J. J.; this would be his decision. They showered, shaved—some even sprayed cologne—and headed out. J.J. was with them; however Prof said he wanted to see Roman ruins. If Carmine wasn't within ear shot, the boys would have sent an endless supply of jokes Prof's way.

The seven men walked into the bordello and were greeted by the madam. Carmine had to remember that he was in a liberated war zone to put it in perspective. It was similar to peacetime whorehouses. The place was clean; there were candles burning and fabric draped over windows and in doorways. They each paid five American dollars and waited. Carmine had argued that the steep price was a good investment. The women would be worth the extra dollars. Carmine purposely went last. When the woman motioned to J.J., Carmine said, "E la sua prima volta." *It is his first time.* J.J., with his shoulders back, walked behind the woman.

Carmine liked the woman he had drawn. She was in her late 20s and respectable looking. Carmine greeted her in Italian. It was a business transaction for both. They removed their clothes and she lay on the bed. Carmine was more attentive than he would have imagined; he had attempted to satisfy her. Carmine, never a man with stamina, ended abruptly.

As they dressed, he asked her name. "My name is Angelina. I am grateful that the Americans liberated us. The Germans are not soldiers—they are devils. The stories I have heard and the things I have seen have angered God."

J.J. was waiting when Carmine walked out. By the side glance J.J. had given him, he suspected it had gone well. "I have one question, Sergeant. What did you say to her?"

Carmine looked puzzled and said, "I don't remember." The next day, J.J. and Prof set out to see Roman ruins. J.J. now walked with a swagger that humiliated his teacher. They saw the Coliseum, the Spanish Steps, the Roman Forum and the Trevi Fountain where people threw coins in the fountain and made the same wish.

J.J. asked, "What are those figurines with two babies standing under a wolf?"

"That, J.J.," said Prof, "represents the mythical story of how Rome began. Twin baby boys were floated down the River Tiber in a basket. Their names were Romulus and Remus. A female wolf found them and nursed them; that's what the figurines depict. Rome gets its name from Romulus."

J.J. held up his hand to get Prof to stop. "I'll be right back. I want to buy two figurines—one for me and one for my parents."

On Saturday they drove to the Vatican and Prof told him the history of the place. Prof was a veritable font of information on the Catholic capital, even though he was a Presbyterian. They both bought prints of the Vatican from merchants with pushcarts. J.J. had one regret . . . he did not have film for his camera; but he had his portrait sketched by a street artist.

Meanwhile, Carmine did a little shopping of his own. He did not have an easy time speaking Italian with the Romans. They didn't fully understand each other; but they shared enough of the language to haggle over prices. Maybe he was overly sensitive; but he read their body language and deduced that they looked down on his southern Italian dialect. Did they also look down on their American liberators? He bought jewelry for Rachel, a tablecloth for his mother, and trinkets for his Brooklyn aunts.

He did not buy anything for Tessa. Tessa was his past; it was over. He did not want to mail gifts to Bruno's address; he feared that the Army would infer that he was part of a black market exchange; or at least, that's what he told himself. Tessa had thrown him out; but Giovanni, Pina and even Nonno thought he had abandoned them. He tried to clear his conscience with the knowledge that Bruno and Yolanda would give the family security and care. After the war, he would find a way to get in touch with Giovanni.

That night he wrote to his wife.

***

Italy, June 1944

Dear Rachel,

I guess you have heard all the good news. We landed at Normandy and pushed the Germans back. It won't be long now. The soldiers are getting the job done. Please be patient. I'm coming home to you. I sent you jewelry, a necklace, a bracelet and earrings. I bought my mother a table cloth, and my aunts some trinkets. You can buy everything here—I think you can guess where I am now.

Darling, I'm going to be moving around, so I don't know how much mail you are going to receive. But I am writing, I promise. If you could see me, you would be

148

relieved—I put on some weight. I guess it's
all the good Italian food I'm eating, and I'm
getting some rest. I haven't had another
malaria outbreak. I would like to think that
I'm cured. I like where I am now—even the
air smells better.

When are you going to send me some
new photographs of yourself? You keep
promising but I haven't received one picture
this year. Maybe someday we'll take a trip
to Italy—but not for about 10 years. The
only trips I want to take when I get back
home are to Coney Island and Atlantic City.
I'm having my war bonds dropped, so soon
you'll be getting 80 dollars more in your
allotment. Let me know if it goes through;
but remember, things like that take time. Tell
your father that the farther north I go in
Italy, the better it looks. He's right—it is a
beautiful country. But I still prefer the
U.S.A.

Give my mother the big news that I was
blessed by Pope Pius XII. I said prayers for
all of my family in Saint Peter's Square. My
parents did not see Rome or the Vatican; but

149

here I am thanks to Uncle Sam. It is
beautiful; tell the people in Brooklyn that
the Vatican survived with little damage.

I am going to close this letter now. I
can't think of anything else to write. I love
you more each day. You and my mother will
be glad to hear I have been going to mass.

Love, your husband,

Carmine

***

J.J. found his way back to the brothel twice in the following week. He requested the same woman, *Bella*. He knew now that the sergeant had told her it was his first time. He understood because looking back, she had done all the work and had guided him into her. J.J. wasn't the first virgin Bella had transitioned; he was grateful. He was also grateful that no one back home would know. With his next visit she had given him more silent instructions.

On his last trip, he asked Prof to join him, and he agreed. Before they left, J.J. asked the sergeant how to say: *It's his first time* in Italian. J.J. would see to it that Prof benefited from his experience—but he would not share Bella. Bella would not be someone the two of them would ever discuss in that way. Prof went in first; but not before J.J. delivered the sergeant's words.

Prof was more frightened by this woman than by all the air raids combined.

Bella came for J.J. minutes later. Prof was waiting for J.J. afterwards and said, "I'm starving. Let's go eat a big bowl of spaghetti, and then get drunk. My treat." J.J. and the Sergeant made it their business to let the boys know about Prof's visit.

Carmine also had return engagements to the brothel. Like J.J., he requested the woman he had seen before. He was tempted to ask Angelina the question men always want to ask prostitutes: "How did you end up in this line of work?" But Carmine did not question her. They did not have sex; they made love. Carmine was at a loss to explain all of it. His whole body relaxed, and he ached for more. They spoke for a few minutes about the war. She loved the *Eternal City*; she cried when she said, "I am frightened the German monsters may still return." Carmine held her, kissed her forehead, and left.

***

The next day dawned with new plans on the horizon. "Okay boys," said Carmine, "The party's over. Write to your girlfriends and wives. There won't be time for writing love letters later; we'll be on the move and busy. I just spoke to the captain. There's a big push on and we need to issue the troops extra supplies. Just think of it this way: the war can't last much longer. We need to finish them off."

CHAPTER EIGHT

France, Belgium and Germany

September 1944-October 1945

Carmine found an attic that they could use for quarters. He made it comfortable for the boys; he even hooked up lights. They did their own cooking; the dinner meal was either chicken or steak. He did not speak this country's language or understand its culture, and he found most of the French disagreeable. Sleep did not come easily in France. He would lay awake thinking of Pina and of the soldier Bruno had killed; it haunted him. The soldier's family would not welcome him home or at the very least, bury him. Bruno had counseled that the *maiale,* pig, would have raped more Italian girls, maybe 12-year-old girls; and when he returned home he would continue to rape. That usually satisfied Carmine, at least temporarily.

French women. The boys had trouble concentrating on the war; it was *French women* who occupied their thoughts. They walked around the warehouse mimicking bad Parisian accents and singing that old song: *How ya gonna keep 'em down on the farm after they've seen Paree.* Someone needed to tell them that they were not in Paris. They were in a small town; the townsfolk probably had never been to Paris. The one thing in their favor was that they supplied the troops. To supply troops, it is strategically desirable to be close to ports. The ports have a way of attracting prostitutes.

As they did in Italy, they asked the other boys where they might find female companionship for sale. They got a few suggestions; but each soldier who had been to Italy agreed that the Italian women were friendlier. The French women, the soldiers informed them, were hard-core. Carmine's boys were up for a challenge. He told them they were on their own now.

"Remember boys, I don't speak the language; I'm no help to you. Watch your pay." J.J. and Prof did not hesitate to climb into the jeep. When they got to their destination, Carmine thought the place looked and sounded like a bad movie. There were scratchy songs sung by throaty women who put no one in the mood. The cigarette smoke was thicker than the smoke in the boy's room back in his Brooklyn High School.

The entry room made no attempt to look girly; it did, however, sell wine. The women could not be stereotyped; their ages and bodies varied greatly. Carmine suggested to J.J. that he go with the young one in the green dress. The older ones looked like they would shred all his recently acquired confidence. Prof followed J.J.'s lead and walked away with a chubby young redhead.

Carmine found humor in the situation and chose an older woman who probably hadn't smiled since she stole a pair of silk stockings from another prostitute. With the aid of hand signals, she gave Carmine an array of choices. He responded with his own hand signals which alerted her to his preference. His choice, from her *menu*, involved her servicing him; he would not touch her. Carmine was unresponsive; he remained stone face and never spoke. He dressed and waited outside. The only pleasure he derived was the satisfaction of knowing that he was colder than she; but it was not worth the price of admission.

J.J. and Prof bought two glasses of wine and looked like they had found a temporary distraction from the war; but Carmine suspected that they favored the Italian brothel. The next night, one of the soldiers and Carmine went to a different brothel. On his next visit, he chose a woman who was pleasant and didn't wear a pound of makeup. She was a good choice, except for her awful perfume. Tonight was also for his pleasure only; but his face had softened and he responded to her touch.

Thanksgiving was a few days off and the boys would have a 20-pound turkey. The French had delicious cheeses, wines and breads; but on that Thursday, November 23, 1944, it would be an all-American feast. The boys ate by themselves, cooking everything but the bird; it was too big for their stove. They had sweet potatoes and corn, and they mashed up bread and mixed it with fried onions and sausage to make a passable stuffing. They ate apple pie and drank cider. Rachel had mailed a box of Fanny Farmer's candy; they savored each piece of chocolate.

J.J. and Carmine explained to the boys that their Thanksgiving back in New York was an Italian/American blend that the Indians would never have recognized. Besides the turkey, their mothers served olives, cheeses, salami, peppers, pasta, artichokes and chestnuts. Then there was a *sweet table,* or dessert table, which featured black coffee with anisette. Afterwards, there were the mandatory card games. The boys added to the conversation and recounted their family traditions. The boys were melancholy; but it was war. They decided to play cards as a tribute to their sergeant.

"A gang just came up today to take over where we are now, so that means we are moving north," said Carmine. The boys burned their letters from home; they needed to carry less stuff. They moved north. They unpacked. They set up. On their second night in their new location they ate at a real French restaurant, and it was a gift for their palate; the French could take simple food and turn it into a feast. Tonight there were no women, no card games, and just two bottles of French wine; tonight the food was the entertainment. Due to wartime restrictions, the menu was limited. Tonight they were offered *coq au vin,* chicken in wine. They couldn't get enough of it; they ripped off chunks of French bread and soaked up the juices. Next, they sampled a large selection of cheeses that they ate with more French bread. A plate of macarons arrived at the end of the meal, accompanied by coffee.

The soldiers sat quietly after dinner and basked in the joy of the banquet. Everyone was in a good mood at the same time—that almost never happened. J.J. and Carmine had one conspiracy that did not come to fruition. The French ate *escargot*, snails. They knew that it might be on the menu tonight; they would not disclose its identity until after the meal was eaten. How would these American guys take to eating snails? Carmine and J.J. ate snails; snails were part of many Italian dishes. Until Carmine was 10 years old, his mother told him the snails were mushroom stems; he ate them unquestioningly; and by the time he learned the truth, he didn't care. They thanked the cook, the proprietor's wife, for the delicious meal and asked her if she would consider being an American Army cook? She smiled, but politely declined the invitation.

Feeling contented and relaxed, the boys were not ready to hit the sack; they decided to see the movie being offered that night. They invited the sergeant. "Not even Ginger Rogers could keep me out of my bed tonight," said Carmine, "besides, that movie-*Top Hat*, is 10 years old. I went to see a movie last week and I almost froze to death; there was no heat. The only movie that could get me there is *Casablanca;* I love that song: *As Time Goes by.* I'll stay in my bed by the stove and write to my wife.

***

November1944

156

France

To my darling Rachel,

How was your Thanksgiving? It was a big feast, I'm sure. We didn't do so badly—we had a big turkey, vegetables and stuffing; and the boys really enjoyed the Fanny Farmer's candy. You know I prefer chicken, but the boys wanted turkey—so my boys got turkey. All that cooking I saw in my mother's kitchen came in handy. These farm boys can fry bacon and eggs and that's about all. I'm the cook. Tell my mother I cook everyday and the boys think I should open a restaurant when I get back. They miss biscuits and gravy. Can you find a recipe?

You asked me if I'm giving the French women lessons? The answer is: no . . . they don't need any lessons. I'm sure by now you understand why you didn't get a lot of letters in July and August; we were busy issuing the soldiers extra supplies for the battle in the south of France. I'm still not sure how much the censors will allow me to write. Thank you for the two shirts; but darling I don't

157

need them where I am now. You can wear anything you want, as long as you're warm. No one gives a damn.

I finally saw sunshine today; it seems like the sun never shines in France. Rachel, I just don't like the French. In my book, they're out. You reminded me of how sick I was in Italy; but I would still rather be there than France. Hell, I would rather be in Germany. Also, darling, of course I wear my wedding ring everyday—and of course I'm being faithful. You don't seem to understand that all I do is work, eat, sleep and watch out for air raids.

Christmas is coming, I am trying to send you a nice present. If I ever get to Paris, I will buy you something swell—maybe a fancy nightgown. I already ordered flowers so I know you will at least get that in time for Christmas. Make sure you have fun on Christmas; don't sit around and be sad because we're apart. The way things are going, I'll be with you next Christmas Eve; and I'll escort you to midnight mass. Then we'll open the little gifts we bought each

other. Don't forget me. You have been so
strong and a good Army wife. It is almost
over, and then I'll come home to you.

I Love you.

Your husband,

Carmine

***

"We're moving north, and before we leave we're going to
requisition extra warm clothes for ourselves. The farther north we
go, the colder it is; and we still have January and February ahead
of us. When are these Germans going to give up?" Once more,
Carmine and the men packed up. As much as they were unattached
to their current location, it would at least it would have been
familiar on Christmas morning.

***

They were settled into their new location by Christmas Eve.
They headed over to the Red Cross. A soldier had chopped down a
tree and Carmine made a wooden stand for it. They ate a turkey
dinner and someone sang Christmas carols. Carmine had
convinced the men not to open their gifts from home until
Christmas Eve. Now it felt more like a holiday with the men
ripping open packages and sharing favorite Christmas cookies.
That night, drinking was the only cure for their homesickness; and
they drank until it no longer hurt. The next day they went to mass

and gathered for a Christmas feast. The chaplain prophesized, "Someday when you're old and gray, you'll look back on this day with affection." Somehow, Carmine believed him.

He allowed himself to consider Bruno's house. Yolanda cooked for days; Pina busied herself with Neapolitan pastries. Did Giovanni celebrate Christmas? He was certain that the boy would not refuse presents. Was Nonno content living under Bruno's roof? For the first time, he realized that Tessa would probably have a man in her life. He imagined that there was a rich man—possibly one of Bruno's associates—who bought her beautiful presents. He had a momentary twinge of jealousy but he was really indifferent to her. How he missed Giovanni; but he knew that Bruno loved the boy. Bruno was the boy's guardian angel. What strange relationships a war produces! As soon as thoughts of the dead soldier entered his head, he stood up, put on his jacket and went for a walk. The cold air hitting his face helped erase the unwelcome memories.

The war pushed north, and the boys followed the war. The news reported these days was good and it gave the men hope that the war was coming to an end. They were cold and they were tired. They traveled by truck over roads that were, at times, heavily damaged. On this day the truck slid into a drainage ditch and it almost toppled over. They jumped out and spent hours getting the truck back on the road.

After traveling a few miles, Carmine saw a house that looked occupied. He ordered his soldier to drive closer to the house. A civilian opened the door and waved them in. The only word the French man repeated was *Americain*. The men were so worn out that they accepted the man's hospitality recklessly; there could have been Germans inside.

The risk paid off; the house was free of Germans and there was a fireplace. No one spoke French so Carmine's Italian would have to suffice; but it was clear that the old man and his wife were giving them a place to spend the night. Carmine instructed Fish and Mac to get five of Rachel's canned foods and eight blankets off the truck. Carmine handed the man money and gave the old woman the five cans of food. With her arms surrounding her treasures, she rushed into the kitchen and placed the food on an ancient wooden table. Then she pushed the gray strands of hair away from her face, wiped her hands on an over-sized apron, reached for a knife and began cutting up potatoes. She served the Americans hot soup with French crusty bread. The steam from the soup rose to warm their faces, giving them a gentle comfort. Carmine would later say that no soup he would ever drink would taste as good.

After the meal, the couple retreated to their bedroom and the soldiers laid their blankets down by the fire. Carmine insisted that one soldier stay awake to stand watch. In the morning there was coffee and biscuits for the soldiers. Carmine thanked the couple and the men reluctantly boarded the truck and went back to the war. Just before they took off the old man ran out and handed them a bottle of wine. Carmine would need to reassess his opinion of the French.

Carmine and his men rolled into Antwerp, Belgium. The Allies had liberated Belgium earlier; however, while the port at Antwerp was under Ally control by September, it was not functional until mid-November. The Antwerp port was vital to the Allies because it was large and their ships, carrying much needed supplies, could reach the harbor. Carmine and his men would remain in Antwerp, supplying the troops, until Germany surrendered.

Carmine's next letter to Rachel would be written from Antwerp, Belgium; but the censors dictated that the heading on his letter not mention his location.

It was a brutally cold night and Carmine wrote his letter standing just inches from the woodstove.

***

APO no.3929

Hello my darling Rachel,

It can't be long now. Even the Germans
want to quit. I know I want to quit. I'm no

*good to this Army anymore; I'm finished.
Patriotism has worn off. I don't how I'll
behave when I get back because I don't
know myself anymore.*

*You asked me about the French girls.
Where I am now everyone looks half
German or half Swiss to me. They don't look
like the French. Today I ate two pounds of
real Swiss cheese; the guy wanted a pack of
cigarettes in trade. Boy was it good. You
wrote in one of your letters that you bought
a pair of shoes. You should see the shoes
these people wear. Wooden shoes, yes, all
wood like you see in pictures of Holland. I
thought only the Dutch wore them; but they
wear them here too. Of course the rich
people don't wear them; they get whatever
they want. I don't know if the censor is
going to cut this out. When you write back,
tell me if the letter was cut up.*

*When I get back I want to buy a brand
new Buick. Do you think we can afford it? In
a few years I would like to have our own
home; the G.I. Bill will give us a good deal.
Should we buy a house in Brooklyn or move*

163

somewhere where there's grass and a big backyard? I'll let you to decide. Get ready— we'll need to fill that house up with kids!

I am sorry this letter is a little angry. Rachel, I just want to come home to you. I'm cold, fed up, and lonely. But we are winning the war; we just have to get them to surrender.

I promise my next letter will be better.

Don't forget me.

Love, your husband,

Carmine

***

They were constantly stocking and re-stocking supplies; but they knew they had to push through their exhaustion and help supply the troops. The supplies were needed by the soldiers advancing to Germany —and that was the end of the line. Winter turned to spring, and the warmer weather lifted their spirits. For the first time in two years Carmine and J.J. attended Easter Sunday mass in a Catholic church, not in a chaplain's tent. It was a reminder of home; and they told each other that next Easter they would go to mass in their own parish.

Carmine liked the Belgians much better than the French; they were friendlier and they appreciated the American presence. Of course, Prof instructed them on Belgium's connection to New York City. He said, "Many of the people in Belgium are Walloons; they have Dutch roots. The Walloons were instrumental in settling New Amsterdam." J.J. invited Prof to visit him in New York after the war; together they would explore the Walloon roots in Manhattan. Carmine decided that besides Jimmy Rizzo, he would keep in touch with J.J. He wanted to keep his friendship; J.J. had been a loyal friend and companion.

***

The Germans surrendered on May 7, 1945. The headline in The New York Times, May 8, 1945 read: "THE WAR IN EUROPE IS ENDED! SURRENDER IS UNCONDITIONAL. V.E. WILL BE PROCLAIMED TODAY…" Carmine usually received the war news from the captain; but today the roar in the camp told him the Germans had surrendered. Everyone went wild; but then it all faded away when the boys became fearful that they would be sent to the Pacific.

Carmine calmed their fears, "I don't think the Army would send you to another theater; hell, you've been serving overseas! Besides, that part of the war will end soon. We are headed for Mannheim, Germany, so pack up." Carmine had no idea if they would be sent to the Pacific; he refused to ruin this day for them. There was a party that lasted all night, and the boys forgot about the Pacific. They drank. They sang. They danced. And in the privacy of their beds, some cried.

***

June 19, 1945

Mannheim, Germany

Dear Rachel,

Well honey, I'm coming home. The war is over and Hitler is dead. It took a long time, but the suffering is over. The prisoners of war and the wounded men are coming home first. The men with 102 points and over will come home this month. The boys with over 85 points were really happy; and honey, I'm one of them. I have 94 points, so I'll be home in a few months. Maybe I'll be home by September; who can tell? The papers say thousands of men are leaving everyday; but I haven't seen one man leave yet. Maybe there are so many men over here that it's not noticeable.

It's tough sweating out the waiting. I had another physical and I'm still 1A even with all that malaria. I've moved to Germany— what a deal this is. We are just like

*prisoners, only with no guards watching
over us with guns. We could get court-
martialed for fraternizing with the enemy, so
we can't move around much.*

*News of what the Germans did is coming
out now. How could German soldiers carry
out those orders? I don't care what they say-
they're as guilty as Hitler. Too bad he killed
himself; I would have liked to see him go out
the same way Mussolini did, and with his
mistress. Don't send any packages; I don't
know how long I'll be here. As soon as I
hear what I'm doing, I'll write to you.*

*It's over my darling, and we have to
restart our lives.*

Love, Carmine

***

Carmine tried to keep himself calm; but the stories about the Jews tormented him. All he could think about was Giovanni. If Bruno saved that kid from death, then he could be canonized as a saint in Carmine's book. What about Giovanni's parents? Are they alive? Should he write to Bruno when he returns home? The waiting was unbearable.

***

October 3, 1945

Mannheim, Germany

Dear Rachel,

This is it; I am shipping out in three weeks. I'm on my way. I'm the happiest man in the world. Don't worry about buying me clothes or having a party. SEEING YOU IS MY PARTY.

Here I come.

Love,

Carmine

Chapter Nine
New York
November-December 2018

Dear Cia,

My name is Ruby Dalton. My mother, Maria Dalton, is Nevada3. I am sorry this response took so long. I have not logged into Ancestry for a few months. I think I can add some clarity. One of the names you listed was Trotta. Are you related to an American WWII soldier Carmine Trotta? If you recognize that name then I believe he is at the core of your mystery. There had always been whispers by my great-Aunt Pina, that Carmine Trotta was my mother's father. In 1944 he was stationed in Naples; Maria was born in Naples in 1945. My mother told me that her mother, my Grandmother Tessa, had never denied Pina's gossip. I will wait

for you to confirm your relationship with
Carmine Trotta before I continue.

Again, I apologize for not getting back to
you sooner. Are you ever in Manhattan?

Sincerely,

Ruby Dalton

***

Cia stared at the screen for 10 minutes. Holy shit, Grandpa Carmine! It looks like you didn't spend every moment fighting the Germans; you seem to have found some down time. Don't worry, I am not judging you; but did you have to leave it to me to tell Sophia? Cia tried to absorb Ruby's news. What would be her next move? Who should she talk to first? Her two options were Jacob and Nicholas. Jacob would read her body language and determine if she was covering up her distress; he would comfort her. Nicholas would think she was engaging in histrionics and just roll his eyes; but it was Nicholas's lineage too. She also needed him to take the news to Sophia, the news that would kill their mother.

In the end she went with her instincts and decided to talk to Jacob; but first she put on her coat and drove to Starbucks. If she was going to wake him up and dump this news on him, she would at least bring him strong coffee and a croissant. He was awake when she got back. She sat on the edge of her seat at the kitchen table and waited for him to complete his continental breakfast.

170

"Okay Cia, tell me; I know if I put you off any longer your body will start shooting off rockets." She held his hand and guided him first to the computer and then to the Ancestry message post.

"Read." Jacob remained silent. He was afraid to respond. He needed to stay calm and think.

"Well, at least your mother wasn't adopted. I think that would have been the worst news. You should prepare yourself for the fallout. Get Nicholas involved; he has a way with her."

"Just say it, you won't offend me: she favors her golden boy. But before I present my findings to him, I'm going to tap my new cousin for more data. I want to bring this to Nicholas with more of the puzzle pieces in place."

***

Dear Ruby,

*Yes, I am very familiar with the WWII
soldier, Carmine Trotta. He is my
grandfather (I guess our grandfather). I live
on Long Island; could we meet in the city?*

Cia

***

Dear Cia,

*I live in Soho. Come for lunch. Send me
your e-mail address and we will set up a
date.*

Ruby

***

The cousins would meet on Thursday the following week at
Ruby's Soho apartment. Cia checked out the Soho address online.
It confirmed what she had suspected: Ruby was affluent. Uncle
Tony had said, "If they have money, then they found themselves a
family." In spite of being alone in the house, she laughed out loud.

In preparation for the meeting, Cia shopped for clothes, got a
manicure, and changed her hairstyle. She kept her distance from

Sophia and Nicholas; but on some level she wanted to share the news. Next Thursday couldn't come soon enough.

***

Finally, it was time to leave for Soho. She took one final look at her reflection and put on her coat. Jacob drove her to the train station in silence; he instinctively knew that her thoughts would be otherwise engaged. She boarded an almost empty train car and took her seat. In her hands she clutched a large envelope that she had filled with family photos.

Who should I be today? Cia wondered. *Should I be a sweet Brooklyn woman who has hung tightly to her southern Italian roots? Am I a sophisticated New Yorker who has a reserved edge about her? Am I someone indifferent to the DNA results and just placating her mother? How should this scene be played*? Outside Madison Square Garden, she bought flowers; then stood in line for a taxi. She announced the address to the driver and sat back. She was filled with dread. *Why*?

The lobby was elegant; the elevator was elegant; the women on the elevator were elegant. *It's going to be a long lunch.*

"Cia, please come in. Thank you for the flowers. I love white roses." Yes, and of course, Ruby was elegant. She was about five feet nine inches, mid to late 30s, with auburn hair, a toned body, and a pretty face that strongly suggested Irish DNA.

After a moment they both spontaneously burst into laughter. When Ruby caught her breath she said, "How awkward is this? There will be plenty of time to see what shakes out of Grandpa Carmine's family tree; let's eat." The hostess had ordered lunch. There was a fruit and cheese platter, salad, and an assortment of gourmet breads. "I opened a large bottle of Italian wine; we can toast our ancestors until its empty."

They shared a light conversation, mostly focusing on Manhattan restaurants and the holidays. Christmas was rapidly approaching—only a few weeks away. Then Ruby put off the inevitable family business by giving her new cousin a tour of the apartment and introducing her to Gulie, her miniature golden doodle who had been confined to the office while they ate. The view was breathtaking, but the décor was high-end plain. Mostly white—with not one antique on display. She could have guessed at the simplicity of the furnishings before she entered; it was basic and unadorned like so many other apartments of wealthy New Yorkers. "I love living in Soho," Ruby said. "I enjoy walking in my neighborhood with Gulie. Mostly I just people watch."

The social niceties out of the way, it was time to unravel the mystery.

***

"Is *Cia* your given name?"

"My baptismal certificate says *Cecilia*; but my birth certificate says *Cia*. They named me after my father's mother, Cecilia. My mother was against the name; she thought it was too old school. She took the first letter and the last two letters of *Cecilia* and built me a name. My husband and I will do something similar. Our first child, boy or girl, will be named Cameron to honor Carmine; and no, I'm not pregnant."

Ruby smiled. "I'm also named after my father's mother, Ruby Ann."

It was Cia who broke the awkward silence. "You would have loved Grandpa Carmine; he was the most influential person in my life. He loved me unconditionally. He would talk to me about his childhood, but he never spoke of his war years. Now I understand his reluctance to share his war stories. I have some pictures with me; he looks so handsome in his uniform."

Ruby took up the photos, one by one. "Yes he is handsome; you bear a strong resemblance to him. Cia, I think this is more emotional for you than me. This has blindsided you; I was raised with the saga of Carmine and Tessa."

"Thank you, Ruby; it is unsettling. I loved Carmine. He found comfort as a young soldier, far from home. I understand. It's my mother's reaction that I am dreading. Let me give you a little background to put things into context.

"Carmine Trotta married Rachel Borgia in 1942. He was married before he was drafted. After the war Rachel had many miscarriages. She finally gave birth to my mother, Sophia, in 1954; there were no other children.

"Our family has its roots in Brooklyn. Sophia married my father, Guy Crispo, and had two children—my brother Nicholas is five years older. My parents divorced when I was 17 and my mother took back her maiden name. Today Sophia is 64. My brother is still single. My husband and I have an antique business on Long Island."

"Our story," said Ruby, "has more detours and intrigue. I will try to simplify it; over time we will add details to the story. These are the basics:

"Tessa and Carmine were lovers in Naples in 1944. Their love affair produced a child: Maria, my mother. Carmine returned to Brooklyn after the war.

"Tessa was bitter, she never spoke of Carmine. Tessa married a man named Vito Napolitano, who raised Maria as his own.

"Tessa had a sister, Pina. Aunt Pina would tell her niece, Maria, that her father was Carmine Trotta, an American soldier. My mother thought it was true. To her way of thinking, he had abandoned her; and that was the end of the story.

"When my mother was 23 she met an American naval officer, Patrick Dalton. He was stationed in Naples. They married and moved to Virginia. My father passed away eight years ago. My mother lives in Virginia now; she is 73.

"I was born and raised in Virginia. I'm 38; an only child.

"I attended Georgetown University where I met my husband, John Shanahan. After graduation, we married and he entered his family's Manhattan real estate business.

"That's the basics; I think we need more wine." Ruby lifted the bottle to refill their glasses, but Cia declined. She was emotionally drained and ready to go home.

Neither one wanted to add more to the story that afternoon. They would fill in the blanks through e-mails. They made plans to see each other after Christmas. Cia imagined Ruby would be skiing in Aspen for the holidays. They said their goodbyes and Cia took the elevator back to the lobby, heading back to her life that would never be quite the same again.

***

Always dependable, Jacob was waiting for her at the Hicksville train station. Cia climbed into the car. After giving Jacob a quick kiss, she launched right into an update on her visit with Ruby.

"I'm okay. It's confirmed: Grandpa had a daughter, Maria. I wonder if he knew about his daughter in Naples? How is my mother going to respond to the news? Could I keep this from her? How would she benefit from knowing about Maria?

"Ruby was friendly and rich. I think she wants to help me put the pieces together. Her family knew, or at least suspected, that Maria's father was an American soldier. She invited me back after Christmas. That was nice of her. The family tree has connected us; but I don't predict a close bond.

"I remember Linda, the antique dealer, telling me about her experiences with new Ancestry cousins. She said there isn't the foundation there that you have with cousins you knew from childhood. Linda said the relationships drop off. That's enough talk for one day; I want to go home and binge watch something mindless."

Jacob smiled at her as they headed home.

***

Good morning Cia,

I enjoyed our visit, and I look forward to more visits. I'm sorry I didn't know you when you had your surprise birthday party. John and I have eaten at Sammy's restaurant. I wonder if we were ever there at the same time?

*I checked the Ancestry matches this
morning and of course, we are matched. I
see you manage your mother's site too. I
manage my mother's and my Uncle Angelo's
site. He is actually my cousin but I refer to
him as Uncle Angelo. Just to clarify—you
are not related to Uncle Angelo. Uncle
Angelo is Pina's son. He is 73 and still lives
in Naples. There have always been questions
about his lineal father; but that does not
involve Grandpa Carmine. Uncle Angelo
had his DNA tested last year while he was
here with me. I think he needed a little
encouragement. My mother had her DNA
tested in the summer along with my husband
and me. My mother did not protest and I
wondered at the time if she was curious
about Aunt Pina's gossip?*

*I don't think I'm as apprehensive as you
about sharing the news with my mother; but
I am hesitant. Do you think the two sisters
would want to meet? We would need to step
lightly around that topic. By the way, you
said that since my mother's code name was
Nevada3, your brother was going to check*

179

the Nevada directory for Trotta. That would
have been futile. Nevada is the name of my
mother's dog and he is 3 years old. I would
like to meet my cousin Nicholas; please ask
him to join us next time.

Did Grandpa Carmine ever mention a
boy named Giovanni?

There's more to unravel.

Fondly,

Ruby

***

Since meeting Ruby, Cia's curiosity about Grandpa Carmine
had been growing. She realized that she had overlooked a key
source of information about her family's past: Jimmy Rizzo,
Grandpa Carmine's best friend. If anyone knew her grandfather's
secrets, it was his buddy Jimmy. Jimmy was 96 and his mind was
sharp. He could still remember the names of the officers he served
with in Burma over 70 years ago. She called him and set up a visit.

First things first. She would need to buy sausages, peppers,
Italian bread and sugar-free cannoli. She wanted to bring Jimmy
the type of food that wasn't served at his assisted living residence.
She was certain he'd enjoy some good home cooking.

The day of the visit, he greeted her in the lobby, dressed in a suit and tie and looking very handsome. They walked to the dining room, where Cia laid out a fancy place setting and served him his Italian specialties. After the meal, they drove to a coffee shop where they could talk in private.

Unlike Carmine, Jimmy liked to talk about his war days. Cia was losing her nerve; this was a touchy subject to broach. She was prying into the private bond of two men who had shared a lifelong friendship.

"Jimmy, my mother had her DNA or bloodline checked and there was one big surprise. It seems my mother has a half sister."

"Maria?" Jimmy asked. And there it was—laid out like a red carpet. How could one word say so much? It told Cia that the story was true. It also told Cia that her grandfather knew he had fathered a child, and that her name was Maria.

"So he knew about his daughter? Did he ever meet her?"

Jimmy was silent. "Cia, war turns everything upside down. Nothing is normal. Young men see things no one should see. War changes men, and when they come home they're not the same. Carmine was a good man. Yes, he broke his vows to Rachel. Carmine and Tessa spent more than one night together. When he left Naples he did not know she was having his baby.

"A few years after the war, he went to Naples to settle his father's inheritance. I went with him. That is when he learned about his Maria. Yes he met her; we both did."

Cia asked, "Did he contact her or the family when he came back?"

"No," said Jimmy. "He said he would write to her family, but he never did; and he never returned to Naples. He intended to return; he even kept a house there for many years. In the end he gave the house to his cousin Mafalda's two sons.

"Cia, he would cry to me, especially after a few beers; he was filled with guilt. Carmine wanted to be a father to Maria. Twice he decided to go get her and bring her back to Brooklyn and Rachel could go to hell if she didn't like it. But he never went; both times he lost his courage. Carmine would pound his fists and say that the bitch, Tessa, better be good to Maria. The day he buried his mother he confided in me that he should have told his mother about Maria; he kept her granddaughter from her. When Sophia was born I thought he would be happy again. It was worse. He felt more guilt. He imagined that Maria wanted him to hold her and not her sister Sophia. He took care of one daughter and abandoned the other.

"By the time you were born, he was older and he had pushed his guilt to the back of his mind. He gave you all the love he couldn't give Maria or Sophia. He was not a perfect man; but he was a good man."

"Jimmy, I loved Carmine and these stories make me see him as a young man, not as a grandfather."

Jimmy's face softened and his thoughts were in the past when he said to her, "Your grandfather called you his *gentile vecchia,* his gentle old woman, because even as a little girl you were a kind old soul.

"Did Ruby mention Giovanni?" asked Jimmy. "Your grandfather found him by the side of the road. The poor kid was starving, and Carmine helped save his life; but that's a story for another day."

Cia stood. "It's time to go. Thank you, Jimmy, for being the one person Carmine trusted with his whole story. I'm jealous of you. I wish I could have gone to Naples with the two of you to see his story unfold."

Cia drove Jimmy back to his assisted living residence, then headed home, lost in her thoughts.

Chapter Ten
Brooklyn, New York & Naples, Italy
May-June 1951

Men spoke in whispers, drank hot coffee, and set up their fishing lines. There was an eerie but peaceful component to being on a pier at 5:00 in the morning. Carmine arrived at Sheepshead Bay before Jimmy Rizzo; he valued this alone time. He had been home for over five years now, and life had settled into a routine.

The excitement of being back home with his young bride had not lasted. Rachel was his friend and partner; she was not a woman who aroused or delighted him. Three weeks after he had returned home, his father laid out a plan for the two of them; it would define the direction of his life.

"Carmine, with these hands I can build anything. I know how to bring in the customers. I draw sketches of the completed work for them. They like to see pictures, and I don't cheat them. You, my son, are good with workers, numbers, inventory and getting the jobs finished on time. We are a good team. We are *Trotta & Son.* What do you say?" Carmine's father looked at him expectantly.

Carmine smiled. "You've got a deal, Dad; and I'll apply for a G.I. loan to get our business started."

The venture was successful. Five years later, Trotta & Son employed 12 men—all of them veterans. Jimmy Rizzo was the first veteran to be hired. After the war Jimmy had joined the 52 Club, a program set up for returning veterans. It allotted the men $20 a week and helped them find jobs. Jimmy found work in a tool and die factory, but it was lousy work.

He thanked Carmine for rescuing him from the factory. Jimmy was the first foreman at Trotta & Son Construction. Carmine finally realized that his quartermaster position had given him useful skills. Also, he had regained his strength, the malaria had not recurred, and the workers called him *Sergeant.*

Carmine roused himself from his memories when he heard footsteps on the pier.

"Good morning Carmine," said Jimmy, my mother wants us to catch eels for tonight's dinner. Before you ask me, yes—I checked my shoes for scorpions. I can't break the habit; I check every morning. My wife filled up my thermos. Here, have some coffee." "Thanks, you can bring your mother the eels; I want to bring back porgies. My family doesn't eat them; but my neighbor put in a request," said Carmine as he brought the hot coffee to his lips.

They found a spot on the pier far away from the other men and cast their lines into the bay. Most of the morning passed in the silence that good friends can share. It was when they stopped to eat the pepper and egg sandwiches that Rachel had packed for them that Carmine began to speak.

"Before you got here this morning, I thought about the first time we met after the war. It was my big idea to meet by the Parachute Jump in Coney Island. You had written to me about making silk sheets from the parachutes, so I thought it would be funny to meet there. We took one look at the parachute falling to the ground and it reminded us of all the bad war stories. We left and went to a bar; that was the day I told you about my time in Naples.

Jimmy, my father's older brother, Zio Anthony, just died in Naples. They sent my father an official notice that said he inherited two houses and a factory. I volunteered to go there and check it out. Maybe I'll just sell everything. I want you to come with me. You're lucky; you'll get to see Italy in peacetime. My father will make sure your wife gets a paycheck while you're over there. What do you say?"

"It sounds like fun, said Jimmy. "Naples without Germans shooting at me; and my wife can't squawk. I'll tell her Mr. Trotta wants me to help sell his property—and I'll be getting paid. Yes, I'll go."

"Thank you, Jimmy. I want to look up Giovanni when I get there; he's about 16 now. I never wrote to Bruno; I didn't want

Rachel to find letters that mentioned Tessa. I can't lie to you; I want to go there to find Giovanni. I need to get answers."

"I hear you," said Jimmy.

Carmine continued. "There's something else. My father's Italian Club wants me to speak at their next meeting. They want me to talk about my experiences in the war. I hate the whole idea, and I am not a good public speaker. What can I do? If I say no, my father will be disappointed. Will you sit in the audience?"

Jimmy agreed. The following Sunday they walked to the Italian Club. Carmine didn't take 10 steps into the room before the older members approached him. They asked Carmine if he had fought in their Italian villages. They kept throwing names out at him. The last guy asked him to talk about the beautiful scenery. Carmine tried to be gracious. His father introduced him and he walked onto the stage. Carmine had stage fright; and to compound his tension, he didn't want to talk about Naples. In a rushed low voice, he spoke of his deployment to North Africa where he contracted malaria. Carmine told them he was sent to Italy, France, Belgium and Germany.

He was silent; then he announced, "My friend Sergeant Jimmy Rizzo served in the Pacific; join me in welcoming him." Jimmy understood; his buddy needed help. Jimmy walked on to the stage and addressed the audience.

"I was drafted in 1942 sent to Camp Crouder in Missouri for basic training," Jimmy began. "Then I was sent to Louisiana. My final destination was Burma, where I spent all of my military service. I was a warehouseman, similar to Carmine.

"The Burmese jungle was treacherous. Not only were the Japanese bombing us; but we had to worry about typhus, scorpions, and tigers. The bugs were a constant torment. I had the most fear when I was on guard duty. It was pitch black and I was always afraid that a tiger would leap out at me.

I had to deliver generators to the British doctors, which meant I had to travel on the Burma Road. The Japanese knew the Burma Road was the major supply route, so that's where they dropped their bombs.

"Burma was isolated; reporters and entertainers rarely showed up. There was no place to go. There was no Rome or Paris to visit—there was nothing. One day I was in a warehouse when the captain said in a steady voice, "Get Out." I ran out just as a Japanese bomb destroyed the warehouse. On another day, the tent next to me was bombed, killing a soldier right in front of me. I saw Frank Merrill of Merrill's Marauders. And Earl Mountbatten greeted us when we first arrived in Burma.

When the war was over, I was happy to get back to Brooklyn. Even now, every morning before I put my shoes on, I check the inside for bugs. I go dancing in Manhattan every Friday night at the Arcadia Hall; it helps me forget about Burma. Thank you."

Jimmy and Carmine walked off the stage. The audience gave them a standing ovation.

***

They sailed for Naples three weeks later. Jimmy was excited; Carmine was apprehensive. His plan was to just show up at Bruno's house. He had told Jimmy everything. He remembered Jimmy's response: "I'm surprised you found time to fight a war."

The journey to Naples would take 10 days. Their accommodations were tourist class, or the cheapest passage. Four men to a room, two sets of bunk beds, and a bathroom down the hall. The two strangers in their cabin spoke only Italian; Carmine and Jimmy pretended not to understand the Italian language so they could eavesdrop on the men's private conversations. The two conspirators listened to the strangers complain that Jimmy and Carmine snored and had body odor. "Hell, said Carmine, as long as they don't say they find us attractive, I don't care. In fact, I'm not going to shower until the last day. Fuck them."

While on board, the two friends spent their time eating, drinking, singing, and finding their way back to their cabin; they repeated this routine each day. The routine worked well for them. They liked it. Neither one admitted that they liked the idea of being unburdened for a few weeks.

On June 16, 1951, they stepped off the ship at the Port of Naples. The port was more welcoming this time—it actually smelled like sea air and not burning rubble, and the people had lost their wartime expression of defeat. Carmine purposely inhaled deeply to signal his brain that the war was indeed over. Naples was still rebuilding five years after the bombs devastated its land. But it was spring: the hills were green, the air was fresh, and women had planted flowers. Naples, like spring itself, was in rebirth mode.

Carmine's cousin met the ship and drove them the 32 miles to Cervinara. The two Americans weren't quite sure which was worse—the man's driving or the condition of the roads. He hit bump after bump; but he never stopped smiling, which irritated his passengers. The car coughed and grunted as it made its way northeast; at one place, outside of Nola, it overheated. They had to sit and wait for the engine to cool down before Jimmy could pour water into the radiator.

It was two hours before they arrived in Cervinara. They were hot, thirsty and irritated and wanted nothing more than to have a drink and then take a bath and a nap; but they had to sit and eat with the relatives. The Americans were treated like celebrities because they were Americans. To the relatives, all Americans were rich; and being rich made you worthy of special treatment. Jimmy and Carmine sat at the outdoor table and were treated to a feast. First they ate fresh pasta, southern style with tomato sauce. Today there was sausage and chicken slow-cooked in a red wine sauce and eggplant dipped in flour and egg and fried with onions. Also on hand were artichokes with breadcrumb and garlic stuffing and loaded down with extra virgin olive oil. There was a seemingly endless supply of wine being poured into half-empty glasses. The salad was served at the end of the meal.

Then the women competed with each other for top honors in baking. Pastry, cakes and anisette cookies covered the table, served with espresso, anisette and small sugar cubes. Today there was no talk of business; today was for feasting. The serving of the espresso signaled the end of the party. Carmine and Jimmy were shown to a room in the back of the house where they would spend the night. They found the beds uncomfortable and smelling of mildew; but they still fell into a welcoming deep sleep.

On Thursday, Carmine toured the closed macaroni factory. His uncle had worked all his life at the factory and Carmine would not disparage its worth. Next he visited the two houses; they were small but structurally sound. Jimmy and Carmine slept in the larger of the two for the remainder of their stay.

On Friday, he borrowed a relative's car and drove to Bruno's house. Jimmy stayed behind; Carmine would need to talk to Bruno alone. He drove to the port first; he could find his way north from the port. He found the house. His heart beat like a battle drum. He wanted to turn and run. He fantasized that Giovanni would be working outside; he would see him and run to him. Instead the house was quiet. Two armed men approached the car and asked him what he wanted. "I am here to see Bruno Falco, my name is Carmine Trotta." They told him to wait.

After a moment, Bruno burst through the door and greeted him with a kiss on both cheeks. "Come inside, I thought maybe you had died in France." Yolanda rushed over and hugged him; she then introduced him to a small boy; his name was Angelo. "Yolanda," said Bruno, "Carmine and I will go outside, keep Angelo in the house. He's a good boy; he'll listen to you."

Outside, Carmine shot Bruno a questioning look. Bruno nodded. "The boy belongs to Pina. Yes, he is from the attack. He looks like a German. When Yolanda was sure Pina was with a baby; she kept her with us. Yolanda, of course, delivered the baby. When Pina saw him, she said he looked like an angel and named him Angelo."

They paused on their walk. Carmine leaned against a wall for support. "How is Pina?" he asked cautiously.

"She survived because of Yolanda," said Bruno. "Pina did not understand that what happened to her brought a child. Pina was excited to be pregnant; she wanted a baby. She is a good mother— maybe more like a big sister, but she has us."

"Make no mistake Carmine. Pina was never hurt by wicked tongues; and we love the boy. Pina is at the bakery; I opened a bakery for Pina and Yolanda after the war, just like I told you I would. What can I say? They like to bake. There is another bakery in the village; I do not put it out of business because the owner helped Giovanni during the war."

"Nonno saw the baby before he died. It was a heart attack. His heart was broken—too much sadness." Carmine looked around and realized they'd made their way back to Bruno's house. Carmine was relieved when Yolanda called them in to eat; he had questions, but he was afraid of the answers.

Angelo was beautiful; he looked like Pina but with blonde hair and light skin. Carmine stared at the boy and wanted to be outraged by the events; but the little boy just brought him joy. He sat Angelo on his lap and sang to him.

After lunch, Pina came home. She no longer looked childlike; she appeared mature. "Carmine," said Pina, "Bruno sent word that you were here. I rushed back; I didn't want to miss you. You look good, Carmine. What do you think of my Angelo?"

"He looks like you; I can see you are a very good mother."

Pina beamed. "Yes, I am." Carmine imagined that Pina would survive the brutality that had been visited on her. Once more Bruno and Yolanda had been guardian angels.

Carmine shifted restlessly. "I must be getting back; but I need to ask about Giovanni. Is he living with you?"

"No," said Yolanda. "He is with his uncle in Rome; but he visits us in the summer. When you return, I will tell you his story;

but be content to know he is well. I will tell Tessa you will be here. When will you return?"

"Monday," said Carmine.

He was grateful for the solitary trip back to Cervinara. The day had unfolded like an old newspaper, giving five-year-old news. It was impossible for his mind to absorb it all; instead he focused on his uncle's properties. Jimmy had spent the day packing up the contents of the larger house so they would have room to walk around.

On Sunday, the Trotta clan gathered for another feast. Carmine began to put the pieces in place. His cousins wanted him to turn all the property over to them. One cousin said, "I can't believe he left everything to his rich American brother." Carmine listened. He did not speak. His father had given him free reign; he would make the decisions. After dinner, the women and children left the table; the male cousins remained seated.

One by one, each man declared his claim to the inheritance. Their words began to collide in Carmine's head. His understanding of their dialect had weakened; and the subtle phrases were lost on him. Carmine and Jimmy drank their wine and stood. They said good night and left in the borrowed car. Later that night, Carmine asked Jimmy for advice.

Jimmy's response was direct. "I understood most of the words; they resented your uncle's decision. Your uncle had one brother and he wanted to honor his younger brother. Also he wanted to show his American brother that he attained some wealth too. They can just all go to hell." Again, Carmine listened but did not speak.

***

Monday morning, Carmine drove out to Bruno's house. This time he remembered the gift he had bought him. There was coffee and Pina's anisette cookies on the table when he walked in the door. Pina was at the bakery; Angelo was with her.

"Bruno, I remembered that you played that scratchy record of *Torna a Surriento*, *Come Back to Sorrento*, when I would visit. I brought you a new copy from America; and Yolanda, I brought you a music box that plays that melody."

Bruno's eyes twinkled. "Wonderful! I will play it right now. Thank you."

Yolanda turned the crank on the dainty music box. She and Bruno shared a smile. "Mille grazie, Carmine," said Yolanda.

The three of them drank coffee, ate anisette cookies and listened to the haunting music on the *Victrola*. Carmine tried to wait for the couple to talk of Giovanni; but they sat quietly. Yolanda stared at the door. Was Giovanni going to surprise him? Carmine broke the silence by asking about Angelo. They responded like two grandparents: he was very smart and he was a good boy. He liked to help his mother bake and covered himself completely in flour. Then it was back to silence.

There was a knock at the door; it was Yolanda who reached the door first. Tessa walked in. Yolanda's voice held rage.

"Tessa, you came alone?" Tessa shot back, "Yes Zia Yolanda, I told you I would come alone. I brought the Communion dresses I made for the poor children. Now every girl will have a pretty white dress when she receives Communion. Give them out at church."

Yolanda accepted the bundle from Tessa. "That is kind of you; but we are disappointed that you are alone, come . . . say hello to Carmine." Carmine was not taking this Neapolitan Opera scene seriously. He suspected that the two strong-willed women antagonized each other. Yolanda should realize this was not sweet Pina.

Now it was time for the obligatory overview of Tessa. She looked beautiful, but with a sharp edge that Carmine did not like. Yes, he was aroused; he would have taken her to the bedroom if he could. She excited him in a way Rachel could not; but he did not want Tessa as his life partner.

He spoke first. "Hello Tessa, you look good; how are you?" Before she could answer, Bruno and Yolanda left the house.

Yolanda walked back in and said, "Tessa, I hope you will return to the house later; talk to Carmine. Bruno and I will go to my sister's house."

Tessa sighed and rolled her eyes as Yolanda quietly closed the door behind her. She turned to Carmine. "Zia Yolanda wants us to talk; so I will tell you my story. The Army sent you to Rome; I was left here with the family. Bruno and Yolanda took care of us; it was a sad time. I could not take care of Pina; all I did was cry. Yolanda took over or Pina would have died. Giovanni was no trouble, he was my helper. Nonno became weaker every day; he blamed himself for Pina's attack. He would cry to her and say he was sorry."

"I wanted more than this awful life; and when you abandoned me, I looked around for a man. I chose one of Bruno's business partners, Vito. He was powerful and rich and he would give me the things I wanted. He is 14 years older than me. I moved into his house and continued to sew my garments. I abandoned my family the way you abandoned me."

"When the war ended, I married Vito. His family did not approve of me, but we did not care. Vito found a job for me on Capri. I made elegant clothes for rich European women; I no longer wanted to go to America. I didn't need you or America."

Carmine calmly said, "I am glad you got everything you wanted; now you have money and no responsibilities. Why do you and Yolanda have bitter words? Does she disapprove of your husband?" Tessa laughed in his face. "Disapprove? She cares nothing for me or my husband. She did not want me to show up here alone today. She wanted me to bring Maria."

Carmine's looked puzzled. "Who is Maria?"

Four words sprayed out of Tessa's mouth like snake venom. "Maria is your daughter."

Carmine did not move; he replayed the sentence in his head. He looked at Tessa. "I have a daughter?"

"Yes, it was your parting gift to me. I named her after Nonno; his Christian name is Mario; he saw her before he died. Angelo and Maria are only weeks apart; Pina and I were both left with swollen bellies. We told Vito's family that the baby was his, that we wanted to wait until after the war to get married. I don't know what his family believes; but they are good to Maria. She was born January 19, 1945. Angelo was born January 3, 1945."

"Where is she?" mumbled Carmine.

"You will never see her," Tessa snapped. "I sent her to a friend's house. You will go home to America without knowing your daughter."

Carmine, stone-faced, stayed seated in his chair; his left leg shook uncontrollably while his hands gripped the edges of the table. Then with a rage that held no boundaries, he got to his feet and charged across the room. He slapped Tessa's face with a force that echoed across the room; she stumbled backwards, falling to the floor. Her newly-sewn Communion dresses also fell to the floor, spreading out in an unholy mass of crumpled fabric.

"Be careful Carmine, my husband is a ruthless man."

"Is he more ruthless than you?" he shot back. "Are you sure she is mine?"

"Yes, she is your baby. I did not sleep with Vito until months later. Vito can count on his fingers; but he wanted a young beautiful wife, and so he accepted all of it. I guess he will want me to give him a son one day. But I will not make my belly swell again."

"Where is she? Where is my daughter?" Carmine cried.

"Why don't you hit me again?" Tessa challenged.

"Just go back to your house or your palace, Tessa; I'll wait here for Bruno." Tessa walked out, her bitter defiance trailing in an angry wake behind her.

While he waited, Carmine helped himself to Bruno's wine. He drank sparingly; he wanted to grasp the reality of Tessa's words. Did she make the whole story up to torment him? He wished Jimmy was here with him.

When Bruno and Yolanda returned, they asked if Tessa would be back. "I don't think so. Tell me about Maria."

It was Yolanda who spoke first. "It is true; you have a daughter. I demanded that she bring her here today; but you saw how she refused. Tessa lived here for months after you left; we all stayed close to Pina. There was no other man. I told her that she looked pregnant to me. I knew before she knew.

"Poor Nonno, I was the one who finally told him. If they didn't bring their war to our door, none of this would have happened."

"Carmine," counseled Bruno, "you cannot bring this child home to your wife. Maria is loved and cared for and she thinks of Vito as her father. It is best to go back to America and leave this here. What else can you do? I will try again to convince her to bring Maria to you; but Tessa is spiteful. Maybe you can return to Naples in a few years and she will no longer be so bitter."

Yolanda handed Carmine a photo of his daughter, taken at her christening. He tried to sear the picture into his brain before he returned the photo to her. Carmine cried openly at their table. "I want to know about Giovanni, but not today. I can take another trip out here on Thursday. Maybe Tessa will come around by then. I need to get back." As Carmine drove off, he rolled down the windows to let the wind whip his hair—and help dry his tears.

***

Jimmy had trouble keeping all the pieces together. Carmine has a daughter? Rachel had had two miscarriages since her husband returned home. Was he sure the baby was his?

Jimmy took a pragmatic approach. "Carmine, Rachel will never accept this baby, and Tessa will keep her from you. Walk away. The child's life is here; your life is in Brooklyn. Do you think you are the only soldier with a war baby? The baby is cared for and Bruno and Yolanda will watch over her. Maria will be better off with her mother and Vito, her *father*, and maybe future siblings. That is a better life than knowing her father was a soldier who did not marry her mother and left them." Carmine listened; he knew that Jimmy's words made sense; but . . . *he had a little girl!*

The next day, Carmine and Jimmy drove to the center of town and looked up Signore Maretti. "Buongiorno, Signore. Bruno Falco sent me to you. I inherited the macaroni factory. I was told you would offer me a fair price for the property."

Signore Maretti looked thoughtful. "Yes," he said, "Signore Falco is correct. I would be happy to discuss with you the sale of the macaroni factory."

Carmine said, "I return to America this Saturday; I would like to complete the sale before I leave."

"Understood," said Signore Maretti.

Carmine knew that without invocation of Bruno's name, this business transaction would have been a bloodbath. Of course, Signore Maretti made him understand that with Carmine's demand for a quick sale, there would need to be a discounted price. Carmine did not haggle; he wanted his relatives to know he'd reached a decision.

When the purchase and sales agreement was signed, he said, "Thank you. I will have Signore Falco read it over, and I will be in touch with my father's bank. I would like the money transferred before I leave." The two men shook hands, and Carmine and Jimmy headed to their car.

"Now Jimmy," said Carmine, "let's have some fun. We're going to Rome." They did not return to the house first or stop anywhere to eat; they just drove straight north. Carmine's idea was to show Jimmy Rome and to buy gifts for his family; but he also wanted to retrace his days with the Army.

They arrived late, checked into a hotel, and found a restaurant. Next, they went to Mussolini's balcony where, a few years earlier, he had climbed the balcony and given a speech for the entertainment of the people below.

"Wait until I tell J.J. I came back to the balcony," he laughed.

They threw coins in Trevi Fountain and Jimmy walked around the Colosseum. Before they went back to the hotel, they drove to the Appian Way where Spartacus was crucified. The next day they bought gifts: Vatican souvenirs for their parents and jewelry for their wives and Maria. Carmine bought toys for Angelo, Maria, and his cousins' children, and antique coins for Giovanni. He kept an eye out for Giovanni's face in the crowd. Their shopping and sightseeing done, they headed back.

They arrived in Naples at 2:00 in the morning. They awoke later in the morning to the sounds of wood being chopped. Carmine's cousin had sent his sister's sons to the house to make repairs. Jimmy took the axes out of their hands and made them coffee. The boys were 15 and 17. Carmine learned that their father had abandoned them during the war. Their mother took in laundry and mainly relied on the charity of her family. Carmine paid them and sent them back home. The men dressed, ate breakfast and headed out to Bruno's house.

They knocked on the door and Carmine braced himself for another confrontation with Tessa. Yolanda opened the door and blocked the entrance.

"Maria is inside; her mother and Vito are not with her. Here . . . she likes little pink cakes; you can give them to her."

"How did you convince Tessa to allow this?" Carmine asked in amazement.

"Bruno told Vito that it would be a good idea. Vito agreed. I don't know how long Maria will be with us. Go. Take the cakes in."

Carmine took a deep breath and walked in with the plate of little cakes. Maria and Angelo were running in circles; Carmine watched as their heads bobbed with laughter. Yolanda was right behind Carmine; she made a little noise and pushed him forward.

Carmine said, "Maria, I brought you little pink cakes. Will you share them with Angelo?"

Maria grabbed for the cakes and handed one to her cousin Angelo. Carmine retreated; he and Jimmy found chairs and sat facing the children. Jimmy winked at his friend. Carmine knew why Jimmy winked; it was obvious Maria was his daughter. She had the same brown curl that fell in front of his left eye. Plus, she looked like all the other little girls running around his cousin's house. The contrast between Maria and Angelo was striking. Maria was a child of Italy; Angelo was tall for his age and blonde.

Carmine just sat, transfixed, with a bright smile on his face. It was Jimmy who took the reins. He asked Maria the questions adults ask children.

"How old are you? Do you know any songs? Do you go to school?"

Carmine tried to memorize the sound of her voice; then he asked her a question. "Do you like to play with dolls?" Maria nodded, and Carmine presented her with a doll dressed in a fancy white bridal dress and veil. Maria's face glowed. Carmine gave Angelo a toy truck, which he grabbed immediately.

Bruno entered the room and Carmine thanked him for his visit with Maria. Bruno shrugged the shrug that was older than the Roman ruins. "What can I say; Vito saw it my way. Vito wanted to come today and meet you but I told him to stay away." Bruno, Yolanda, Jimmy, Carmine and the two children sat down to dinner. Maria was seated next to her father. There were no formal introductions; Yolanda just called the men by their first names. Carmine watched how she picked up her fork, how she wiped off her face; every movement was a miracle to him. Carmine's fork and knife never left his hands for fear that he would reach over and pick up his daughter. Maria would be fearful and run from him; that would break his heart.

After they ate, Carmine asked Yolanda if Maria's toes were a little different. "Yes, the two middle toes on each foot are stuck together halfway up."

Carmine smiled broadly. "They are my mother's toes. They pass from the mother, to the son, to the daughter. There is no doubt; she is mine."

Jimmy played with the children while Carmine drank coffee with Bruno and Yolanda. "Thank you," said Carmine. "It is the best day of my life. But I also know it will be followed by sadness; I have to leave her here."

"War is a terrible thing," said Yolanda, "but babies will be born when they are unexpected—even in America. We will watch over her. This way everyone has a chance at a good life; and it is a blessing for me because I am a grandmother twice." Carmine smiled at Yolanda, stepped around the table, and gave her a gentle kiss on the cheek.

Then Carmine sat back down and switched topics. "Bruno, I have other business. I have sold Signore Maretti the factory; I brought the purchase and sales agreement with me for you to review before I finalize the deal. Then I need to follow up with the bank before I leave for home." Bruno nodded his understanding and took the paperwork as Carmine handed it across the table.

"Also," said Carmine, "do you think you could find work for two of my young cousins? I was thinking they could help out in the bakery."

"Yes, I could use two young men," Bruno said. "I want to start making bread again for the people, not just fancy little pastries. They will learn the bread trade. Or would you prefer they learn the fishing trade?"

"The bakery is better," said Carmine. "It is inside, the work is easier, and they will be able to bake bread for more years than they can fish. I will send them to you. Their father was a bum who abandoned their mother. Thank you Bruno, you have my respect." Bruno lifted his head in response.

Yolanda looked at the front door, alerted by a sound; she announced that Tessa was there. Carmine walked outside.

"Tessa, she is beautiful. I am sorry I doubted you. She is my child. Too bad she will not carry the Trotta name."

"Do you think I care that you are sorry?" Tessa spit back. "This was not my idea. Bruno rules the province. Even my tough husband behaves like a girl in front of him."

Carmine shook his head in bewilderment. "Tessa, what happened to you? I think that sweet Tessa at the egg man's house was all an act. You are a conniving bitch." Tessa glared at him in response.

Carmine continued. "I will give you my word that if you harm one hair on my daughter's head, I will come back here and cut your throat. Remember, Bruno and Yolanda will be watching you."

Tessa walked up to his face and said, "I'm a bitch?" Then she spit in his face. Carmine cupped her face with his hand and threw her backwards to the ground. Bruno's men rushed over and separated them.

Bruno raised his voice. "This will not go on in front of the children. Tessa, go home. My men will take Maria to you later. Carmine, go inside." Carmine walked toward the house, but then turned and said to Tessa, "I will say it again—harm one hair on her head and I will make the trip across the ocean and leave you dead." Tessa stalked off, her head held high.

Carmine felt emotionally drained. "Bruno, I want to hear about Giovanni."

Bruno clapped Carmine on the shoulder. "I will come to your uncle's house tomorrow night; I will give you back your paperwork then we will drink wine and I will tell you Giovanni's story."

Before Carmine and Jimmy left, Carmine handed Yolanda a tiny gold cross. "Yolanda, I would like you to give this cross to Maria next year when she receives her first, holy, Communion.

Perhaps you can tell her it's from you? Also, I bought Giovanni antique coins." Then, he leaned over and gave his daughter a kiss on both cheeks and held her tightly; he cried into her hair. Jimmy patted Carmine on the back; they thanked Bruno and Yolanda, said goodbye to the children, and walked to the car.

***

On Friday afternoon, Carmine and Jimmy went to the cousin's house. Today all the cousins would learn how Carmine would divide his uncle's property. There was plenty of food and homemade wine; there was also a priest present to bless the bread. The little girls played hide and seek; Carmine saw Maria in each of their faces. He would be carrying home a tear in his heart that would never heal.

After the meal, the women set out fruit, cheeses, and nuts for the men. Was the priest there to suggest to Carmine that he do the right thing? His presence annoyed Carmine; he chose not to acknowledge him. He placed a cigarette in his mouth with his usual ritual; he lit the cigarette, then shook the match three times, threw it to the ground and stomped it out. It was clear to Jimmy that his friend had no use for these people and wouldn't give them a dime.

When it was clear that Carmine had their attention, he began to speak. "My father and his older brother, Zio Anthony, loved each other. The inheritance was passed to my father as a gift; my father wanted to honor that gift. He sent me here to assess the property and make a decision. The macaroni factory was sold to Signore Maretti; the payment will be wired to my father's bank and that is the end of it. Zio Anthony left two houses; I have given these properties much thought. The larger house will be given to cousin Mafalda and her two sons. She is without a husband or an income. In this way my father and his brother will care for her. I have spoken to Bruno Falco; he will teach the boys to bake bread; they start Sunday. The smaller house I will keep; it will remain in my family. I will pay Mafalda to keep it in good condition; she will receive a payment each month. The smaller house has a larger parcel of land. I will allow all of you to plant crops to supplement your income. Mafalda can plant crops on her property; it is her house and her land. Now it is final."

Silence weighed heavily in the room. The cousins did not comment; they did not move a muscle.

"Carmine," one cousin finally spoke up, "it was our understanding that the factory would remain with us. We would try to bring it back to life or sell it. We would divide the money and our children would have a better life. Can we strip the factory of its metal?"

Carmine said, "No. Zio Anthony could have left the factory to you; he did not. I know all of you have helped Mafalda; now she can walk with dignity and have easier days." Before he left, Carmine signed the house over to Mafalda and told her sons to work hard. He also gave his cousin 50 dollars for the use of his car. The mood was dark; Carmine's extended family was clearly unhappy with the way things had worked out.

Even so, Jimmy and Carmine thanked them all for their hospitality and left. Before they reached the car, Mafalda ran out with cheeses and salami for their long voyage back to America. The night was clear and the sky full of stars. Jimmy and Carmine sat outside the smaller house, the one he would keep for himself, and drank homemade wine. Bruno showed up with a driver; the driver was loaded down with sweets for their trip home. Carmine wished that Maria would have taken the ride; but it was not to be.

Bruno handed him the purchase and sales agreement that Carmine had asked Bruno to read. "What's this?" asked Carmine.

"It's the final price Signore Maretti paid you for the factory," said Bruno.

Carmine adjusted his eyes and said, "It's 300 dollars more than he quoted me."

Bruno nodded. "Yes I know. Signore Maretti decided this was a better price." Carmine thanked him.

"Bruno, should I write to you? I don't know what to do. Rachel could see the letters and I don't want to explain Tessa. She is not stupid."

Bruno shook his head. "No, do not write. This is your family's homeland; visit your homeland and the people you left behind. It is better than letters." Bruno gestured to the small house that Carmine was keeping. "This is now your house. Come back, visit, and lay your head in your house."

"Thank you Bruno, you are a good friend to me and to all that I love. If Maria ever needs anything, give it to her. I will see that you are repaid."

Bruno said, "She will always be well taken care of. Do not worry."

Carmine sighed and smiled. "Now, it is almost midnight; I am leaving tomorrow. Tell me about Giovanni."

"Ah, Giovanni. His name is Giovanni Levi. He is Jewish. Sit back; it is a long story."

Chapter Eleven
Naples/Rome/Naples 1940-45

Naples 1941

All of Giovanni's senses were heightened as he stepped off the train at the Naples station. He held Catarina's hand tightly for protection against the sea of people pushing past him. He was in a strange place, with strange smells and strange sounds. His mother had told him it would be an adventure; but he was afraid of the people's faces, and their unfamiliar language confused his ears.

Rome 1940-1941

Sergio and Stella Levi, Giovanni's parents, owned and operated a hotel in Rome. Its old-world charm and excellent service had made it the preferred choice for the European elite. This year there were guests who would mischievously whisper to Stella that the only challenge with her hotel was the pastries she served. "Now we are all fat," they would tease.

Nine months before Giovanni boarded the train for Naples, Stella had travelled there to recruit a Neapolitan pastry chef. There she had discovered 18-year-old Catarina. While Catarina had followed her father's pastry recipes, it was her skill with their presentation that had attracted Stella. It would be worth the extra bags of sugar she would need to order to keep the guests happy and returning for more.

The negotiations with Catarina's father had been arduous; but Stella finally convinced Signore Lorenzo that Catarina would be protected from the Roman men and she encouraged him to visit Rome to check on his daughter. She also added that most of the girl's paycheck would be sent directly to him. Stella's negotiations finally paid off; Catarina's father gave his consent, and the two women boarded the train for Rome.

Not only did Stella's new young pastry chef bring in new business; Catarina became a friend to little Giovanni. Whenever the boy was out of his family's sight, they would find him, covered in flour, baking with Catarina and licking sugar off his fingers. Sergio said that if they weren't careful Giovanni would turn his back on the university and become a Roman baker.

Of course, Stella had also found her 20-year-old brother Roberto in Catarina's kitchen. The girl was shapely and naïve, which worried Stella. She had made certain Roberto understood that the girl was off limits. "Roberto, I promised Signore Lorenzo that I would protect Catarina's chastity. Rome is a big city; go find another signorina."

Rome in 1940 had become a treacherous city for the Jewish hotel owners. Sergio and Stella Levi's primary concern was their son's safety. The only escape that seemed feasible to them was to send their six-year-old south to Catarina's home. Catarina had only been in their employ nine months; but they had no choice but to trust her. They asked her to hide Giovanni's identity, and they gave her new papers for the boy. Catarina was instructed to tell her neighbors that the boy was an orphaned second cousin and a Catholic. She was sent away with hidden money and jewelry to be used for their son's care. "As soon as it is safe, we will come for him."

Before they left, Stella spoke to her son. "Giovanni, there is trouble in Rome. Catarina will care for you until Rome is once again a happy place for children to play. You must listen carefully to me. No one is to know that you are Jewish; it is not safe to tell anyone. And do not tell anyone about your family. Catarina will speak for you; just remain silent if they ask questions. Now I can keep my promise to you. You will finally see Naples, and there will be many children there. When I return for you, we will go to Pompeii and you will see all the ruins. This is a great adventure with secrets and new discoveries. Momma and Poppa love you. You must not keep Catarina waiting. Be a good boy."

Naples 1941-1945

When Giovanni reached Catarina's house in Naples, he was excited to find so many children. He liked it here; the children played competitive games that made him run and catch his breath. Sometimes he did not understand the children's words, but he followed their lead. That night they found a bed with a table for Giovanni and they stuffed him with pastries and pasta.

Despite their famous bake shop, the Lorenzos were simple people who had no political understanding of the war; they did not read the newspapers. The idea of rich Giovanni not being safe in that palatial hotel was incomprehensible to Catarina's father. He did, through his daughter's whispered words, come to understand that Rome—and also Naples—were no longer safe places for Jewish children. They must hide Giovanni's Jewish heritage from everyone.

Signore Lorenzo collected all the money and jewelry his daughter was given and added it to the family's finances. He suspected that when they came back for their son there would be a substantial reward for hiding him. He would see that Giovanni was returned well fed and healthy; he would expand his business with Roman money.

Signore Lorenzo wasted no time in putting Catarina and Giovanni to work. "Catarina, you are home now and there is work for you and many pots to wash. This is not a fancy hotel with a big staff. You are not this boy's mother; you cannot spend your day caring for him. He must work too; he can sweep and stock the shelves. No one is a guest here; if you eat here, you work here. The only good part of this war is that the soldiers have money for my pastries; otherwise maybe we would all starve."

As three full years passed, Catarina tired of caring for the boy; she wanted to spend her free time with her friends—especially Michael. Her father too, thought the boy would be gone by now and a reward would be in his hands; but Signore Lorenzo would not give away the boy's secret. The Germans were animals; he saw with his own eyes how ungodly they were. The boy would be safe under his roof.

Giovanni imagined he had done something wrong. Catarina and her family were kind to him when he first came to live with them; but now they wanted him to work and not eat so much. He wanted Rome to be safe again; he missed his mother. Here the other children had mothers; but he was alone and far away. Even Catarina no longer wiped his tears or took him to the river to fish.

Each night he would talk to his mother. "Momma, I miss you; please come for me. If Rome isn't safe I will play in the storeroom where no one will find me. I don't want more toys; I want you to cook for me and teach me about Pompeii. I do not want to come home with Catarina; I think I did something to anger her."

When Giovanni turned nine years old; he was abruptly sent to live with a family by the church. It was Catarina's mother who demanded the child leave their house. The wagging tongues of the old women sent her into a rage. Signora Gallo told her of the scandal. "Signora Lorenzo, I hear many things at the market. Even at church tongues are sharp. The women accuse Catarina of having a baby without a husband. They say she hid the baby here and then moved away. Now she is back with a boy that is her son. She will never find a husband; no one will want a woman with a boy."

Catarina's father listened and then spoke evenly to his wife. "That makes no sense. The boy is too old for Catarina to be his mother; and where did we hide the baby before she left? You listen to the tongues of old crazy women."

His wife countered, "Old crazy women can ruin Catarina's life; this gossip will haunt her. Send him away."

Giovanni's few belonging were put into a bag; and he was sent off to live with another family. Signore Lorenzo promised to give the family five loaves of bread each week to contribute to his care. The family was poor and the bread would help feed them. The boy's religion was not mentioned. Signore Lorenzo felt bad for the boy; but his wife was relentless. He would find a way to collect the reward for the child; he had put too many meals into the boy's stomach.

Giovanni slept on a dirty mat laid out on the floor. No one spoke to him. The older boys grabbed the food he was given until he learned to hide it behind a bushel. Each day he awoke and was handed a sack. His job was to look for dry twigs to build fires. No one beat him; but no one took an interest in him, either. He cried at night until the other children complained. Then he would cry while he searched for his twigs.

He still talked to his mother at night; but now he spoke to her with urgency. He told her that he did not care if Rome was not safe; he would rather be in Rome than away from her. He wanted her to wash his face and sing him songs.

Signore Lorenzo came to see him once. Catarina never came to see him. One day while collecting twigs he met an American soldier, Carmine. Carmine found a home for him with Nonno and then with Bruno. "Sometimes," he told Zio Bruno, "I worried that Catarina would come for me; but I knew you would not allow her to take me. Everyone is afraid of you."

***

The ringing of church bells was the first sign. Then everyone began shouting; the American soldiers started honking the horns of their Army trucks. The war was over; the Germans were defeated. It was May 7, 1945. Giovanni continued to live with Zio Bruno; life did not change for him.

Roberto, Giovanni's uncle, had been in hiding since 1943.When he was confident the news was correct; he left the farm that had sheltered him and traveled to Naples. He prayed that Lorenzo's Bakery had not been bombed; and in its place he would find a pile of rubble. "Buongiorno, Signore Lorenzo, do you remember me?" asked Roberto.

"No," said Signore Lorenzo, "I do not remember you. Do you wish to buy something?"

"I am Roberto; your daughter Catarina was the head baker at my sister's hotel in Rome. I was introduced to you when you were a guest at the hotel. I am here for my nephew, Giovanni. My sister sent him here with Catarina; she was to care for him."

The man's hesitation frightened Roberto. He braced himself for the words that would leave this man's mouth. "Giovanni is not far from here. He is living with another family; I will take you to him. I will give you my address for your sister. We kept your nephew safe for many years."

Giovanni froze when he saw his uncle. Was he looking at a ghost? He walked slowly up to him and touched his arm. "Is that you, Zio Roberto?" When his uncle said "Yes," Giovanni released the tears that had been stored in his heart for his short lifetime.

"I want to go home," he told his uncle. Yolanda invited Roberto to have lunch with them. While Giovanni played with Angelo, the two men spoke. They encapsulated the last few years. Roberto thanked Bruno and Yolanda for saving Giovanni's life.

"Signore Falco, I do not know what I will find in Rome; but my nephew and I will learn together what happened to our family.

The two of us are not alone; we have each other. I will never leave him."

Bruno shook his hand and said, "I would like you to bring Giovanni back for visits; I will miss him. Will you go to America?"

"No," said Roberto. "We will live in Rome for now; eventually we will settle in Palestine."

Bruno arranged for one of his men to take them to Rome. Yolanda packed up Giovanni's few possessions and prepared food for the trip. Yolanda saw Bruno give money to Roberto and hand him a letter.

"Tell my Roman friend, Signore Tomanelli, that I would be most appreciative of any help he would give you." Roberto nodded his thanks.

When it was time to leave, Giovanni held on tightly to Bruno; there were more tears. Giovanni was settled in the car when he suddenly jumped out and ran into the house. He picked up Angelo and stood like a statue holding him. "I love you Angelo. You are my little brother. I wish Maria was here, will you tell her that I will come back to visit? I will bring my mother and father with me. But I must go home now."

In the months that followed, Signore Tomanelli got word back to Bruno. Giovanni's parents had been sent to a concentration camp. They did not survive.

Chapter Twelve
New York
December 2018-January 2019

"Tomorrow is the last night of Chanukah," Cia told Nicholas. "I waited until Sunday to have a traditional dinner since you would be here; it will be more festive with my brother at our table." Nicholas smiled at her. Cia continued. "Jacob is at the store, so we have plenty of time to review our revised family tree.

Nicholas looked over the new family tree. "I like the way you charted the family tree; you could begin a new career as a genealogist. It's the human stories behind the DNA matches that capture my interest."

"Jimmy Rizzo told me he met Maria when he went to Naples with Grandpa," said Cia.

Nicholas shook his head and said, "You mean even after Grandpa died, Jimmy kept his secret? I think you need to pay Jimmy another visit. What other Neapolitan operas is he concealing?"

"Who knows?" said Cia, smiling.

"So," said Nicholas. "Mom and I are coming for Christmas dinner; I suggest we sleep over. Then on December 26, we sit Mom down and tell her that she isn't an only child. By the way, I'm single again; so I won't be bringing anyone.

Cia sighed. "Nicholas, women are not library books—you can't return them after 21 days. What are we going to say to Mom? Let me rephrase that: what are *you* going to say to Mom?"

Nicholas said, "I haven't worked out the details; actually I think I should see how Mom's state of mind is on Christmas and the next day. If she's relaxed with a holiday glow, she may be more receptive to Grandpa's story. If, on the other hand, she's stressed and exhausted from shopping and baking, it wouldn't be the right time to approach the topic and add to her stress."

"That makes sense Nicholas," replied Cia. "But I hope we can get this over with to lessen my stress. Oh, Uncle Tony will join us for Christmas. He's also sleeping over, but he has to leave early the next morning to celebrate St. Stephen's feast day at his church. I have kept him updated about Maria. Believe me; he wants to leave before Sophia detonates."

***

Nicholas and Cia watched as Jacob lighted the Chanukah candles at sundown. Cia presented her husband with a gift on each of the eight days of Chanukah; tonight she gave him marble bookends that he had admired on their last trip to the Hamptons.

Then they ate latkes, soup, brisket, carrots and sweet potatoes—a traditional holiday meal in Jacob's family.

Later, Cia drove her brother to the train station; but she did not go straight home. She pulled into the parking lot of her church and turned off the engine. The church was closed; but she was comforted by the proximity of her spiritual home. Cia cried. She cried the deep, sorrowful tears of little girls; she cried for Sophia. Sophia, who wanted the love of her father; instead she was met with distance and indifference. Sophia had wanted to be cherished and pampered by her father, but no . . . he would not yield. Carmine could not show love to one daughter and abandon the other. It was Carmine's guilt that had made Sophia *broken*.

In later years Sophia watched with sadness as her father showered her daughter, Cia, with attention. Where was *her* attention? Where was *her* affection? Cia knew that she had stumbled upon the reason for her mother's antagonistic relationship with her. Sophia was jealous of the bond her daughter shared with Carmine. Why didn't he love his own daughter? Why was Cia cherished and Sophia not worthy of the same love? Cia also understood why her mother favored Nicholas. Sophia did not compete with her son for her father's affection.

At some point, did Carmine think of Cia as the daughter he left in Naples? Was Cia a replacement for Maria? Cia dismissed those questions; she knew her grandfather loved her above all the others. Cia cried for herself. Carmine had set into motion her caustic relationship with her mother; it was always there beneath the surface. Carmine had also set into motion the resentment Cia felt toward her brother. When Cia stood back and watched her mother's exchanges with Nicholas, the adoration on her mother's face was palpable. Not so with Cia. And Cia cried for Maria— Maria, who was abandoned by her father. Did she cry for him at night? Maria had moved to America and had not looked for Carmine Trotta. Ruby would have told her.

Cia made a pact with herself. She would blame all the tears on the war and not on her grandfather. She knew that from time to time she would revisit this contract. Then she started the car and drove home.

***

At the same moment in time, Nicholas was on board a Long Island train headed west to Brooklyn. His thoughts were unsettled, too. World War II ended in 1945. Many American soldiers returned home to the arms of their loved ones—and to nightmares that would haunt them for the rest of their lives. Post-traumatic stress disorder was a diagnosis for the future. Nicholas understood that the fallout from war never ends. The adverse effects of war can plague not only the soldier but his children and his children's children.

His mother felt unloved by her father, which caused her to compete with her daughter. In turn, her daughter could never trust her mother to be emotionally supportive. His family paid a small price compared to the children who endured alcoholic or physically abusive former soldiers; soldiers who had served their country and had come home *broken*. War destroys more than bodies and property; it destroys the fabric of our humanity. As soon as Nicholas was back in Brooklyn, he headed for the nearest bar.

***

Cia's last stop was to the local liquor store. If Cia was to get through Christmas, wine would have to be an essential addition to the dinner table. With the aid of wine she would enjoy Christmas and not obsess over the day after and Sophia's impending fury. For now, Cia would focus on the fun part of the holidays: baking, cooking and setting a festive table that would impress even Martha Stewart.

On Christmas Day, Cia did her best to put on a happy face.

"Merry Christmas Mom; I love your Christmas sweater." Cia, with a glass of wine in her hand, leaned in and kissed her mother on both cheeks. "When you're settled, I want you to taste the tomato sauce. I have the grated cheese, salt, and pepper on the counter; you always add more." She turned to her brother.

"Merry Christmas Nicholas. I see you drove; I wouldn't be a Long Islander if I didn't ask about the traffic."

Nicholas laughed. "Merry Christmas Sis. The house looks beautiful—and don't ask about the traffic."

Cia busied herself in the kitchen; Jacob carried his mother-in-law's overnight bag into the guest room. Nicholas, rarely demonstrative, placed his arm around his sister and kissed her. Cia appreciated the support he was conveying through his body language.

Uncle Tony arrived loaded down with presents and Italian pastry. His first words were about food. "Cia I brought you *sfogliatelle*, your favorite pastry." Cia loved her Uncle Tony, her father's brother. He was always in a happy place. By contrast, her father was solemn and distant; when Sophia and her husband divorced, she cut off all ties with her in-laws. But Cia refused to give up Uncle Tony. Her father's sisters were another story; they had the same lackluster love of life as her father.

Sophia gave Cia a cameo that belonged to her mother. It had been a gift from Carmine; he sent it to Rachel while he was stationed in Naples. Cia did not mention that Carmine had given her his mother's identical cameo. Sophia gave Jacob and Nicholas imported Scottish scarves; she gave Uncle Tony a bottle of anisette. Cia gave her mother a designer handbag; Jacob had procured a rare book for Nicholas. For Uncle Tony, Cia had a shirt, a tie, and a sweater. Her uncle had never married; he needed a woman's touch in the wardrobe department. Uncle Tony gave

Sophia, Nicholas, Cia and Jacob leather gloves. Nicholas presented the four of them with gift cards.

After exchanging gifts, it was time to eat. First, Uncle Tony said a prayer. Then Cia served antipasto, artichokes, pasta with braciola, roast beef, and an assortment of vegetables heavily seasoned with garlic. The wine and a relaxed conversation flowed.

When dinner was over, they agreed they needed a little time before they could start on dessert. They walked into the living room. Cia asked them to stand by the Christmas tree. She pointed out ornaments that had special meaning for her. Some she had made in grammar school; others were gifts from family members. Her most cherished ornament was a snowman made of yarn. Cia made it in second grade and had given it to Grandpa Carmine. When he died, Cia found it in a wooden box on his workbench; she reclaimed it. She asked Uncle Tony if he had a Carmine story. Uncle Tony sat down, folded his hands on his lap and smiled.

"Rachel's brother told this story to me. Today it's funny; at the time, it was anything but funny.

"During World War II, Carmine mailed a package home to his wife, Rachel. He sent her a souvenir: a Nazi flag that he had ripped off a building after a battle. Rachel didn't understand the concept of war trophies. So Rachel did what she did with every piece of dirty fabric that came her way—she washed it. After which, she

228

opened her fourth-floor window and hung the flag on her clothesline." Eyebrows raised around the room.

Uncle Tony continued. "Now, while Rachel was born here, her father and older brother were born in Italy. They were in this country legally, but they were not citizens. Remember—at the beginning of the war, Italy was an Axis power; Italy was on the side of Hitler. Italian immigrants, like Rachel's family, were looked upon with distrust by their neighbors. The neighbors questioned their loyalty to America; and her father and brother lived in fear of being deported.

"So one day, Rachel's brother is walking down the street in the middle of the afternoon. He looks up and sees a Nazi flag waving in the wind over his house. All the blood drained from his face; his 250-pound frame flew into the house and he took the stairs two at a time. He opened Rachel's door, pushed her out of the way, and opened the window. He pulled that clothesline toward him with such force that he had rope burns on his hands. He took the flag downstairs to the backyard, started a fire in a trash can, and burned it. Then he admonished his sister with the words: 'Tell your husband—no more souvenirs!'"

Uncle Tony had them all laughing. Rachel's family never knew if any of the neighbors had seen the flag flapping in the wind. Whenever the doorbell rang, the family expected to see government officials with deportation papers in their hands.

Sophia said, "It feels so unfair when you think that my father was an American soldier who had ripped that enemy flag off a building." Nicholas nodded; but he doubted Grandpa had actually been in any battles.

After that story, everyone was ready for dessert. Sophia made a pot of espresso and Cia placed the *sfogliatelle*, *struffoli*, and anisette cookies on the dining room table; Cia brought out anisette and tiny cubes of sugar for the espresso.

Later they changed into pajamas and watched old Christmas movies.

"Mom, you'll sleep here in the guest room, and Uncle Tony and Nicholas will be in the office; Jacob set it up for them.

"Well, childless couples certainly have plenty of room," said Sophia. Cia, Nicholas, Uncle Tony and Jacob stiffened.

And there it was . . . the warmth and comfort of the day was replaced by a nor'easter. Cia reacted the way any rational person reacted when faced with a storm—she ran for cover. With Uncle Tony's arm tightly affixed to her shoulder, she turned wordlessly and walked into the kitchen. Jacob and Nicholas retreated to the office. Uncle Tony put on the tea kettle.

With all the tea rituals accomplished—boiling water in the tea kettle, searching for cups, steeping the tea in china cups, spooning out sugar from an antique bowl, dispensing the precise amount of milk and finally stirring the brew—uncle and niece sat across from each other and savored the medicinal properties of their hot tea. They sat in silence.

In the end, Uncle Tony's first word put a smile on her face. He whispered, "*Karma.*" He was referring to the crashing news that would come Sophia's way tomorrow. They drank their tea, reviewing the good memories of the day. Then they stood, held each other briefly, and said good night.

***

"Are you sleeping?" asked Jacob as he entered their bedroom.

"No," said Cia," but I'm okay. I decided to ignore her words. Besides, Uncle Tony reminded me that tomorrow my mother will hear words from us that will torment her. Karma is a bitch. There is even a little slice of irony. My mother spoke about my lack of a child; tomorrow she'll learn about an added child. Yes, karma *is* a bitch." Jacob gave Cia a gentle kiss and they settled down to sleep.

Cia awoke to the aroma of coffee drifting through the house; the digital clock displayed 6:43 a.m. She reached for her robe and walked into the kitchen. Uncle Tony was sipping coffee and nibbling on anisette cookies; Italians love their continental breakfast.

"Good morning, Uncle Tony. Are you getting out of Dodge before the bullets start flying?" Cia teased.

Uncle Tony smiled; but she knew she had interrupted serious thoughts. "My little Cia, I was up most of the night; I didn't know if I should add your father's name to this dreadful day. I'm going to go ahead with my words. I want you to open your heart and your eyes to your father. Your mother and father's marriage was not good. My brother was quiet and distant, but he was never cruel. Sophia was cruel. She demeaned him until he believed he was worthless. I was always silent when you complained about her; but I say these words today for my brother."

Cia kissed her uncle on the forehead. "I love you Zio Tony; and I am happy you spoke for my father. Your words make sense. We'll talk soon. I promise. Now go home before she starts screaming and the neighbors call the police."

Jacob, Nicholas and Cia huddled in the office while Sophia showered. Nicholas had decided to go ahead with the plan to tell his mother. "You can't deliver the news with a solemn expression," said Cia. "I wouldn't smile, but I would talk with a matter-of-fact demeanor. Jacob, I'll text you at the store when she either calms down or leaves."

Cia stood and started pacing. "We've put this off long enough. She's had breakfast; after her shower she'll dress and then join us. We'll sit in the living room and wait for her—and don't mention Grandpa's friend Jimmy Rizzo. The man fought in the jungles of Burma; he doesn't need to be interrogated by Sophia."

Jacob said his goodbyes. He kissed Cia gently. "Good luck. Don't worry so much; things will work out." Then he walked out the front door, closing it quietly behind him.

Nicholas and Cia moved to the living room; they sat on the comfortable sofa, trying to mask their edginess. After a few minutes, they heard the door to the guest room open, then Sophia's footsteps as she walked into the dining room.

"Mom, we're in here," called Nicholas. "Come and sit down. Before we head back to Brooklyn we need to give you an update on your Ancestry match."

Sophia let out a soft sigh as she sat in the richly upholstered armchair. Nicholas feigned a casual tone and continued. "Remember that close match on your Ancestry site and you asked me what it all meant? Cia and I followed up with *Nevada3*; and it turns out the two of you are a very close match."

"How close a match?" Sophia cut in. "What does that mean?" She leaned toward Nicholas.

"Mom . . . let me speak first then I'll answer all your questions. There is a woman in Virginia named Maria Dalton. She is 73 years old. She is your half sister."

If silence really were golden, they would have been swimming in riches in that moment.

Nicholas continued. "Grandpa Carmine is her father. When he was stationed in Naples he had a relationship with a woman and Maria is the child of that relationship."

More silence, deep and still. Then Sophia exploded out of her chair.

She stood and paced the room; then she faced Cia. "Did you know about this woman? Did your grandfather confide in you? Is that why I needed your ridiculous Ancestry test? You just can't let things alone. Maybe it's my fault, it was the one time I checked my Ancestry page."

Cia began to speak, "Mom . . ."

Sophia shut her down. "I always knew he was no good. He was a disgrace. Look what he did to my poor mother. You both adored him, especially you Cia; and now you know he was an unfaithful, evil, godless man. I know he loved this child; he laughed in my face and my mother's face. I will have nothing to do with her." Sophia glared at Cia.

It was Cia's turn to stand. "He was a wonderful man," she shot back at her mother. "I loved him as a child and I love him now. I don't care how upset you are, you will not disrespect his memory in my house. No one can force you to meet her. Let's not forget that this was not her fault. And to answer your question: no, I did not know of her when I bought you a DNA kit."

Sophia whirled on Cia and countered, "You defend him? He slept with whores and then returned to my mother's bed—and you defend him?"

Cia turned her back to her mother and walked away as calmly as she could manage. She walked the length of the main hall of the house to her bedroom and, in a childish response, slammed the door. The tears she had held back now left her body; they were gentle tears, not deep sobs. She walked into the master bathroom and washed her face. She stared at the reflection in the mirror and spoke to the woman staring back at her.

"My mother is hurt; she is lashing out at me. It will get easier for her. This house is my sanctuary; I will not be vanquished by her words." Cia sat on her bed and watched the nightstand clock tick off 30 minutes. Then she washed her face again and walked into the living room.

Nicholas was speaking softly to his mother. When Cia was within earshot, she heard Nicholas reciting the Ancestry events chronologically. Sophia listened quietly. "Cia," said Nicholas, "I am explaining to Mom how this news came about, step by step. I have reassured her that she has no obligation to meet Maria or Ruby."

Cia nodded; she did not look in Sophia's direction when she quietly spoke. "I think it's time for Mom to go back to Brooklyn. It will be easier for her to reflect on your words in her own home;

and I would like to be alone in my home." Cia took the silence in the room as assent, and went into the kitchen to clean up the morning's dishes.

Cia kept herself busy with inconsequential household things while Nicholas packed the car. As she opened the front door for a little fresh air, she saw her neighbor Pat, walking her dog. Cia engaged the woman in conversation and waived to Nicholas and her mother as the two walked to Nicholas' car. She would be forever grateful for the distraction. There were no long, awkward *goodbyes*. Jacob received her text before Nicholas' car turned the corner.

Mom was told. She went Medieval. She left. I'm going back to bed.

Jacob sent back: *Cia, there are some clients in town for the holiday. They want to look at our inventory. I set up private appointments. We don't want our good clients to meet each other. We'll be busy for the rest of the week which I think is a good thing.*

Cia appreciated the fact that Jacob was sticking to business. *I agree. Just so you know, I invited Uncle Tony here for New Year's Eve, so don't book me after three. Thank you for avoiding the 800-pound gorilla in the room.* She headed back to her room for a well-deserved nap. The week could only get better.

As it turned out, the week was hectic, but lucrative. It was also social: out-of-town clients they had known for years insisted on

236

taking them out to dinner. By Monday, New Year's Eve, Cia was happy to be home in her sweats.

She had promised Uncle Tony a traditional Italian seafood dinner; but she was tired, and the meal was a lot of work. The linguini and red clam sauce she made as soon as she walked in the door. The rest of the meal would be catered. She had placed her order two days earlier; Jacob picked it up from Long Island's south shore. Living on an island with a large Italian population had its advantages. Uncle Tony drove out with champagne and an overnight bag.

They sat down to a meal of linguini and red clam sauce, lobster tails, shrimp, scallops, and fried calamari, scungilli, and eels. In the authentic tradition, the salad was served at the end of the meal. They drank wine and laughed easily. At midnight they watched the ball drop and toasted 2019 with Uncle Tony's champagne. They were all yawning; it was time for their heads to meet their pillows. They said goodnight.

On the first morning of 2019, Jacob busied himself in his office; he knew his wife and her uncle needed to talk. Jacob realized that it was her uncle, not her husband or brother that Cia needed to console her. Jacob was fine with Cia's choice; he never understood Sophia. A mother who hurt her child was alien to him. In the past, he had suggested to Cia that she just stay away from Sophia; but Cia would get angry and say she couldn't cut her mother out of her life. Cia would end each argument with the same

237

words—*As she gets older, she'll mellow.* Jacob saw no signs of a mellowing process.

Uncle Tony sat at the table, drinking coffee, and talking about the house his sister bought in Congers, N.Y. near Bear Mountain. Then the topic turned to his parish priest who had recently retired. The topic he fervently avoided was Sophia; he was having difficulty controlling the anger that was rising inside him. It was Cia who finally opened the conversation.

"It's been a rough week; I've kept my distance, but I can't hide from my mother forever. I'm afraid that the next time I see her she'll continue to blame me for uncovering her father's betrayal."

"Don't see her until you are ready to deal with her anger," said her uncle. "She had no right to attack you; you did nothing wrong. She's your mother. She should act like a mother instead of a self-centered bitter woman."

Cia reached for his hand and said, "Don't be so hard on her; she suffered an almost lethal blow. So much comes into question; everything she knew about herself and her family tree has been rocked. I will admit, I didn't expect her total condemnation of Carmine. I thought she would be most upset about not knowing.

"There was even the slightest sliver of hope that she would welcome a sister. Throughout my childhood she had shared with me her wish of having a sister. And I'm sorry I went all-out to defend Grandpa. He did have affairs and left a baby girl in Naples.

He was flawed; but I understand that you cannot expect twenty-something soldiers to be away from their wives for years. Sex may have been the one release from a war that raged all around them."

Uncle Tony shrugged ever so slightly, gesturing at Cia to continue.

"I'll just keep my distance for awhile; I'll have Nicholas guide her through the Ancestry results. But at some point today I am obligated to wish her a Happy New Year. That's what Jacob doesn't understand; Mom will remain in my life. I can try to build an imaginary wall around my emotions; but I cannot physically retreat. Today I am most grateful that I am not an only child; I have Nicholas taking the lead."

Uncle Tony nodded. "I agree you cannot bar her from your life. I am sorry that she is not a kind woman; but I would not blame all her hostility on her bad relationship with her father. She is not a happy person. Why don't you call Sophia now while I'm here? This way you can say a few words and then pass the phone over to me and Jacob?"

Cia laughed and kissed her Uncle on the forehead. "That would be worse; she'd be annoyed that you were invited and not she."

"Okay then," said Uncle Tony, "I'll sit quietly while you call her; that will give you courage; and I'll be here if there's fallout." Cia smiled and nodded her agreement.

Cia walked into the office and told Jacob she was about to call her mother, and added that she is not to know Uncle Tony is here. "I'll hand you the phone at some point," she warned her husband. Jacob gave her a thumbs-up.

Prepared for the call, with reinforcements at her back, Cia dialed her mother's number.

"Good morning Mom, I hope I didn't wake you. I want to wish you a Happy New Year…Yes, I know I could have called at the stroke of midnight; but I wasn't sure you would be awake…Yes, I was busy all week; Jacob and I had to cater to out-of-town clients. We will be busy for the next few weeks. Please hold on—Jacob wants to wish you Happy New Year; and I'll say goodbye now." She walked down the hall, handed the phone to her husband, and walked back to the kitchen.

She looked at Uncle Tony. "I knew I had to make it a short conversation. In my world, more words lead to conflict. Thank you, Uncle Tony, for making me laugh and stroking my hair when I cried."

Uncle Tony spread his arms wide. "Come here, you." Cia walked to him for one last restorative hug.

Jacob carried her uncle's overnight bag to his car and once more they wished him a Happy New Year. They walked back into the house and closed out the world behind them. They had a rare lazy day of reading, watching television, and napping. It felt good.

For the next few days, Cia stayed home. She took down the Christmas tree, the outside lights, and packed away all the decorations. There is a certain satisfaction in getting your house back to its pre-Christmas status.

***

Two weeks after Christmas there was an e-mail from Ruby.

***

Hello Cousin,

We returned from Virginia where we spent the holidays with my mother. I probably gained 10 pounds! I told her about Sophia; there wasn't much of a reaction. I will share with you exactly what she said. "Carmine was married when he met my mother; so of course he would go back to his wife after the war and start a family. I am surprised I only have one sibling. I think I met Carmine once, but I am not sure. Sometimes people tell you stories and after awhile they become your memories. My Aunt Pina told me Carmine met me when I was five years old. I think I remember a man hugging me and crying in my hair; but I just don't know. I am 73, I do not want to meet a

*half sister at this point in time; but I would
like to see pictures, especially of Sophia as a
young girl. I will admit that I am curious to
see if there is a resemblance. I would also
like to see photos of Carmine. If you and Cia
begin a friendship, you have my blessing."*

*She did not even bring it up again while
we were in Virginia; but she did give me
photos that might interest us.*

*Did you break the news to your mother?
I hope it did not ruin your Christmas
holiday.*

*I would like to show you the photos; and
I am interested in knowing more about my
Grandfather Carmine. And while you're not
related to Angelo; I want to tell you about
his parentage. It goes back to the war when
Carmine was stationed in Naples. It's sad;
but again you are not related to him.
Carmine is not his father.*

*I'd like to invite you back for lunch; do
you think Nicholas would like to meet me?
Next Wednesday about noon would work for
me.*

Love,

Ruby

***

Cia laughed to herself. Here she thought Ruby was skiing in Aspen, when she was actually in Virginia with her mother. Not as glamorous as Cia had envisioned. She spoke with Nicholas; he agreed to meet Ruby.

***

Dear Ruby,

Nicholas and I would love to meet with you next Wednesday. He rescued all the old photos when our grandfather died; he has a stack of photos to show you.

Yes, my mother was told about Maria; it was a shock for her, to say the least. I am looking forward to hearing about Angelo.

I will see you soon,

Love,

Cia

Chapter Thirteen
New York
January-February 2019

It was cold in Manhattan. Cia stood in front of Macy's at the corner of Seventh Avenue and 34th Street waiting for Nicholas. He pulled over to the curb; she opened the door, sat down, and quickly closed the door before drivers started honking their horns. Manhattan drivers were not patient, but they were quite vocal. "Thank you, big brother, for picking up the flowers for Ruby; it saved me time. I think you'll like her. I can't say I feel a family tie, but she is friendly and supportive."

He nodded as he checked his rear-view mirror and inched forward. With his eyes fixed on the traffic ahead, Nicholas said, "When you told me Ruby extended her invitation to include me, I agreed to join you. Afterwards I began having second thoughts. I'm a history professor and I'm not even sure I want to learn more about Grandpa's WWII years. But here I am—and yes, I am curious. Ultimately, Cia, I based my decision on the premise that what I hear today doesn't necessarily have to be passed on to Mom."

"I agree Nicholas, Mom is at her limit. Who am I kidding? She's over her limit of family secrets. Jacob has asked me why these Ancestry results have been an obsession with me. I'm not sure it's an obsession; but I think it brings me closer to Grandpa. I see him as a young man, younger than I am today. Imagine being older than your grandfather? I feel even closer to him."

After 40 minutes, the car reached Spring Street. With street parking unavailable, they pulled into a parking lot, gasped at the exorbitant prices, and handed over the car keys to the attendant. This was a section of Manhattan that neither of them knew well; as they walked toward Ruby's building, they took mental screen shots of the *old New York* upscale neighborhood. The warm air of the lobby greeted them as they entered. Cia led the way to the elevator, pushed the button and the two siblings stepped into the empty elevator. In a soft voice, Cia said, "Was I exaggerating, big brother? How rich do you have to be to afford this address?" They got off at Ruby's floor and walked down the hall to her apartment.

A strange woman answered the door and welcomed them by name. She was about five foot eight, on the thin side, thirtyish, with a pale, freckled, intelligent face. There was a wiry energy about her. Cia was clearly confused.

"Hi there! You must be Cia and Nicholas. I'm Phyllis Shanahan, Ruby's sister-in-law. Ruby is running late; she had to sign some papers at my brother's office. Let me take your coats and put the flowers in a vase."

In an effort to fill the silence, Phyllis grasped at topics of conversation. "Ruby is married to my brother John. Two years ago, I decided to move to Manhattan and join the family business. John found an apartment for me in his building; I live two floors up. I like being near Ruby and John; I felt so isolated when I was living in Boston."

Cia had to suppress a smile. She could tell that Nicholas was mesmerized by her. She was a redhead; Nicholas liked *gingers.* She decided to help her brother out; after all, he had been so supportive of her lately.

"It's so nice to meet you," said Cia. "Is your husband also in the family business?" Subtle.

Phyllis waved her hand. "Oh, no; I'm not married. There are millions of people in New York; but I haven't met anyone special. When I lived in Boston I didn't date much either; I spent most of my weekends touring haunted houses all around Boston." Nicholas and Cia looked at her with surprise.

"Don't judge me; yes, I believe in ghosts." Cia kept her eyes straight ahead; she dared not look at her brother. *Ghosts!* Nicolas believed in ghosts. He believed the spirit of Nikola Tesla haunted Bryant Park. Oh, this was too good.

Before Cia could pull her brother into the conversation, Ruby walked in. She was full of energy and apologies. Cia and Nicholas followed few of her words; their thoughts were on Phyllis.

Ruby extended her hand to Nicholas and hugged Cia. "You must be starving; I'll have lunched ready in five minutes. It's so good to see you. Phyllis, would you mind taking the dog for a walk? She behaves with you."

Phyllis must have been prepared for this request because her coat was on the chair. Nicholas helped her on with her coat and asked if he could walk with her.

"I would love the company," she said.

When they closed the door behind them, Ruby and Cia giggled like girls in middle school. Ruby put her hand on Cia's arm like a willing co-conspirator. "I have a confession Cia. When John asked me to go to his office, I turned him down. Then I remembered that your brother is single, 35, and a college professor—and I changed my mind. I knew if I simply asked Phyllis to drop by and meet the two of you, she would say it was an intrusion. So I helped John and introduced Phyllis to Nicholas—and do you know what the best part is? They're not related." They both smiled.

Phyllis, Nicholas and the dog, Gulie, returned from their walk, looking grateful to be off the cold windy New York streets. Ruby had ordered in soup and sandwiches; she also kept the conversation moving. "Phyllis, did you tell Nicholas that you named Gulie after the Spring Street Ghost?"

"No," said Phyllis, "not yet, but it's on my list of topics. If it's okay with you, I invited Nicholas to my apartment after lunch." Ruby and Cia nodded their agreement.

Nicholas and Phyllis left after lunch; Gulie stayed. Ruby carried in a tray of cookies. "I have a gift for you, compliments of my mother. She baked her great Aunt Pina's anisette cookies. They have been in my freezer since I came back from Virginia.

Cia reached for one. "This is Pina's recipe? So that's where he got the recipe; it has connected our family since the war. In my family we call them Grandpa Carmine's cookies. He said he brought the recipe back from Naples. I do know it is a common Neapolitan cookie. Do you think Grandpa conjured up visions of Pina and Tessa when he baked them?"

"I don't know," said Ruby. "But they do taste like home."

"That they do," said Cia. "Let's look at the pictures."

They spread the photos out on the dining room table. They weren't sure what they hoped to discover, but they had plenty of pictures to go through. Ruby suggested they look for childhood photos of their mothers. Was there a resemblance? Both Sophia and Maria had olive skin, brown hair and eyes. They needed to go deeper and look for bone structure and the shape of their eyes.

Photos of them at roughly the age of 14 were the most revealing. They had Carmine's cheekbones and saucer-shaped dark brown eyes. It was their hair that made the two daughters laugh;

Sophia and Maria's curly hair adorned their faces in the same untamed fashion.

Ruby gave Cia a few pictures of Maria at different stages of her life. Today, Sophia's hair was dyed red and Maria's was blonde. Sophia was heavier than Maria. Maria was older; she had a few more lines on her face. Ruby noted that Cia resembled Carmine more than she did.

Cia showed Ruby photos of Carmine taken during the war. She did not offer any to Ruby; she was reluctant to share her grandfather. At that moment, her mother's anguish came into focus.

Ruby interrupted Cia's reflection. "Cia, I have an idea. Our mothers do not want to meet each other; but I am certain that at some point, they would watch a video of each other. I have my video from Christmas; I actually recorded my mother singing *Silent Night.*"

Cia nodded. "I think that's a great idea. A video would give them so much more insight—and they could hear each other's voices. I have my video from Christmas, too. In it, my mother is opening gifts, laughing, and—of course—serving food. You're a genius!"

They set the photos aside and stopped for a coffee break. Cia put her cup down and hesitantly announced, "Carmine did meet your mother when she was five years old. I believe that is the only time he saw her. We have a gift in the form of Jimmy Rizzo, Grandpa's closest friend. He lives on Long Island, and I spoke to him recently. He also saw Maria. He will be a wealth of information for us; he's 96 and still remembers the names of the war buddies he served with in Burma. Why don't we make plans to visit him together? You could have lunch at my house and then I'll arrange for us to see him. Does Saturday work for you?"

Ruby nodded and was about to speak when Nicholas and Phyllis walked into the room. Cia asked if they wanted to join them at her house this Saturday. "I'm sorry, sis," Nicholas said. "Phyllis and I are going to visit some haunted houses up in Boston. We're leaving Friday after work and we'll be back late Saturday."

It took all of Ruby and Cia's restraint not to look at each other. It was Phyllis who broke the silence that followed. "I didn't tell Nicholas about the Spring Street Ghost yet. I'll tell him now; that way Cia can hear it, too."

Everyone got comfortable to hear the story.

Phyllis began. "On the evening of December 22, 1799, 22-year-old Gulielma Elmore Sands was secretly meeting with her lover, Levi Weeks. Gulielma's cousin would later testify that Sands and Weeks were going to elope that night; she may have been carrying his child. That was the last day she was seen alive. Less than two weeks later, her body was found floating in a well in

Lispenard's Meadow. Today that is two blocks from here, on Spring Street.

"It was determined that she had been strangled. Her lover, Weeks, was accused of the crime but was found not guilty. He had a pretty good defense team: Alexander Hamilton and Aaron Burr. I guess the two lawyers weren't dueling back then.

"Since her death there have been sightings of her in a white dress. It is said that she cries out for justice. The well was rediscovered about 40 years ago at 129 Spring Street. Gulie and I look for her whenever we walk by that building. They say animals are more sensitive to apparitions; maybe she'll lead me to her namesake."

"Sometimes I forget the rich history of New York City," said Nicholas. "Imagine being represented by Aaron Burr and Alexander Hamilton! Phyllis didn't know that Nikola Tesla lived here and fed the pigeons in Bryant Park. Next week we'll visit the park; I told her the kiosk there sells the best hot chocolate in New York." Nicholas and Phyllis exchanged smiles while Cia and Ruby surreptitiously did the same.

Cia and Nicholas gathered their photos, thanked Ruby for her hospitality, and said goodbye. In the privacy of his car, Cia began her inquisition. "Do you think you might be moving too fast? What is she like? Is she rich? How old is she? Are you going to tell Mom?"

Nicholas, for his part, ignored her questions and said, "I like her. I really like her; and I realize how awkward it will be for Mom. I want to keep this relationship between Phyllis and me. I don't want to jeopardize it with you and Ruby getting involved. Please Cia; this is important to me. I don't want to screw it up."

"I understand, Nicholas. We'll keep things quiet."

"Thank you," said Nicholas. "I appreciate that." He dropped her off at Penn Station and headed back to Brooklyn.

***

All of Wednesday night and into Saturday morning, Cia obsessed over Ruby's visit. The view from her Levittown window was far less impressive than the view from Ruby's 5 million-dollar Soho apartment; but in the end she talked herself into counting her blessings. She would enjoy the day and not compare their lifestyles. Jimmy was looking forward to meeting Maria's daughter and showing her his pictures of Carmine.

At 10:15 Saturday morning she drove to the Hicksville train station and waited for Ruby's train. They greeted each other like two sorority sisters, all gushy and giddy. Ruby was balancing a laptop, a manila envelope, her handbag and a cake box. Cia helped settle the cake box in a stable spot in the back seat, and they headed back toward home for lunch. They would have the house to themselves; Jacob was in Rockland County at an antique show.

The chatter in the car mostly focused on Nicholas and Phyllis. Cia tried to toe the line and resist the temptation to share in the excitement, remembering her promise to respect her brother's privacy.

After two cups of coffee and a croissant, Ruby opened the manila envelope. "This is Tessa, my grandmother, on her wedding day; she married Vito Napolitano. That's Pina; she was the maid of honor. Maria was born before her mother married. Don't you think Tessa and Pina were beautiful?" Cia nodded.

Ruby continued. "According to Pina, Tessa refused to give Vito a child and because of that, Vito's family never visited their house. Maria grew up hearing the stories of Carmine and sometimes wishing he would come and rescue her. Their mother/daughter bond was weak. Maria said her mother was cold and distant not only to her but also to Vito, Pina, and Angelo.

"Vito eventually opened a high-end dress shop for her; Maria said she liked visiting the store because it was the only time she saw a smile on her mother's face. Maria, my mother, met my father in Naples. He was an American Naval Officer stationed at NATO. My father, Patrick Dalton, married Maria before he was sent back to the states. They settled in Virginia. He was a career officer and a good man. He passed away on March 11, 2006." After all that information sharing, it was time for lunch.

Ruby walked through the house with Cia; she admired the antiques and said she loved the house's country charm. *Country charm? Was that code for provincial blue collar homes?*

Today's lunch consisted of ricotta spinach pie and green bean salad. Cia wanted to emulate Ruby's light lunches and at the same time impress on her that she had prepared the meal herself. They had a quiet lunch, making light small talk and just enjoying each other's company and the delicious food. When they were finished, Cia served Ruby's cake and they went back to the photos. Ruby looked through them and chose one of a boy.

"Cia, Jimmy mentioned Giovanni: this is a picture of him taken in Rome on his Bar Mitzvah. Today he is 83 years old and living in Tel Aviv. Angelo keeps in touch with him; Angelo still lives in Naples.

"Giovanni was a 10-year old boy when Carmine found him by the side of the road. He went to live with Tessa, Pina and my great-grandfather. Giovanni had a secret: he was Jewish. They cared for him and kept his secret. After the war Giovanni's uncle came for him and took him back to Rome; Giovanni's parents had perished in a death camp.

"Giovanni really loved Carmine. Angelo said Giovanni wanted to go to America and find Carmine, but it was never the right time. Giovanni moved to Israel in the 1950s, married, and had two sons."

This revelation unsettled Cia. The Holocaust was personal history now. Grandpa helped save Giovanni; Giovanni's parents had perished. Cia's mind blended Giovanni's face with that of her Jewish husband's face. If Jacob had been alive in the1940s and living in Europe, he might have suffered the same fate as Giovanni's parents. Her body trembled. Ruby noticed Cia's distress and did not comment. Ruby had been brought up with stories of Giovanni's childhood. She understood Cia was hearing the stories for the first time. When she was composed, she said, "Tell me about Angelo."

"Angelo's story is also heart-wrenching. Angelo and my mother were born only weeks apart. Maria was conceived by two young lovers; Angelo was the product of a rape. Pina was child-like. Her mother had died giving birth to her; the midwife tried, but there were complications with Pina. Her mental capacities never fully developed. This was 1926; there wasn't a doctor on call to assist with the birth. My mother guessed Pina's mental age to be about 13.

"When Pina was 18, she took the back path to visit a neighbor's house. It was raining and Tessa asked Carmine to catch up with Pina and take her a coat. Carmine and a friend, Bruno, followed the back path and found a man on top of her. Carmine pulled the man off Pina and the man took off. Bruno fired two shots at him as he ran into the woods. The bullets missed their target. Pina remembered Carmine calling him a Nazi.

"Carmine's friend was Bruno Falco, a powerful man in Naples. He was married to Yolanda Falco, a midwife. Bruno took Pina back to his house to be cared for by his wife. In the months that followed, Yolanda discovered that Pina was pregnant. Pina, Tessa, their father and Giovanni went to live with Bruno. Bruno had guessed at Giovanni's secret and wanted to keep him and the others under his roof. They would be safe with him.

"The first time Pina saw her baby, she said he looked like an angel. She named him Angelo. The boy could have looked like Pina and her family, but it was not to be. Angelo had blonde hair and fair skin; he looked German. If it weren't for Bruno's powerful presence, the people in her town would have accused her of being a whore for the German soldiers. I don't know what the gossip was behind Bruno's back; but no one dared say an unkind word out loud. Bruno Falco was never a man to cross.

"Under Bruno and Yolanda's watchful eye, Angelo grew up in a loving environment. Bruno sent him to the university, where he became an architect. Pina never married; as far as anyone knows, she never took a man to her bed. She was too traumatized by the assault she endured while still in her teens. After Bruno and Yolanda passed away, Angelo took total care of his mother. Pina lived with Angelo and his wife until the day she died.

"If my mother guessed correctly, and Pina had a mental age of 13, that might explain her constant need to gossip. Was she behaving like a middle school girl in a locker room? She kept nothing to herself. She told Angelo that he was a product of a rape by a Nazi. She told Maria all she could remember about Carmine. Yet my mother said she was not mean-spirited, just a gossip. Mom would say it was like she relished the idea of knowing events and facts that were unknown to others.

"Angelo only needed a mirror to know the rape allegations were true, but he was curious—not about his lineal father—but about who he was. What was in his genetic code? He confided in us that he would not have children because a son might grow up with his grandfather's inclinations for violence toward women. Angelo, I can assure you, is a kind, intelligent, and a gentle man; and that, Cia, is the story of Angelo."

Cia did not move or speak. What could she say? She needed time alone to absorb it all—Nazis, rapes—it was all too much. She couldn't get time alone right now, with Ruby as a guest in her house. She couldn't retreat to her bedroom and pull the covers over her head. Having your DNA researched, she conceded, came at a price. Was it worth it?

Finally, Cia said, "Ruby, that's a lot of information to take in-in one sitting. I need a little time to process this. How about some fresh coffee?"

Cia made a fresh pot of coffee and served more cake. "Ruby, there is so much sadness in your stories. Grandpa must have been devastated when he found Pina on the ground. I knew him; I did not know Giovanni, Pina or Angelo. It is Grandpa's pain that is unbearable to me." Ruby put her hand gently on Cia's arm and they sat quietly for a few minutes, sipping their coffee.

Eventually, the two cousins went back to the topic of Nicholas and Phyllis. They laughed and both agreed it was a good match. Ruby leaned toward Cia conspiratorially. "Can you imagine what would happen if your brother and Phyllis decided to marry? Your mother would be forced to attend the ceremony. My mother is close to Phyllis, so I know she would want to be part of the celebration. We would be compelled to step in and have them meet before the big day. It wouldn't be fair to the bride and groom to have the potential disaster on the day of their wedding."

Cia mulled this over. "My mother would not be happy with the circumstances, but she'd be happy he finally got married. Do you realize that if it weren't for our grandfather they never would have met? Let's see, Nicholas would be your cousin and your brother-in-law; and you and Nicholas would share the same in-laws. We're one big happy Ancestry family. Speaking of Ancestry, what happened when Angelo read his DNA posts?"

"That, my dear Cia, is a new story." They settled in, and Ruby began.

***

"It started when Angelo visited last year. He and my mother are very close; they grew up more like fraternal twins than cousins.

258

He's my cousin; but I call him Uncle Angelo. They were born only weeks apart and Maria spent most of her childhood at Angelo's house. When Maria moved to America each promised not to abandon the other. My mother still had friends in Naples; so she did most of the traveling. A year ago he did travel to the U.S. and my mother and Angelo spent three weeks with me in Manhattan. Then the two of them went to my mother's home in Virginia where he spent the rest of the summer.

"They are closer now that they both lost their spouses; they comfort each other. I'm so grateful that she has Angelo in her life; I just wish he would move here, for mom's sake, and to keep a closer eye on him. He had talked about having a DNA test; and while he was at my home, I ordered his kit. The kit arrived a week later and on that very same day I mailed out Angelo's saliva sample for the DNA test.

"When the results came back, it confirmed that he was half German. I managed his site, and I decided to drive to Virginia to gauge his reaction. I can't imagine living with the knowledge that you were conceived by a violent act against your mother.

"Angelo, then 72, finally saw the reality of his conception on the screen. He showed interest in his *Ethnicity Estimate*, but did not want to research family trees. He stood, shut down the computer and announced that the topic was closed. My mother said he never spoke of it again.

"I have my laptop with me, so we could view the family's Ancestry sites. Let me pull up Angelo." Ruby navigated through several screens. "Okay, take a look at his chart. Most of his DNA is either German or Italian, with minimal percentages from Eastern Europe. I did view his Ancestry site last year, but I didn't research the family trees."

Ruby navigated the Ancestry screens easily. Ruby and Angelo were matched as second cousins. She then looked for people who were related to him but not her; some had lengthy family trees posted. Ruby saw long German surnames and a sprinkling of given names that were right out of German fairy tales—Helga, Gretel, Helmut.

They changed their focus and concentrated on German relatives who posted their photos. Did anyone resemble Angelo? That was a dead end. "Well," said Ruby, "Here's a cousin that at least has a pronounceable name. Otto *Winter*. Let's look at his family tree. It lists his grandfather, another Otto Winter, the grandfather's three sons Hermann, Otto and Hans Winter and . . . What is it Cia? You have the oddest expression on your face."

Cia walked into the dining room and dumped all the photos on the table. She spread her hands quickly through the pile until she grabbed one photo and went back to the computer. In a trembling voice, she said, "Ruby, I think our world just turned upside down. The name *Otto Winter* sounded familiar, but I couldn't connect it at first. One of Carmine's war photos was taken in Naples with four of his buddies. On the back he wrote their nicknames with their full name in parentheses. From left to right there's Carmine Trotta, Fish (Joseph Fish), Mac (Mike Warren), J.J. (Jerry Joseph Miello) and Otter (Otto Winter). Otto Winter? What does it mean? It's the same name; it doesn't make any sense. Could Otter, an American, be a descendant of this German family? I think we need to see Jimmy Rizzo. I'll get your coat."

***

They rode in silence, but their minds were in a storm of confusion. What does it mean? Who raped Pina? Could this be a coincidence? Winter is a common name. As they say on the detective shows, DNA doesn't lie.

Jimmy was happy to see them. He liked showing off his guests to the residents. He embraced Ruby and said, "I met your mother when she was a little girl." Rudy kissed his cheek and Cia asked if there was someplace private they could go. He led them to a vacant sitting room. Cia slowly presented the events of their afternoon research . . . and waited. Jimmy, at 96, did not believe in wasting time. He spoke up.

"I have kept Carmine's secret all these years. Three men committed violence that day; today they are all in the ground. Otter was one of Carmine's soldiers. They served in North Africa together. Otter was transferred out of Carmine's unit shortly after they reached Naples. Carmine never liked him; Otter was lazy. The other boys would get the job done to make their Sergeant look good, but not Otter—he was never loyal to Carmine. Worst of all, Carmine thought he cheated at cards but he could never prove it.

Otter's parents were born in Munich; he spoke German. That made him essential to the Army. He went where he was needed; but when he could, he came back to Carmine's camp for card games. The day Pina was walking to her neighbor's house, Otter was on his way to her grandfather's house for a card game. It was Otter who raped Pina. Carmine found him on top of her and pounded his fists into his face while Bruno held down Otter's shoulders. Then Carmine reached for his side arm to shoot him; but Bruno stopped him.

Pina heard Carmine call Otter a Nazi because of his German background. Carmine picked Pina up and started walking away; it was Bruno who shot and killed Otter. Bruno's men disposed of Otter's body. He was never found. Otter's family believed he was a casualty of war. They probably think of him as an American hero.

Bruno killed Otter; but that did not mean that Carmine wasn't haunted by Otter's murder. Otter was an American soldier and his family could not bring him home and bury him. That night changed Carmine. He was the one who had convinced Pina's father to hold the card games. Pina would not have been raped if he had not encouraged the games. He didn't protect her.

Carmine also felt guilty that Otter's family lost their son. I think that is why he only went back to Italy that one time. He couldn't face Maria and Angelo; and he knew pieces of Otter were in Naples. That is the story. It can still hurt Angelo, Otter's family and your family."

Ruby and Cia had questions, but Jimmy was drained. They hugged him and said they would be back soon.

They closed the car doors and fastened their seat belts. Cia drove away, lost in thought. It was Ruby who spoke first.

"I just can't wrap my mind around this. An American soldier raped Pina, an American with German DNA? I want to go back in time and kill him myself. Angelo is the son of an American; it's too bizarre."

Cia came away with a different primary outrage. Her words were those of calm fury. "Carmine had to live with the guilt of Pina's rape and the knowledge that an American family's son would not return home, not even his dead body. Ruby, don't go back to the city tonight; stay with me. Jacob is staying at the hotel where the antique show is being held. He'll be home tomorrow."

Ruby agreed to spend the night. Cia pulled into the Target parking lot; Ruby needed to pick up a few overnight essentials. Cia stayed in the car and had her one smile of the day. Cia could not imagine Ruby buying underwear and toiletries in a suburban Target. Cia texted her brother while she waited in the parking lot.

You need to come out to my house tomorrow; and come alone.
There's another Ancestry tsunami. Nicholas texted back that he'd
be there late Sunday morning.

The key turned into Cia's front door lock; the women entered
the house in a trance-like state. Cia and Ruby took off their coats
and sat in the living room, each occupied with their own thoughts.
It was their bodies that propelled them into the present. They were
hungry; they had not eaten since lunchtime. Cia willed herself to
stand and walk into the kitchen. She made grilled cheese
sandwiches as a bedtime snack. After they ate, the two women said
goodnight and headed to bed. Cia collapsed on her bed. First she
cried; then she showered. Finally she texted Jacob: *I'm home. Ruby*
is sleeping over. Nicholas will join us tomorrow. Awful day! I love
you.

She was still awake when she heard Ruby at the door, asking if
she could come in. They sat on the bed and hugged each other.
Then a floodgate of words poured out of them. They spoke into the
air; not waiting for the other to respond; and at times speaking over
each other. Their thoughts were fragmented.

"It was an American soldier?"

"An animal."

"Did Pina know?"

"Did the Winter family look for answers?"

"Did the other soldiers know?"

"Did the Army investigate?"

"Did Otter know he was raping someone close to Carmine?"

"I want to rip him apart."

"What do we do now?"

"Angelo's father was German but not a Nazi?"

"Is that better?"

"Did Angelo hear whispers of the truth?"

"Poor Carmine."

"I would like to know who knew."

"If Bruno's men got rid of the body, did they ever tell anyone who they buried?"

"Did Carmine know where he was buried?"

Clearly, they had more questions than answers; but they felt better for having gotten those questions out.

Ruby said goodnight for the second time and stumbled back to the guest room. Cia closed her eyes.

In the morning Cia awoke to the smell of coffee brewing and eggs frying. Cia admonished herself. *Give Ruby a break. She is kind and normal even if she is rich.*

She walked into the kitchen with a smile on her face. "Thank you Ruby. My mother says my coffee is dreadful, so it will be wonderful to have a good cup of coffee." The mood was much lighter this morning for both cousins. They ate their eggs and then decided to reopen the cake box. They cut two large pieces of chocolate cake and left barely any crumbs. It tasted much better today than yesterday.

A short time later, Nicholas arrived with a box of cannoli and two bottles of wine. "Your text sounded ominous; I wasn't sure two bottles of wine would be enough to sustain us."

The two women started pouring out an update of yesterday's events. They saw confusion on Nicholas' face, and realized they were throwing words at him in no sequential order. In time, it came together and the awful truth began to come clear. Ruby questioned whether Angelo had a right to know. Nicholas asked, "Do we have an obligation to inform Otter's family?"

That was a very good question with no easy answer.

They spent most of the day at the computer. They looked more closely at Angelo's family trees and reviewed Otto's military history. They all agreed on one thing: they would not contact Otto Winter's family. If they did, the family would learn the whole truth about their beloved American hero—that he was a rapist. That would certainly not bring them comfort, and it would also bring into question Carmine's role in the murder.

The three cousins were not in agreement whether Angelo should know that his father was an American with German DNA. Ruby and Nicholas argued that Angelo already knew his mother was raped. He had a right to know his truth, and they could tell him the name of his father. Cia held an opposing view. Angelo was a child of rape; at 73, he did not need to tear bandages off old wounds. "Besides," Cia said, "If we tell Angelo, we have no guarantee he won't contact the Winter family or the Army."

By the end of the day they had formulated a plan. Ruby would deliver the information to her mother, who would make the final decision. No one was closer to Angelo than Maria. Nicholas, Cia, and Ruby made a pact that there would be six people entrusted with the secret: Nicholas, Ruby, Cia, Jimmy, Maria, and Angelo. Ruby had no issue withholding the secret from her husband, but Cia would have chosen to tell Jacob. He would have been a comfort to her. But Cia gave her word; Jacob would not know. The day was at a close and they were wiped out. Nicholas kissed his sister goodbye and said, "The next step is for Maria to learn the news." Then he turned to Ruby and said, "I'll drive you home. I'm going to dinner with Phyllis." Cia closed and locked the door behind them and then, with deliberate steps, walked out to her backyard. She sat down on a cold stone bench and willed her mind to go blank. When it became unbearably cold to remain outside, she walked back into her house, collapsing on her couch.

***

It was 11:30 by the time Jacob walked in the door Sunday night. Cia greeted him with a smile. "Do you need me to help you unload the car, Jacob?"

"No, leave it; I'll unload the boxes tomorrow morning. The traffic was heavy and there was an accident on the Mario Cuomo Bridge; it took me 2½ hours to get home. Fortunately, there was a Starbuck's in the hotel and I had coffee and a sandwich before I left. I'm going to kiss my wife, use the bathroom and then fall into bed, in that order. Are you coming?—to the bed, not the bathroom."

She smiled. "I'll take the kiss; but I fell asleep on the couch earlier so now I'm wide awake." They kissed and then he headed for the bathroom while she headed for the kitchen. At times like this, when she needed to release built-up tension, Cia baked. She baked corn muffins and three loaves of raisin bread. And when her baked goods were cooled and wrapped securely, she took a long shower and then gently opened her bedroom door. Jacob was asleep. She gingerly crawled into her side of the bed; and in a voice barely audible, said, "Good night Jacob, I love you."

By the next morning, Cia had a story ready for her husband when he asked about yesterday. "Oh Jacob, listening to what Jimmy Rizzo faced in Burma was difficult to hear. It really upset Ruby and me." In the future she would bring up the secret pact to Nicholas and Ruby and ask if Jacob could be included. Was she naïve? Did Ruby run straight home and tell John?

***

The next day she went back to see Jimmy Rizzo. He was waiting for her at the front desk; they walked to her car. "Jimmy, that last visit was a drain on you. I saw your face tighten when you talked about Carmine's secrets. I was selfish. I was only thinking of my anguish, and I apologize. Today we'll just be two friends enjoying a day out. First we gamble." She looked over at him and winked.

There was a casino near Jimmy's residence; Jimmy liked to play the slot machines. The two sat side-by-side as they lost their money. When they'd lost enough, they headed back to the car. Cia said, "I have a good place to eat—and it's not a diner that's close to your residence. I'm taking you to a restaurant where local fishermen go to eat. It's on the south shore and it's Italian. You can eat calamari, scungilli, or eel."

Jimmy raised his eyebrows. "Eel?" he asked.

"Yes, eel like you and Carmine caught in Sheepshead Bay. Sound like a plan?"

"You bet," said Jimmy.

He ate his fish and curled his linguini with a fork and spoon and was in heaven. She had put an awful burden on him two days ago, and she vowed never to go down that path again. "Jimmy, you told me that you served in the Pacific, in jungles. Have you ever been honored for your service?"

"No," said Jimmy. "After the war an Italian club had me stand up and tell my story; but it wasn't anything special."

Cia shook her head in amazement. "Everyone should know your military record; we'll start writing it down. Look for your Army pictures."

"Okay," he said. "In one picture I'm holding a monkey."

"Perfect," Cia said.

It was after nine when Cia got Jimmy back to his residence. He was tired. And he was happy. Cia walked him to the lobby. Jimmy gave her a big hug and said, "Thanks for dinner. It was absolutely fantastic."

"You're welcome, Jimmy," said Cia. "It was the least I could do. I really appreciate you sharing the stories; I know it wasn't easy. We'll talk soon. Take care." Jimmy smiled and headed toward his suite.

Alone in her car, Cia announced out loud: "I'm going to give this warrior the honor he deserves."

***

It was three weeks later when she saw an e-mail from Ruby.

***

Hello cousin,

Wow! What a rollercoaster!

*I drove down to Virginia. I had to
deliver the news in person. Mom was
shocked to learn the truth about Pina's rape.
She broke out in hives; I was afraid she
would need medical attention. She wept; I
know she was crying for Pina and Angelo. I
know Pina was violated, Angelo was the
child of a rape and Carmine felt guilty for
Pina, Angelo and that soldier's family; but I
feel most sorry for my mother. She is
heartbroken.*

*She said Angelo must be told. Whether
it's the correct decision she doesn't know;
but Angelo would want to know. She wished
she had the energy to go to Naples and tell
him in person, but a telephone call will need
to suffice. My mother said Angelo would
never talk to the Winter family or the Army.
He would want to know, but he is a private
person. It will remain with him.*

*My mother has told him about how you
reached out to us, and he likes hearing
about you and Nicholas. He wrote to
Giovanni about our meeting; Giovanni
loved Carmine and he would like to write to*

you. May I give him your e-mail address? He invited Angelo, Mom and me to his 50th wedding anniversary, but no one wants to make that trip to Israel.

By the way, I bumped into Nicholas on the elevator yesterday. It was 7:15 am! It looks promising. John's mother is thrilled; she wants her baby girl married.

Love,

Ruby

***

Hi Ruby,

I can't believe you met Nicholas on the elevator! He was probably embarrassed; but you never know with him. I would like to get to know Phyllis better, but for now I'll take my cues from my big brother. Yes, I want to hear from Giovanni, as long as he doesn't have more secrets to share. I will enjoy hearing about Carmine when he was a soldier.

Love,

Cia

Cia spoke to Carmine's picture. "Grandpa, I am so proud of you. You saved Giovanni. You are my hero."

Chapter Fourteen
New York & Tel Aviv
February-June 2019

St. Charles Cemetery in Farmingdale was only 20 minutes away. It was a comfort knowing Carmine rested so close to her home. Cia dressed and was on her way to the cemetery by 9:30. She stood huddled in front of the joint headstone. First she greeted her grandmother and told her she missed her. Then she spoke to her grandfather.

I believe you were by my side when I discovered Maria. I know it broke your heart leaving her in Naples. I am sorry. Mom is upset, but she will come around. I think you brought Nicholas and his future wife together; Nicholas is one happy man these days. You harbored so many secrets; too many for one young soldier.

Grandpa, the story of Pina's rape 73 years ago still has ramifications. Jimmy filled in the blanks; he is one loyal friend. He said Otter's family haunted you until your last day. I can't speak for Nicholas or Ruby; but I now carry your secret with me. It's like a thin layer of soot that I can't wash off. Otter was the criminal. If you didn't find Pina when you did, he might have taken her life. I

*doubt it was his first rape; but it was certainly his last. I am proud
of you. You were a righteous man and you were instrumental in
saving Giovanni's life. I will reach out to him, and I will comfort
Mom through the turbulence. I know that is what you would want
of me. I brought you a gift. I love you, Grandpa.*

Cia reached into her bag and removed a garden spade and a
photo of Maria in her Communion dress with a tiny gold cross
dangling from her neck. Cia knelt down and dug into the hard soil;
she gently placed Maria with her father; and covered up the photo.
She wiped her tears and said goodbye to her grandparents.

Alone in her car, Cia listened to the voice in her head. It
suggested she reach out to Giovanni and have patience with her
mother; but it also demanded that she include Jacob in all the
unraveling events. Was she shutting him out? Cia would begin by
confiding in him. No more secrets. She would tell him about Otter.
Nicholas and Ruby would learn of her broken promise in the
future; there would be no added drama this winter.

Her e-mail inbox had a strange domain listed. It was common
to see *@gmail* or *@aol;* but never *@ieee.* The subject was listed as
Carmine Trotta.

***

Dear Cia,

*"Allow me to introduce myself. I am
Giovanni Levi, a friend of Angelo Salvatore*

275

and Carmine Trotta. Angelo has told me that you are Carmine's granddaughter; and that you have reached out to Ruby. I want you to know that I loved my American soldier. I am sorry that I never saw him in the years that followed. I would like to meet you; I see you as an extension of Carmine. You could talk to me of Carmine's life in peacetime. At 83, my health will not permit me to travel to America. My wife and I are celebrating our 50th wedding anniversary at the end of May; we would love for you to be at our side. Do you think it's a possibility? I will send you a formal invitation. I understand your husband is Jewish; has he ever been to Israel?"

Sincerely,

Giovanni Levi

***

"I understand your husband is Jewish." The words circulated in her head. Could she pull this off? She called Jacob's mother.

At dinner, Cia was all smiles. "Jacob, you're in for a treat. I made stuffed peppers and I baked rice pudding, your mother's recipe."

"Did you total the car—or worse, invite your mother to live with us?" Jacob was looking slightly alarmed.

Cia waved the question away. "No Jacob, can't I just appreciate my husband?" He was still clearly suspicious—but he was also hungry. While he enjoyed the rice pudding, Cia spoke.

"First of all, I want to apologize for taking days off from the store. I know my absence has caused more work for you. I'm back! I am breaking my promise to Nicholas and Ruby to tell you another war secret."

Jacob put down his spoon and held up both hands. "Stop right there, Cia mia. I don't want you to break your promise to either of them. It must be serious for the three of you to keep it a secret. I will honor that decision; besides, you may feel guilty after you tell me. Let it drop, but thank you."

Cia didn't know whether to feel disappointed or relieved. She nodded and went on.

"There's something else."

"There's more?" asked Jacob.

"Yes," said Cia. "Giovanni invited us to his 50th wedding anniversary in Tel Aviv. I would like to accept his invitation." Cia could see Jacob's mind at work.

Jacob was quiet for a few moments. "You know my cousin Harold lives there; I would love to see him. I have to speak with my mother. Wait, what about the store?"

"I'm way ahead of you, husband. Nicholas' school term will be over. He's agreed to run the store Thursday through Sunday. It will be closed the other days. Your mother spoke to Harold; he's already making plans. It's too late to call him tonight; Israel's time is seven hours ahead. Why don't you talk to your mother?" Jacob went into his office and called her. Cia smiled and started clearing the table.

***

Jacob emerged from his study about 20 minutes later. "Okay, Cia. Mom said Harold would like me to fly to Egypt with him; but the problem is he can't take a vacation until the third week in June."

Cia had it all planned. "Your mother told me; she also told me how you and your cousin Harold spent half your childhood at the Metropolitan Museum. You knew every inch of the Egyptian exhibit. Harold has never been to Egypt either. The plan is this: we arrive in Tel Aviv and stay with Harold and Sheila. I'll come home about nine days later to take care of the store. You and Harold can tour Israel and then fly to Egypt. In all, you'll be gone about seven weeks. Jacob, I want this for us." Cia looked at him expectantly.

Jacob walked up to her and wrapped her in a hug. He kissed her forehead. "Well, if you insist."

There was much to plan, but the basics were settled. Next she e-mailed Giovanni.

***

Dear Giovanni,

It was wonderful receiving your e-mail. My husband Jacob and I will be attending your anniversary celebration. We will be staying with Jacob's cousin who also lives in Tel Aviv. I will send you all the specifics when they are finalized; I hope we can set aside some time to talk about Carmine.

I am looking forward to discovering this ancient land.

Sincerely,

Cia

***

One last e-mail . . .

***

Dear Ruby,

*"This has come about in a flash—Jacob
and I will be going to Israel for Giovanni's
celebration! I wish you would change your
mind and join us. Thank you for the
Christmas video with your mother; I
forwarded it to Nicholas. I'll send my video
out to you later today. Have there been any
sightings of Nicholas on the elevator?"*

Love,

Cia

***

Now it was time to call her mother. The phone was always a good choice. If Sophia was incorrigible, Cia could announce that there was someone at the door and abruptly hang up.

No answer. She left a message:

Hello Mom. I remember you said you wanted to start baking for the church's bake sale. I'm going to drive into Brooklyn tomorrow and help you. I'm sure there are a lot of apples to peel; they love your pies! I'll be there about 10:00. Love ya.

***

A drive to Brooklyn was always an adventure. On this morning the Belt Parkway was backed up due to flooding. Grandpa

Carmine would often say, "If it's raining, the Belt Parkway is flooding."

With 10 pounds of sugar balanced in her arms, Cia greeted her mother with a wide smile. She was determined to have a civil day; she would be satisfied with civility on this gray, dreary morning.

"Mom, the sugar is my donation to the church; and to you I'm donating a day of help." Her mother thanked her; and with first things being first, she poured her daughter a steamy cup of hot chocolate. The overused mantra *it's complicated* jumped into her head; yes, their relationship was impossible to define. The mother rolled out dough while the daughter peeled, cored and sliced apples. Then Sophia skillfully placed the dough on the bottom and sides of the pie pans. Next, she mixed the apple slices with sugar and spices and filled the pans, added a top layer of dough, cut slits to vent the steam during baking, pinched the edges of the dough together, brushed them with an egg wash and put the pies in the oven.

The aroma of pies baking, the sound of raindrops splashing on the outside trellis, and working in her childhood kitchen all added to Cia's sense of serenity. When they stopped for a lunch of minestrone soup, Sophia's first topic of conversation was Nicholas.

"Do you know he has a new girlfriend? He told me he doesn't want to say too much because he doesn't want to jinx it." *Jinx it?* Cia could not believe her brother stooped to using superstition to avoid details; but it made sense to Sophia. "He also said he may not renew his lease; he's thinking of moving into his girlfriend's apartment in downtown Manhattan. At first I didn't like the idea; but then I thought I would have a reason to take the train to Manhattan."

Cia knew she had to say something; she couldn't remain mute. "I had no idea he was thinking of moving out of Brooklyn."

"Yes, he said if it doesn't work out, he'll stay with me until he finds a new rental."

"Wow, Mom, this is big news." They dropped the subject of Nicholas. Cia half expected her to say, *Maybe he'll be the one to give me a grandchild*; but she was, in this instance, kind. She allowed the subject to drop.

Five hours and two shriveled hands later, Cia loaded the pies into her car; she would drop them off at the church where they would be stored in a walk-in freezer. "Mom, I know you and your church friends are going away for Easter; I want to make plans for Mother's Day. I could make lunch and then drive you to the cemetery; you could visit your mother's grave. We'll buy her pink roses and wish her Happy Mother's Day."

Sophia said, "I would also be visiting her husband's gravesite; I think I'm ready to say prayers for my father. I have reached out to Father MacNamara for counsel. He said I should begin with prayer."

Cia knew she had to leave before this moment deteriorated. "Mom, look at the time; please call the rectory and tell them I'm on my way."

She called her brother.

"I'm driving home from Mom's house. It went well; no verbal skirmishes. I don't want to *jinx* you or anything; but what's this about moving in with Phyllis?"

"Sis, I'm not looking forward to telling Mom about the Phyllis/Carmine connection. I thought I should begin the process slowly and build on it over the next few months. You know mom is superstitious; the jinx part was easy.

"Cia, I have to move in; I'm afraid I'll lose her if I'm not aggressive. Besides, moving in is not the same as taking vows; we can end it without lawyers. If living together was not an option, I would marry her tomorrow. That's how fearful I am of losing her. The good news is she says she loves me. I don't want Mom to be upset, but I will not jeopardize what I have to placate her. A student just walked in; I'll talk to you soon. Gotta go."

***

The next few weeks were a whirlwind of activity. The itinerary for the Israel/Egypt trip was set. Nicholas came out to familiarize himself with the store. Mother's Day came sooner than they expected, with lunch at Cia's house.

The *Pastiera di Grano* Easter wheat pie hit the table like a 10-pound bag of cement. Sophia had been away for Easter, so she made the pie for Mother's Day. Her children could never bring themselves to confess their dislike for the pie. It was thick, bland, dry, and not sweet. As young adults they started taking a closer look at the ingredients. The recipe called for nine egg yolks and a pound and a half of ricotta cheese. They dutifully ate small pieces which fulfilled their cholesterol allotment for the month of May.

At lunch Sophia spoke of the wonderful time she had over Easter weekend. She and her church group were invited to stay at a former parishioner's home in New Jersey. Sophia said, "We attended Easter Sunday mass at the local church; the altar was filled with flowers from local gardens. The priest's sermon was joyful; we all came away with a sense of spiritual renewal."

Nicholas, for some reason, felt obligated to antagonize his mother. "Mom, isn't that woman's home just three miles from the Atlantic City casinos?"

"Yes, that's right Nicholas; on Saturday night we had dinner at the Borgata." Cia suppressed a smile and suggested they head out to the cemetery.

At the gravesite, the children stood back while their mother put pink roses on their grandmother's grave. Sophia was intermittently reciting prayers and speaking to her parents. The only words Nicholas and Cia overheard were, "Did you apologize to

Momma?" They waited patiently until finally, she turned back to them and said, "Would you like to say a prayer with me?" They obediently stepped forward and made the sign of the cross.

Later that night there was an e-mail from Ruby.

***

Hi Cia,

I'm in Woodbridge Virginia helping my mother plant flowers. Every Mother's Day we spend time together covered in mud. She agreed to watch the video. Mom said Sophia has many of the same mannerisms as she, and their voices sound similar. That was the extent of her interest.

Mom told Angelo the truth about his lineal father. She said she wished she could have spoken to him in person; she could not gauge his reaction. His only words were, "An American soldier would do this?" She made up her mind to visit him this summer. Maybe I'll go to Naples with her.

Have a wonderful time in Israel. Please send my love to Giovanni.

Love,

***

Ten days after praying at Carmine's gravesite, an El Al jet carried Cia to Giovanni's homeland. Jacob and Cia finally made their way out of Ben Gurion Airport and into Harold's car. The two Americans tried to feign excitement for their host, but the trip had exhausted them. Sheila greeted them and was graciously low-key. She said, "Harold and I are going out; it will give you the freedom to relax and unwind. I stocked the refrigerator—help your selves."

They were too restless to nap; instead they showered, unpacked and snacked on yogurt and fruit. Jacob had a suggestion. "I don't know how much privacy we're going to have in the next week. I want to take this opportunity to make love to my wife."

Cia responded with one weary word: "Now?"

Jacob tried a dramatic approach. "I'm a son of Israel; I want to make love to my wife in my ancestral home. It is considered a blessing."

Cia stared him down and asked, "Do you want me to lie down in the desert?"

"No, just in the guest room." The couple fit in two *blessings* before their cousins returned.

That night they feasted on chicken, olive salad, hummus and for dessert, chocolate babka. Harold said, "Our son will not be joining us; he's in the military. His goal is to be in the Paratrooper Brigade."

Sheila added, "I'm proud and terrified at the same time."

Yankee and Met's jerseys, along with a print of the Brooklyn Bridge, were pulled out of Jacob's suitcase and presented to his cousins. The hours spent agonizing over what to buy Harold and Sheila were not wasted; the gifts were well received. They laughed and tried the jerseys on over their clothes. Now sleep would not wait; Cia and Jacob said goodnight.

The next day, they planned out the itinerary. Sheila and Harold were both accountants, but worked at different companies. Sheila had more flexibility in her schedule; but for today Harold would be their host and Sheila would go to her office. Cia had plans to visit Giovanni while Harold and Jacob explored Tel Aviv.

Harold's car pulled up in front of Giovanni's building and Cia stepped out; she was not at all comfortable with her decision to come alone. Jacob reached out his car window and squeezed her hand. "You'll be fine. Enjoy your talk with Giovanni." He tugged her hand and brought her down for a quick kiss. "Now go."

Cia walked up to the building and stepped into the lobby. A man was waiting at the elevator. He said one word: "Cia?" That one word, said with such warmth and gentleness, melted away all her anxiety. Giovanni led her into his apartment and introduced her to his wife Jacqueline. His wife handed her a cold fruit drink and told Cia she was beautiful; then she announced that she would be back later with the children. Giovanni and Cia sat down in the living room.

Giovanni leaned toward Cia. "Where do we begin? Tell me what Carmine did with his life." Cia did her best to convey her grandfather's successes in business and his love for her and his family. She backed up her claims with a family photo album featuring all the milestones in his life. The album was a gift for Giovanni. He was delighted with the album and scrutinized each photo.

"You look like Carmine. Do you know that the last time I saw him was 73 years ago? But I remember him clearly. He saw a skinny boy by the side of the road and rescued him. I was fortunate. Besides Carmine, I had Bruno and Nonno as protectors. In a time when the world was upside down and full of hate, I found love and protection.

"After the war my Uncle Roberto brought me back to Rome. We looked for my parents; but Bruno's friend Signore Tomanelli checked with the officials and they told him that my parents were dead. Ten-year-old boys should not hear such things, but in 1945 many children heard these words.

"Uncle Roberto and I came to Israel in 1955; I have not been back to Italy. I had a good life. I became an architect; Angelo also became an architect. In Bruno's house we liked to build houses out of boxes; Italians are builders."

They had been talking for over an hour. "Where are my manners?" said Giovanni. "Join me for lunch." After they ate their salad, Giovanni brought out a box and placed it on the floor. He took out an American flag with 48 stars that Carmine had given to him. He also showed her two stamp albums that were mailed to him by her great-grandfather.

"Cia, the flag is dear to me; I cannot part with it. But I want to give you and your brother the albums. They were passed from your great-grandfather, to Carmine, to me. It is time they were returned to America."

Cia thanked him and held the albums gently. Then Giovanni began to weep. She did not speak. She did not reach for his hand. She remained rigid and silent. Cia imagined his mind's eye was replaying the horrific scenes and emotions he had experienced in Italy. She wanted to give his thoughts privacy. Words, to her way of thinking, were useless. Eventually he stood up, walked into the kitchen, and brought her back lemonade. She thanked him and sipped slowly.

Giovanni took a deep breath before he began. "I must tell you that I have spoken to Angelo. He told me the secret. He thought I knew. I did not; but I did hear words whispered in Bruno's kitchen one night. His men were talking about a soldier they buried. I was a child, and there were many dead soldiers. Was it this soldier? I do not know."

"Carmine loved Pina like a sister; he believed he did not protect her that day. It was not his fault; he could not have predicted what would await Pina on that path." Then Giovanni whispered, "It was a godless time, filled with atrocities. I will not repeat this secret. Angelo and I must see each other once more; we must come together." Giovanni seemed to feel that it was time to come out of the past and back into the present. "Okay, now I will show you the gardens; now we will smile."

When they returned from the gardens; Jacqueline was there with a small mob of people. She dramatically announced, "I want to introduce you to Carmine's granddaughter Cia. Without her grandfather you would not be here today. Cia, I will give Giovanni the pleasure of introducing his children to you."

Giovanni was beaming as he made the introductions. "This is my son, Sergio, and his wife Francesca; this is my son Roberto and his wife Lin. Now I will introduce my 17-year-old twin grandsons: this is Aaron and this is Jody. They are fine musicians and they will perform at our party tomorrow. This is my Stella; she is nine years old and sings for her grandfather."

Stella came forward and presented Cia with a bouquet of flowers. She said, "Your grandfather took care of my grandfather. I have a cameo just like the one you are wearing. Welcome to Israel." Cia hugged her and at that moment in time she was grateful that she had had her DNA tested. This one moment more than made up for all the explosive secrets.

Giovanni convinced Stella to sing a song for their guest. She had a lovely voice; of course, Cia did not understand one word of the song, since Stella was singing in Hebrew. The two families said goodbye, saying they looked forward to meeting Cia's husband and his cousins at the party. She thanked them again for inviting Harold and Sheila to the anniversary party.

Giovanni walked her to the elevator. "Did Carmine give you the cameo you are wearing?" Cia nodded. "Angelo gave Stella an identical one. He said it originally belonged to Tessa; it was a present from Carmine. Tessa gave it to her sister. Pina was wearing it when she died. Angelo sent the cameo to Israel when Stella was born."

"Yes, Giovanni, Carmine sent this one home to his mother; he gave it to me after she died. Recently my mother gave me the cameo Carmine sent to his wife. I know southern Italy is famous for its cameos."

Harold's car was waiting in front of the building. Cia waved goodbye, and brought her hand up to touch her cameo. Life was good.

***

The following evening, Cia, Jacob, Harold and Sheila attended Giovanni and Jacqueline's 50th anniversary celebration. As soon as Cia entered the room, Stella ran up to her and proudly pointed to her pendant. "I wore my cameo too; the cameo ladies are twins." Everyone laughed. Jacqueline had seated them with her American cousins. They were from Baltimore, and were considering a move to Tel Aviv.

Cia couldn't escape. She tried to break through; but the feeling held her tightly. She was experiencing a mental time warp. It was 1944 and Carmine, Giovanni and Pina were marching through her thoughts. She was there, too, a mute observer. Jacob knew she was distracted; he knew she was overcome with an array of emotions. Cia's physical responses were appropriate—she smiled, laughed, and danced—but she was not there. She was with Carmine, Giovanni and Pina. The ugliness of war had stolen their innocence. The remnants of their history collected in this elegant room like a heavy, floating mist.

At the end of the evening, Giovanni and Jacqueline kissed Cia goodnight and thanked her for sharing this night with them.

292

Giovanni promised to keep in touch, and invited her back to Israel for Stella's Bat Mitzvah.

Back at Harold and Sheila's, Cia lay sprawled on the bed. She was exhausted; sleep claimed her.

"The Sea of Galilee—it's biblical, it's where Jesus performed miracles, and it's a lake. I want to walk on its banks and breathe its air. Jacob, I'm going home in three days. I don't want to visit all the Christian sites; it's too exhausting. Sheila and Harold said they would both take off tomorrow and drive us to the Sea of Galilee. I even like the way it sounds, *the Sea of Galilee.* It's what I want."

She would get no argument from Jacob. "Okay, Cia mia, then that's what we'll do. I cannot believe how different I feel here; Israel has anchored me. I am caught up in all the history—and I owe it all to you, Thank you." He gave her a gentle kiss.

"You can thank Giovanni and me for your Israeli trip, but ultimately it was Carmine who brought us here; that is my belief. Carmine introduced Nicholas to Phyllis and invited you to Israel. The past and present are colliding by design. However, for today I want to push these abstract thoughts aside and do something tangible like go to a mall. I need to buy a gift and I'm running out of time. Mom wants a piece of jewelry, a necklace with an Eilat or King Solomon stone. Let's go."

Israel is a visual contradiction. It is an ancient land and also the site of modern, state of the art malls. Cia made her way through the upscale dress stores before settling on a simple black dress. "Don't say a word, Jacob, I know I have a closet full of black dresses; but here's the distinction-this one is a summer dress. I saw a jewelry store when we first walked in; I want to buy my mother her necklace and I am going to buy you a pair of cufflinks as a keepsake."

Jacob smiled at her and gave her a quick kiss. "Thank you Cia, I would like that. I think you should buy Uncle Tony a piece of jewelry, possibly a cross? I'll pick up something for my parents when Harold and I tour Israel, and I'm looking forward to buying Nicholas a gift from Egypt," said Jacob. They went on with their shopping. With their purchases in hand, they left the mall—but not before they took a selfie by its front entrance.

The next morning the group of four set out for their two-and-a-half-hour trip to the Sea of Galilee. Cia was awestruck by the beautiful landscape; she imagined it would have been mile after mile of sand. By noon they had arrived. First they stopped and ate a lunch of chicken and olive salad. Cia ate her chicken, but she was desperate for a plate of pasta. Then they made their first stop at the Church of the Multiplication of Fish and Loaves. Cia and Sheila had followed the dress code: no shorts and no sleeveless blouses. The church is said to be built over the site where Jesus fed 5,000 people with just a basket of fish and loaves of bread. Cia found a holy water font, put her right hand in the water and made the sign of the cross. Then she bowed her head and prayed for Carmine, her mother, Nicholas and Uncle Tony.

She didn't stay long—20 minutes—she wanted to experience the holy site, not learn of the church's architecture. The other three followed her lead, and walked out behind her. They made their way to the Sea of Galilee and watched Christians being baptized in the water. "I want to walk into water, just walk by the edge," she said to Jacob and his cousins. Harold found a close spot where she could take off her sandals and step into the water. Cia took three steps into the water and stood motionless and stared out at the far distance, then she abruptly turned and said, "I'm ready to leave."

"Cia," said Sheila, "are you sure you want to go? We have no problem staying; there are many Christian sites for you to visit."

Cia shook her head. "I'm good. I'd like to head back." They drove back without stopping for food. Harold took an alternate route so his guests could have a good view of different scenery.

The next day, Harold and Sheila both went to their offices. Cia and Jacob had a lazy day—they only went as far as the tiny terrace. "It has been amazing, Cia, this ancient land was here and I never gave it much thought. When Harold moved here, I thought he was crazy. He wasn't crazy." Cia looked up and smiled at her husband who, at the moment, looked like a little boy.

On Cia's last night in Israel, Sheila and Harold took them out to dinner at their favorite restaurant. A piano player took a request from Harold and sang New York, New York. To Jacob and Cia's surprise, many patrons began singing along. When the song ended, people walked up to their table and asked them where they were from. One man said, "You brought Brooklyn to me."

Back at the apartment Cia finished her packing, then laid in bed next to her husband. "Cia, we have never been apart more than a few days; I feel empty already."

Cia kissed him and said, "This is an historic and magical time for you, I want you to enjoy every moment. Besides, we can Facetime each other. Let me get some sleep; it's going to be a long day."

Sheila and Jacob drove her to the airport. Cia would miss Jacob. She would miss this ancient land. But she was ready to go home.

Chapter Fifteen
New York
June-July 2019

It was a long flight back to New York. Cia was exhausted when she landed, but happy to be home. Her brother was waiting for her at the airport.

"Thank you Nicholas, I appreciate you driving out to JFK to pick me up."

"My pleasure; how was the trip back?"

"I think the Pilgrims had an easier time on their maiden voyage; at least they didn't deal with security. I'm wiped out. As soon as we took off, the man in the next seat wanted to chat. I panicked. Usually I give one-word answers and stick my nose in a book; but this time my rudeness reached new heights. I refused to answer any of his questions. I just ignored him for the entire flight. Is my store still operable?"

"Yes Sis." Nicholas smiled. I even sold two clocks and a painting. And I made an appointment for you to see a collection in Quogue."

"That's great, Nicholas. Thank you," said Cia.

Nicholas took a surreptitious deep breath. "Mom came out with me. I dropped her at your house and then drove to the airport. She cooked, and was packing the refrigerator and airing out the house when I left."

"That was gracious of her; but when we get back, please don't plan on staying. I want to shower and tell my bed how much I missed it. Jacob said he will roam Egypt until he finds the perfect gift for you."

"Cia, before we walk in the door I have to share some news. I drove Mom to her session with Father MacNamara; he and I had prearranged the meeting. I decided I would drop the *Phyllis* bomb on Mom while you were in Israel. I wanted it to be between the two of us with Father MacNamara acting as referee. I told her the whole story.

"The keys points were:

- I love Phyllis and will not lose her

- She is not related to Carmine

- She is removed from the events

- Phyllis' brother is married to Carmine's granddaughter

- Cia did not introduce us

"I showed her the video of her half sister. She didn't ask to see it, but I wanted to hold nothing back. She didn't think the two of them looked alike."

"Wow that *is* news; so what happened?"

"She asked Father MacNamara to pray with her. Then she said that she has no choice but to respect my wishes. She made it clear that she was not interested in embracing a half sister, but she would be in God's graces when she attended family functions. The sisters won't have a storybook ending; but there is nothing fair about war. Finally, I made it clear that she was not to speak to you about my life."

"Nicholas, I think you handled it perfectly; she wants her son to be happy and she doesn't want to lose his love. Good job." Cia stifled a yawn. "I apologize for yawning; believe me, it's not the conversation." Nicholas just smiled and headed toward Cia's house.

The house was filled with the aroma of tomato sauce; she knew she was home. Cia kissed her mother and thanked her for the warm welcome. Then she gave her the Israeli necklace with its blue-green stones. Sophia was impressed. The necklace was not only striking—it was from the Holy Land.

Sophia served her children the pasta as though it had healing properties. She asked Cia what Christian sites she had visited. "I visited The Church of the Multiplication of Fish and Loaves and

The Sea of Galilee. I tried to imagine Jesus walking on the water and feeding the masses. It was humbling to think I stood where Jesus had walked."

Sophia asked to see photos of the Church of the Holy Sepulchre and the Church of the Nativity. "I don't have any, Mom."

"You didn't take pictures?"

"No, I didn't go to those churches; I did go to the Sea of Galilee."

Sophia's face displayed a look of bewilderment mixed with rising anger. "What do you mean you didn't go? What Catholic doesn't make pilgrimages while in Israel?"

"Mom, it would have been too exhausting. I chose not to go; but I did feel close to my religion. As Jacob observed, Israel anchors you.

Sophia made a huffing sound. "That's all very nice, but what am I going to say to my rosary club? I'm embarrassed to tell Father MacNamara you didn't make a pilgrimage."

"I'm sorry," was her daughter's only response. Dinner ground to a halt.

Nicholas interrupted his mother's rant and announced it was time to head back home. Cia cleared the table while Sophia gathered up her things for the ride back to Brooklyn. They both finished at about the same time, and walked together to the front door. Nicholas held the door for his mother, and the two headed down the walk. Cia waved goodbye, then closed her mind and her front door to her mother. Nicholas started the car, then abruptly turned it off and walked back into the house—leaving Sophia in the passenger seat.

He hugged his sister and told her he loved her. "It's okay Nicholas; I'm annoyed, but not upset. If I ran the Boston Marathon and was the first person to cross the finish line, she would tell me I needed deodorant." The two of them shared a knowing laugh. Nicholas gave her one more hug and headed back out to the car. Cia did not bother to shower; she stripped down and fell into her bed.

For the next few weeks, Cia ate lunch and dinner at the store. The antiques business was as much about networking as store sales. She had to laugh when she read her brother's note about a collection in Quoque. The appointment was with Lance—*Lance the Lecherous*, as she had labeled him; he probably plotted to put a collection together in Jacob's absence. No, that meeting would not take place.

On Wednesday Uncle Tony drove out to the store and brought her lunch. It was a perfect July day with sunshine and a breeze. They sat on a bench just a few steps from the front door. She knew he had cooked peppers and eggs; she could see the oil stains on the paper bag. Lunch was delicious.

"Uncle Tony, I brought you a cross and a chain; and I said prayers for you at the Church of the Multiplication of Fish and Loaves."

"Thank you, Cia. That's so thoughtful of you." He gave her a kiss on the cheek.

Cia continued. "I have something else to say. I want to learn more about my father. I want to see him through your eyes."

"I prayed for this day and today my prayers were answered," said her Uncle. "I would hug you but my hands are filled with peppers and eggs. God bless you."

Then she brought him up to date on the Phyllis and Nicholas saga, adding in the Sophia component. "Every time I think my mother and I are making progress, we crash. I have decided that she doesn't dislike me, she dislikes herself." She held up her hand as Tony was about to protest. "I know what you are going to say— *count your blessings.* I think that I am going to try your approach. You are a wise man, Uncle Tony."

He spent the rest of the day with Cia at the shop, dusting shelves, cleaning the glass on the showcases and winding clocks. He liked being alone with his niece; with Jacob away, he had her all to himself. At 6:00, they closed the shop and went out to dinner. Cia chose an Italian restaurant; she had to make up for all the pasta meals she had recently missed. They both ordered spaghetti with clam sauce. Uncle Tony ordered his spaghetti with white clam sauce, while Cia's clam sauce was red. Both meals were delicious.

When the check arrived, Cia grabbed for it. "My treat," she said. "I want to repay you for all the cleaning you did today; and for being such good company."

Tony gave Cia a warm smile. "Thank you," he said.

"You are very welcome," said Cia.

Outside the restaurant, Uncle Tony walked Cia to her car, kissed her on the cheek and watched her drive away; then he headed for his car. He already missed his niece.

At 9:00 the next morning Cia received a text from Ruby. Ruby asked if she could come out to the house tomorrow. Cia said, "Of course," even though Jacob was due home in two days and she wanted to have everything just so for his return. Cia would not have planned a visit the day before Jacob's homecoming, but she would make it work.

Cia picked Ruby up at the train station the next morning and realized she had missed her new found cousin. *What's that about?*

Ruby gave Cia a quick hug before she buckled her seat belt. "Thank you for agreeing to this last-minute visit. I didn't want to lose my nerve. Tell me about Giovanni." Cia smiled, took a deep breath, and started telling Ruby about the trip.

The drive back to Levittown was filled with talk of Giovanni, his family, and his party. Cia was struck by the easy flow of their conversation. The two women chatted like two close cousins who had grown up together. It felt good. It felt right. At the house they had coffee and muffins; Ruby said she couldn't stay long. Cia brought out an album of Giovanni's party that she had put together for Ruby and her mother.

"Thank you, Cia. My mother will cherish this and she'll be excited to share it with Angelo." Ruby sat uneasily for a few moments. Cia wasn't sure what was going on, but she figured she'd wait a minute before prompting Ruby. Then Ruby said what was on her mind.

"I don't know how to say this, so I'll just blurt it out: would you take me to our grandfather's grave? I want to have his memory in my life. He is no longer some abstract figure; he is real to me—and he brought me to you."

Cia brushed away tears and excused herself. When she returned she was carrying a cameo in her hand. "I want you to have this cameo. I am giving you the one that belonged to your great-grandmother; Carmine sent it to his mother. I have the one he gave to his wife; and Giovanni's granddaughter has the one Carmine gave to Tessa. Angelo sent it to Israel when Giovanni's granddaughter was born."Ruby stared at the cameo without speaking. When she found her voice she said, "Thank you, Cia. This gift makes me feel like I am truly his granddaughter." Then with a slight smile she added, "I'm a Trotta!" The two cousins embraced.

Ruby and Cia wore their cameos to the cemetery. At the gravesite, Cia stood back and gave her cousin privacy. Then they stood side by side and said goodbye to their grandfather.

At the train station, Ruby gave Cia a farewell hug and whispered, "I love you." She touched her cameo and ran for the train.

Alone in the car, Cia cried, "Grandpa, don't ever leave me." Cia wiped her tears and drove away.

Chapter Sixteen
New York
July 2019

Cia had already put in a full day at the shop. Just the thought of now driving to the airport in rush hour traffic deflated her spirit. *Jacob will be landing in two hours, and then I will feel whole again. Just stop whining and smile.* Cia focused on seeing Jacob and celebrating his homecoming; by the time she reached Lynbrook, her spirit was restored. JFK was predictable: polluted dead air, people filling every inch of space, horns honking and cars everywhere. Cia was waiting in the parking lot. Jacob had landed and was picking up his luggage. She had told him where to find her.

Finally Jacob came into view. He shoved his luggage into the trunk and slid into the passenger's seat. They had a quick hug and kiss in the car; then they were ready to head for home. Jacob was feeling edgy after the long flight; but as soon as they cleared the airport his body relaxed.

"We circled the airport for 30 minutes. I wanted to open the door and parachute out. Cia, I missed you. I have so many stories to tell you; but I am just happy to be home. Seven weeks is too long to be out of the country."

"I really missed you. I will never be that generous again and allow you to be away from me that long."

Jacob said, "I don't ever want to be away from you that long again." The traffic had subsided by the time they reached the Southern State Parkway. It was a cool July night and Long Island's landscape was green and welcoming. Jacob was happy to be home.

Cia had a variety of cooked food ready for him; she didn't know if he would arrive ravenous, or too tired to eat. "Are you hungry?"

"No, I'm too wound up to eat; but I guarantee you I will have my appetite back by tomorrow. I missed your cooking, I missed fast food burgers and New York pizza; but I will take a glass of wine." They sat on the couch, Jacob drinking his wine and Cia sipping lemonade. They stole sideward glances at each other; they were reassuring themselves that the other was truly there.

"Did you find gifts for Nicholas and your parents?" Cia asked.

"Yes," said Jacob, "I bought your brother old maps and I bought my parents a print of Jerusalem. I stored the print in my luggage; I hope it didn't tear. I should have carried my parents' gift with me."

Cia smiled. "Jacob, I carried your parents' gift with me when I came back from Israel."

Jacob looked puzzled. "Cia, I don't understand."

Cia was beaming—so happy she felt she might float. "I carried your parents' gift home with me. Their grandchild was conceived in Israel."

Jacob stared at her, baffled for a moment, until her meaning finally sank it. Then he broke into a smile and swept his wife up in his arms.

"I told you it was a blessing."

Rose Warren was born in Proctor Vermont and raised in New York City.

Her essays have appeared in newspapers, magazines and in the Congressional Record.

Treads of the Parachute is her debut novel.

She lives in Long Island, New York with her husband and children.

Cia's journey takes her from today's exclusive high-end dwellings of Soho in NYC, back in time to the ravaged European towns of WWII. An Ancestry dna test will begin to unravel family secrets that have remained dormant for over 70 years. It chronicles her Grandfather's military service in WWII. In Naples, Cia's grandfather, Carmine, rescues a 10 year old boy who is too frightened to reveal his true identity. Carmine must leave Naples, and his mistress, to march up the spine of Italy, to France, Belgium and finally Germany. He is haunted by a war-time rape and murder that he blames himself for not preventing. The final explosive discovery has the potential to tear apart the very fabric of three unsuspecting families.